**I am an Indian.**

I must bow to the laws of the Pueblo, but I cannot accept its ways; I cannot cut the heels off my white man's boots; I cannot cut the seat from my pants and cover myself with a blanket....

**I am an Indian.**

I went to the white man's school and learned to be a carpenter, but I cannot drink whiskey as the white man does nor go where he goes nor live as he lives....I am a man who must find out who he is.

**I am**

**THE MAN WHO KILLED THE DEER**

"Even the reader who does not know the American Indian at first hand can hardly fail to sense the full authenticity of Mr. Waters' book. ...It will live as one of the important pieces of literature on the American Indian."

—*San Francisco Chronicle*

**THE MAN WHO KILLED THE DEER**
was originally published by Farrar, Rinehart.

# THE MAN WHO KILLED THE DEER

•

*by*

**FRANK WATERS**

PUBLISHED BY POCKET BOOKS NEW YORK

THE MAN WHO KILLED THE DEER

Farrar, Rinehart edition published 1941

POCKET BOOK edition published August, 1971

6th printing....................September, 1974

L

**This POCKET BOOK edition includes every word contained in the original, higher-priced edition. It is printed from brand-new plates made from completely reset, clear, easy-to-read type. POCKET BOOK editions are published by POCKET BOOKS, a division of Simon & Schuster, Inc., 630 Fifth Avenue, New York, N.Y. 10020. Trademarks registered in the United States and other countries.**

---

Standard Book Number: 671-78849-3.

This POCKET BOOK edition is published by arrangement with The Swallow Press, Inc. 

Printed in the U.S.A.

To

Mabel and Tony

# 1

THE LAST piñon knot crumpled in the small conical fireplace. Its coals blazed redly alive, then slowly clouded over with a gray film like the eyes of a dead hawk. The whitewashed adobe walls began to lose their pinkish pallor and dim outlines. A rat scampered across the dark earthen floor into silence. There sounded in the room only the rhythmic breathing of sleep.

It came loudly from a woman and a young girl lying on a wooden bedstead; more softly from the man-child wrapped in a serape on the adobe seating ledge extending along the wall. But the man stretched out on floor mat and blankets between them could not sleep. It was as if an invisible hand was pulling at his spirit . . . pulling it out of his chest . . . pulling it outside the great sleeping pyramid of adobe in which he lay.

There were no windows in the room; only a small, square breathing shaft opening in the ceiling above. Yet he heard the October wind prowling along the walls, moaning in the outdoor ovens dotting the plaza like ant-hills. From the willow thickets along the stream rose clear, deep voices. "Hi-yah! Ai! Hi-yah!" They came from young men wrapped palely as ghosts in sheets and blankets who had been singing, hour after hour, at the rising moon. Across the pastures came the sound of a little water drum. But beyond, the dark pine mountain throbbed deeper. It was the shape of a recumbent woman's great soft breast flattened at the point, really incurved like an old buffalo bow. And the beat, from deep within, from the heart of the world, pulsed steadily, inaudibly, like the beat of the man's blood. Each was the echo of the other, indivisible. But they were not quite in tune.

So the man could not sleep. He rose quietly, pulled on his pants. Squatting before the fireplace, he gently turned over the coals with a stick. In the faint glow his ruddy brown chest and shoulders emerged soft, hairless and fleshy, like a woman's, but powerful. His black eyes, big nose, full lips and massive cheek bones were the features of a mahogany mask.

The face was somber and relaxed, yet intent—the rapt face of a man who would see without what he felt within.

As he waited, it came again—a long, wavering but insistent cry from the lower pine slopes. It was the frosty, eerie voice of a coyote. He had heard it thrice before; but now, with the pull upon his spirit, the cry held a summons he could not ignore.

His dark immobile face changed. It was still trance-like, but decisive. He dressed slowly and unhurried: in wool shirt, store boots with the heels removed, a dirty leather jacket and blanket. A waterfall of long black hair poured down his back. He did not wait to braid it with colored hair-strings into two long pig-tails falling to his waist. He bound it simply, the old way, into a chignon tied at the back with a strip of dirty cloth. Softly, so as not to awaken wife and children, he glided across the dark room. His strong, sensitive hands took down a rifle from a pair of mounted deer horns. He opened the door and stepped quietly outside.

The moon was high. A light frost covered the smooth beaten earth of the plaza. The halves of the pueblo on each side loomed up like great lumpy cliffs. There were no lights. Even the dogs were asleep. The young men had gone, and the stream sang alone over the frosty stones.

He reached the corrals outside the town wall. Already fresh evergreen branches were stacked along the logs to keep out wind and snow. The sorrel mare smelled him and hushed her whinny. He bridled, blanketed and saddled, led her outside to mount. She stepped daintily, distastefully, through the cold stream.

At one of the two great ash piles which still slowly rise upon hundreds of years' refuse, broken pottery and old bones, the mare hesitated. But not the rider. He pressed with his right knee, and shook loose the reins. It was as if an invisible cord, the invisible hand upon his spirit, was pulling him to the rocky upper trail.

Beautifully it all spread out below: the narrow valley ascending with the stream, great clumps of paling cottonwoods, thickets of wild plum and chokecherry, corn milpas and patches of open fields. But in the green-gray moonlight trance-like and empty as a dream. The dry pale cornstalks rattled in the wind. An overturned wicker basket left that afternoon by a group of women frightened away by a bear spilled chokecherries across the path.

The man looked up into the clear dark sky. The Deer were up. Some crows were calling. He listened attentively and rode on.

The trail led upward over the sloping thigh of the mountain. It was rough and sharp with black volcanic tufa. The mare shied round a boulder: the one marked with the strange signs of the Old Ones—a circle enclosing a dot. the imprint of a hand, a strange long-legged animal with a longer neck. The rider felt, as the mare, the lingering vibrations of the life that had never died but only lost its nonessential bodily form.

On the shoulder of the mountain they stopped. The mare to stand heaving, with sweat trickling down withers and flanks. The rider to stare dreamily down at the low town wall enclosing the two communal mud pyramids like the halves of a nutmeat within a broken shell; at the stream between them, with its two bridges of square-hewn timbers, flowing through the plaza; the conical outdoor ovens repeating in miniature the pattern of the mountain above; and at the ceremonial round kivas with ladders coming out of the top. But here, from high above and in the moonlight, it was all compressed and blended into a self-inclosed, impenetrable unity. The two opposite halves of the pueblo appeared like the fragments of a great headless drum, like the walls of an ancient kiva unearthed after a thousand years. There was the same dead weight of earth once raised and slowly sinking back. The same indifferent non-resistance. A curious non-aliveness. Not deadness, for nothing dies, but as something living with a slow serpent-pulse in a perpetual dream of time.

When the pull upon the man's spirit tightened he rode on. Through a thick, dark forest of pine and spruce. To the mouth of a steep and narrow cañon. The trail was narrow. Brush scraped his legs and the hanging rifle. He lowered his bare head under outflung branches.

It was high country now. Perhaps nine thousand feet. The shadowy forest dropped behind. Between the tips of tall firs he saw the pale sage desert stretching away beyond the river. And beyond it, the hazy western range wherein lay the Sun's house. But the gentle, insistent pull led him still higher.

The cañon walls drew back. The stream poured whitely down the falls, rushed through small glades, spread into great still trout pools. Here the beavers worked. Felled trees crossed stream and trail. Others on each side stood smooth and straight, but with an X-shaped notch where they were being gnawed in two, and with a talus of fresh chips below.

After a time the man reined up his mare. He stared upward and ahead at the bare granite face of the mountain above timberline. It was calm, expressionless, stoical as his own. There over the lower crest, the in-curved bow, lay the sacred tribal lake. The little blue eye of faith. The deep turquoise lake of life. But now there was no pull upon him. He listened to the deep pulse of the mountain, and he felt it as one feels a drum which has been beating so long that he is no longer conscious of the mere sound. He listened to the pulse of his own blood. They beat together now, in time. And he knew he was to go no farther.

So he waited, sitting patiently on his mare. At the edge of a small clearing. Hidden in the grove of tall pale aspens. The clouds drifted on. The Night People twinkled clearly again. Wind Old Woman blew cold off the first ice above, rattling the pale brittle leaves which fell like flakes of snow. Still he did not stir.

A shadow flitted from tree to tree-top. A deer bounded into the glade. It stood an instant nose forward, the petals of its ears up; then with a flick of its white tail-piece vanished into the brush. The man did not reach for his rifle. His hand lay heavily and calmly upon the neck of his mare. Still there was no sign.

After a while he rode out into the clearing, looked around him, then dismounted and led his mare to the stream. Six paces from the edge she suddenly whinnied and reared up on her hind legs. The man jerked her down with a powerful but steady hand. Before her front feet touched earth, the rifle was in his other hand. He stood bent forward in a crouch, no longer trance-like, but intensely aware.

He heard a muffled moan. It came from a man lying in the shadow of a boulder. He was lying on one side, legs doubled up, arms outspread, his face to the ground. But even as the rider bent down, scratching a match with his thumbnail, the head rolled sideways, and there stared up at him a face whose features were familiar but drained of color to a sallow yellow.

"Martiniano!" the rider called softly and clearly. "I have heard your call. I am come."

As he dropped to his knees and slid a gentle calloused hand under the blood-dried head, the one answered. "Palemon. My friend. It is my head. It makes my blood water, my legs weak. I could crawl no farther." The voice was weak but calm, almost as steady as the black fathomless eyes shining in the match light.

Palemon built a tiny fire. With water from the stream he washed his friend's gashed head. With wet leaves and a dirty bandana he bound it. They smoked a cigarette in a silence too heavily impregnated with mystery for empty words.

Then Palemon called softly to his mount. "She is a strong mare. That you know. I will hold you on," he said simply.

"The deer I killed," replied Martiniano. "You will get him first? Maybe half mile back. You will see where I crawled, the blood also. He is hid in the bushes. Those others, they rode fast away."

A quick sharp look passed between them.

"Those white men I say. They left me dead," added Martiniano.

Palemon did not answer. On foot, leading the mare, he vanished into the darkness.

Dawn was breaking over the mountains when they came down the trail. But down below, dark still held between the two tall adobe cliffs. The faces of the cliffs were seamed with ladders reaching from ledge to ledge. Before the doors, facing the east, stood cardboard figures shrouded in shawls and blankets. On the highest house-tops two others robed in white took up their posts, to stand or sit there till evening dusk.

As the first beam of light struck across the well of darkness, all emptied their hands of corn meal and spoke their prayers to the sun coming out standing to his sacred place. Jets of pale blue smoke began to spout from a hundred and fifty chimneys.

The plaza below awoke with life. Women waddling down to the stream balancing water jars and tin buckets on their blue-black heads. Children, naked and shivering, running after more faggots. Men returning from the corrals to stand in front of ovens or against the sunny walls. Wrapped to the eyes in cheap cotton blankets, rolling corn-husk cigarettes, saying nothing, seeing all. It was the rhythm of Indian life: an unvarying, age-old pattern whose mutations changed regularly and simultaneously with the patterns of day and night.

The rhythm was abruptly changed by the overloaded sorrel mare entering the plaza. One man slumped in the saddle, his feet dangling loosely to the sides, his swaying head tied round with a dirty red bandana. The other, feet in the stirrups, rode behind him. His hands, passed under the arms of the first to hold him upright, grasped the reins. Behind on the rump bobbled the bloody carcass of a deer held by rope lashings.

Something was wrong. It tainted the air. Yet no man, shrouded in his impenetrability, betrayed himself by anxious questions. The women, after one quick look, walked by with averted faces. Children ducked into the willows bordering the stream like baby chickens at sight of a hawk. Only a quick tension rippled through all.

The mare plodded slowly across the plaza, forded the stream, and stopped at an adobe building with glass windows and a shiny brass door-knob behind the pueblo—the Government office of the reservation. An Indian youth with short hair came out, followed by a white man in spectacles. They lifted Martiniano off the mare, and half carried him inside.

Palemon nodded respectfully, then walked his horse back across the plaza. He met his wife coming down to the stream with a water jar on her head. She was a good woman. She had risen to find her husband gone, his rifle gone. His face was grave. Her own was worried as she wondered why he had left her at night, not for deer. But she did not voice her worry, and thus betray her man by lack of faith. She simply greeted him with a look, receiving his curt nod as she modestly lowered her gaze, and walked on to her task.

Palemon rode around the pueblo. Down a rutty road in back, outside the town wall. Across a corn field bounded by plum thickets. He reined up in front of a small adobe hut. To one side was a small log corral. In front stood an old springless wagon. The place revealed drabness and poverty. The drabness was colored with scarlet strings of chiles hanging from protruding viga ends. The poverty was belittled by a huge heap of Indian corn in front of the corral.

A woman was seated before it in the sunlight, shucking the corn. As she stripped off the pale leaves wet with dew, the ears leapt from her hands into another pile: black, blue, red, yellow, white and speckled.

When Palemon rode up she stood. She was a young woman. Work had not yet made her tough, weathered and stringy. Repeated childbirth had not yet made of her long slim body a shapeless sack. She was dressed in a tattered shawl, a dirty gingham and a pair of sloppy shoes laced with string. Bits of corn silk littered her black hair. Ceremonially dressed she might have been almost beautiful. Her lips quivered; and her big black eyes were restless. The play of muscles around both, in her sensitive brown skin, seemed expressive of her Indian name—Flowers Playing. But she waited patiently for Palemon to speak.

"He is safe but hurt," he said quietly. "But not too hurt to send you this meat. See? It is gutted and there has been cut out just a piece. Now I shall carry it, and string it up for you, so you may skin it properly, taking care to conceal the hide and horns from all idle questioning."

He dismounted to do as he had said. He returned and swung back upon his mare. The woman shuffled up to him and laid her hand on the mare's neck. "Is it proper I go at once?"

Palemon smiled—a slow fire that warmed the marrow in her bones. "Why not? But why not wait till his head is washed and properly bound and he can return? As you will. Have no fear. But ask no questions. There will be trouble. Not much, but trouble. It is necessary I report it, and so hold my tongue until it is bidden me to speak. Adios!"

He wheeled his mount and cantered off. Riding back into the plaza, he dismounted in front of the pueblo. An old man was squatting on the ground against the sunny wall, and whittling a cedar stick. His long brown fingers were bony and prehensile as the talons of a hawk. His tattered shirt and trousers tied round with a blanket held skinny, brittle limbs. Perhaps he was the man of whom the old joke was said, "Indians don't die. They just dry up and blow away."

But when he raised his face there was in it something one seldom sees now. Dark and wrinkled, at once kind and indomitable, it held the keen black eyes of a man who has long known all the vagaries of weather and men's passions alike, and who has seen through them to the calm heart of all storms. He was the Governor of the pueblo.

So Palemon stood in front of him in silence. A big man, grave and stern, but with a respectful posture.

The Governor's stare probed his own steady glance. The old man clicked shut his little pocket knife and laid aside his whittled stick. Deliberately he gathered up all the cedar shavings, held them to his nose, and then stuffed them in the fold of his blanket.

"You will come inside, my son."

Palemon flung his reins to one of the boys playing near by with bright pebbles, and followed him inside the doorway. The room with the door shut seemed dark and cold. An old crone was sweeping up clouds of dust from the earthen floor with a handful of popote. The old man drove her to an inner room with a torrent of idioma. When that door too was shut, he seated himself on a low stool in front of a burning twig, and motioned the visitor to the seating ledge.

There was the silence of actors in the moment before the curtain rises. These two men had their roles, but they were not actors. Their roles were the assumption of symbols of a life that had never grown too stale to lose the significance of its drama and its ever-present mystery.

The Governor took out a cigarette paper, smoothed out its wrinkles. Palemon dutifully offered tobacco, and was asked to smoke himself if he desired. As the men puffed, the objects of the room stood out more clearly. The patterns of the cheap cotton blankets and fine old serapes on the seating ledge, the old bows and arrows, the paper Catholic Saints hanging on the walls, the herbs dangling from the vigas, the old carven Santo in its niche.

The Governor threw away his stub.

"It is of that Martiniano you would speak? Now that is for the Outside Chiefs. You will have to report it to the War Captain. But I will listen first. There may be that which concerns us all."

As evening dusk began to blur the two pale splotches on the highest house-tops, a third appeared. For minutes his deep, clear voice sang out sonorously to all below. It was like a summons, like a muezzin's call at twilight. Each man stopped to listen, then continued to his task.

Wood and water were brought. Horses were shut up in their corrals. Burros were herded into their communal log inclosure. The people shut themselves up in the pueblo like a race self-entombed in a pyramid.

Strips of ribs were cut from carcasses hanging from the rafters, cooked and eaten with chile and tortillas. Cheap fresh coffee was added to the morning's grounds, boiled and drunk. Corn-husk cigarettes were rolled and puffed. And now in warm, smoky households, the people sat resting in flame-light.

Children rolled up in serapes and blankets, stretching out along the seating ledges. Women prepared beds and floor mats. But the old men still sat nodding before the coals.

Who knew what o'clock it was? There were no battered clocks, no dollar Ingersolls that kept time. The people likely couldn't read them anyway. They had no sense of time, these people. To them time was no moving flow to be measured, ticked out and struck at funny intervals. Time was all one, ever-present and indestructible. It was they who moved through it. There was only the consciousness of the moment for right action. No one knew how it came. But when it came they obeyed.

So suddenly, all at once, doors began to open. And the old men, drawing their blankets closer over head and shoulders, stepped out into the dark. They walked in their aloneness, slow and silent, across the two squared timbers over the stream. Toward the end of the pueblo where a door stayed open. A trickle of light flowed out upon two men, swathed in blankets, standing against the wall. They would stand here in cold and darkness all night on guard.

A meeting of the Council had been called.

The old men walked in slowly and sat down silently on the ledge running around three walls. Palemon wore a new red blanket and a proud, dark face. Martiniano a white bandage around his head, and a sallow face. Being young men, not members of the Council, they seated themselves close to the door. Beside two, younger still, already there.

It was a big room. Scattered on the plank floor were little wooden boxes filled with clean sand. The white-washed walls were clean and bare except for the silver-headed canes of authority of the Governor and the Lieutenant-Governor hanging below a picture of Abraham Lincoln, their donor. The vigas supporting the roof gleamed dark yellow as honey. A man dipped into the flame a branch of cedar. As it burned in his hand he walked about the room so that its sharp, clean odor filled the air.

In the middle of the room sat a deal table holding one candle stuck in a shiny black stick of Santa Clara ware. The only two chairs in the room were drawn up before it. In one sat an intelligent-looking, middle-aged man in "American" clothes save that the heels of his shoes had been removed and a blanket was wrapped round his middle. He would probably not open his mouth all evening, for while most of those present spoke Spanish and understood English, they would speak tonight only in their own tongue. But this was his usual post.

The occupant of the other chair drew it back closer to the fire. He was a seamed crag that still jutted out, unbroken, into the waves of life. There was snow in his straggly hair, moss on his face. His eyes were like those of a sun-hawk, of a mystic, of an old, old man who really couldn't focus very well on near objects. They were the most compelling things in the room. For while those of the Governor who sat behind him saw through all the passions of weather and men to the calm heart of all storms, these eyes saw farther. They saw the stormy soul of creation within the calm. They were the eyes that watched the sunsets from the highest house-top to make solar observations as the sun left its house mountain between the two peaks on the western horizon, that determined for his people the solstices and the times for ceremonial dances. He was the Cacique, holding hereditary office for life.

On the ledge behind him, on each side of the Governor, sat the Lieutenant-Governor, the War Captain, the Fiscal, and their assistants, and all the Kiva Chiefs. And about them sat the old men with faces sharp as hawks', and old and wrinkled as cedar bark, with blankets drawn up around their shoulders. Nearly forty men, all old, but of whom it was more respectfully said, "Councillors sing, they do not dance."

The door was closed. And still they sat unspeaking, hunching blankets closer. It was a terrible tension, the deathless silence, the dim light, the dark somber faces now shrouded so that only the eyes stared out black and bright as beads. It was as if they had gathered to read from symbols those meanings which were themselves symbols of a life whose substance they felt but could not see, whose edges they touched, like the shape of a door, but could not open.

The Governor broke it. He grinned a little toothlessly, and picked up a brown paper bag from the floor to slide across the table. The interpreter walked with it around the room, pausing before each man. In it was a roll of huge black tobacco leaves folded when damp and now dry and hard. Punche from the mountains of Mexico. Strong as the kick of a horse. A gift from that strange white man, Rodolfo Byers, their favorite trader for over thirty years. So each man chuckled and made a little joke as he broke off a pinch, crushed it between calloused palms, and rolled a cigarette. They sat and smoked and spit into the little wooden boxes filled with sand on the floor before them.

Now the silence, impregnated with smoke, seemed thicker, heavier. And the tension held again. As each man threw away his stub, he leaned back against the wall and drew the blanket up around his head. They might all have been settling for a sleep. Then suddenly the talk. Slow, measured, polite and wary. The Governor began it.

"Martiniano here, and these two boys. They have got themselves into trouble. They have caused trouble in the air. There will be more. There is much to consider. Is not this true? Or has my tongue betrayed me?"

Ai, ai, ai.

"Well then. Let us consider it fully and calmly. Like men. Not old women or chattering magpies. Let us move evenly together. Martiniano here and these two boys. They went into the mountains. A deer was killed. They were arrested. Now let the young men speak. Filadelphio, are you ready to empty your heart? God knows, will help us, will give us medicine."

Filadelphio spoke. Like his companion he was just twenty. With short hair, and better known by his Spanish name.

"This is what I say. It makes two days I started with Jesús here, and Martiniano whom you see also. We went up the low trail, the high trail. We crossed the stream. We entered the cañon that is long and steep and narrow. We went past the Saltillo, past the beaver dams. We came to the small mountain pastures among the aspens. We cooked our meat and our tortillas. And then it was dark. We slept."

Low and measureless his voice went on. "We got up. It was gray and cold. We had nothing left to eat. We thought, We will go back now. The cooking pots are on, the ovens full of bread. But Martiniano saw the fresh spoor of a deer. He said, 'I will just put a shell in my gun. I will just kill this deer. My wife will like fresh meat.' We started forth. Up the cañon, over the ridge. Myself on one side, behind. Jesús on one side, behind. Martiniano in the middle, ahead.

"What man does not know how a deer bounds up the slope when startled in the brush? We saw it. Martiniano shot it. It fell dead. Down to the vega we carried it. The sun was high. It was past dinner time. Two men rode up on horses. White men, Government men. They were angry. They said, 'It is past the Government time for killing deer on Government land. We arrest you. Come now and pay heavy fines.' And one man on his horse led away Jesús and me on foot.

"But Martiniano did not look up. He was busy taking out the deer's insides. He said, 'I am Indian. I am hungry. Why should I hurry for Government men?' We heard no more. We saw no more. We went to the jail. The Jéfe took our names, he looked into our faces. He said, 'There may be heavy fines. There may be none. I would have your fathers come see me.' And we came back as we were bid. And now my heart is empty. This I say."

It had taken him nearly a half-hour; and it took Jesús almost as long to confirm it. But these were the mere details of action. What was the substance of this action? Why did two young men go with Martiniano into the mountains, without food, to stay all night away from their bed? Are we not all in one nest?

Jesús tried not to look surprised. Why did one go to the mountains? What man did not go to the mountains, and if it was dark did not sleep quietly before his fire? There were the stars, the moon, the shimmer of brittle leaves. There was, if the truth be emptied from the heart, the sweet smelling sachet growing so high and which the young girls treasure. Moreover, there was this about the fresh spoor of a deer. One minute a man has no thought. The next minute he has but one thought. Has it not always been so with our people?

Jesús was very modest about these things; his voice was very low. No man reproached him with word or look. But still his heart told him that he had been too confident in his assertions and assumptions, too bold in speaking thus. And he sat down, a little too haughtily to mask his shame, and wondering what his father would say to him tomorrow.

Now Palemon spoke forth. He too was a young man and would so be regarded till he was fifty. But he had wife and children. He worked his land. He obeyed the customs. He did his ceremonial duties. And so he was old enough to empty his heart in proud humility.

"My wife was in bed. My children were in bed. I was in bed. They were asleep. But I was not asleep. So I lay awake and wondered why. I looked this way and that way, into my body, my mind, my heart. You know how it is when there is something in the air. You cannot touch it, you cannot think it, you cannot feel it. But it is there.

"I listened to the heart of my body. I listened to the heart of the mountain. And I knew that something was wrong. So I waited.

"I heard Grandfather Coyote cry. I heard him cry four times. Each time he was more angry because I would not listen to his message, because I would not answer. I went out and saddled my mare. And I listened to the heart of my body, and I listened to the heart of the mountains. And I knew I had done well.

"Grandfather Coyote no longer cried; he was no longer angry. But Grandfather Crow and his brothers were calling; they were calling, 'Pa-le-mon! Pa-le-mon!' And so I rode up to the mountain, and they stopped calling because I had come.

"I rode up the cañon, past the beaver dams, into the tall pale aspens. Above me the Night People came out clear. Morning Star Older Brother showed me the way. So I came to where the trail winds up to cross the crest of the mountains and dip down to the lake. The little blue eye of faith. The deep turquoise lake of life. I could hear the great heart of the mountain. I could hear my own heart. And they were one. So I went no farther. And there I found him. Martiniano. With his broken head. So I brought him down.

"This I say. You know how it is. The things that no words speak, but which live in all our hearts. And now my heart is empty too."

No man applauded him by word or look. They sat faces bowed, eyes downward, wrapped in blankets, swathed in silence. But this silence was pregnant with the ever-living mystery; and the tentacles of mind and heart groped through it to feel its shape and form and substance. And Palemon knew he had spoken well. He slumped modestly on his bench no longer conscious of his new red blanket.

A Council meeting is a strange thing. The fire crackles. The candle gutters. And the old men sit stolidly on their benches round the walls. When a man speaks they do not interrupt. They lower their swathed heads or half close their eyes so as not to encourage or embarrass him with a look. And when the guttural Indian voice finally stops there is silence. A silence so heavy and profound that it squashes the kernel of truth out of his words, and leaves the meaningless husks mercilessly exposed. And still no man speaks. Each waits courteously for another. And the silence grows round the walls, handed from one to another, until all the silence is one silence, and that silence has the meaning of all. So the individuals vanish. It is all one heart. It is the soul of the tribe. A soul that is linked by that other silence with all the souls of all the tribal councils which have sat here in the memory of man.

A Council meeting is one-half talk and one-half silence. The silence has more weight, more meanings, more intonations than the talk. It is angry, impatient, cheerful, but masked by calmness, patience, dignity. Thus the members move evenly together. Now it suddenly thickened. It boiled. It was the taut silence of a hunter the moment before striking.

For it was true what had happened. They had looked at this thing one way, another, before, behind. Now let them look at its center, at its heart.

Ai. Now let Martiniano put out his face and his belly before us, and so speak as to empty his heart. God knows, will help us, will give us medicine.

Martiniano began to speak. He had a cinnamon-sallow, pain-racked face, and a bloody white bandage round his head. He was not as young and Filadelphio and Jesús, or as old as Palemon. He had been to the Government away-school and wore old store clothes and shoes like the former, but hair braids and a blanket like the latter. His face and demeanor showed that he was at once of the old and the new, and that it was not the first time he had been caught between them. His voice was sullen but respectful.

"I went to the mountains and I took my rifle. I wanted to kill a deer," he stated defiantly, but with lowered face. "The Council does not give me the privileges of others since I have come back from away-school. It would not give me my turn at the thresher for my oats, my wheat. So I had to thresh them the old way, with my animals' hoofs. It took me a long, long time—what should have taken but a day. Then my friend, the good white trader, loaned me his machine—for one sack out of ten. Yet it was two days after hunting season that I finished. Should my wife be without fresh meat, a skin for boots and moccasins? Should I go without my rights for two days of white man's law? The white man's Government that took me away to school, for which you now do not give me the privileges of others? What is the difference between killing a deer on Tuesday or Thursday? Would I not have killed it anyway?"

He paused to twang at the Council the arrow of accusing silence. It missed the mark. Or perhaps the mute impenetrability of those rows of covered faces was too sturdy a shield to pierce. And completing its arc, like an arrow shot into the sky and which must fall again to earth, it turned home.

Martiniano resumed. "This I told the Government man who remained with me as you have heard. I did not have to look up to hear his angry voice, to feel the hate steaming from his body. 'You dirty Indian, who kills deer out of season in the Government's National Forest!' he cried. 'I am going to ride up to that old mine for rope to tie you up. Try to run away and I will shoot you like a dog!'

"As he went away I laid back the flap of the skin, I cut off a piece of my deer. I had no fear; I had hunger. I had not eaten since the day before. While it cooked over the coals I hid my deer in the bushes. But before I could eat it, he came back. The rope was on his saddle horn, the rifle raised to my breast. He smelled the meat. His face was red with anger.

"I turned over the meat. What Indian makes a foolish move before an angry white man's gun? I but raised my hands to wipe off my fingers on my hair.

"At that moment he struck. With the iron of his gun. Across my head. I woke up. My head was cracked open. Blood ran down my face. He had taken my knife. My hands were tied behind my back. When he kicked me, I tried to stand up. He lifted me like a sack of meal to the rump of his horse. We started off. I could not sit up, but fell upon his back. Blood ran down his shirt. This made him very angry. He put me in front. Still I bled and kept falling, save for his hand upon my collar.

"Now my thoughts returned. I said, 'There is a thing I must do, which every man does, behind a bush. You understand it is this hurt which makes my kidneys weak.'

"He stopped the horse. I fell off and stood up. 'Pardon,' I said, 'but my hands are tied behind my back.'

" 'Oh no you don't!' he said, and with his rifle butt he swept open the front of my trousers. See? How he tore off the buttons?"

His eyes hard as black obsidian, Martiniano stood there,

one leg forward, showing the gaping flap of his blood-stained trousers. No one looked. They saw it in his voice.

"If he had done more than this," Martiniano stated quietly, "there would be more for this venerated Council to consider. I would have killed him.

"But now"—a shade on the apologetic side to balance his unseemly show of passion—"I went noisily into the bushes. Then I quietly waded upstream against the noise of the falls. I hid in water, deep between the logs of a beaver dam. I heard him call. I saw him plunging through the bushes to find me. Suddenly he rode off. Quickly. In a gallop. Fear pursued him. He had forgotten me, my rifle, my deer.

"For a long time I cut at my rope on the sharp rocks. I was too weak to walk when my hands were free. I crawled back up the trail. I was weak, but the thought of the strength of my deer meat made me vomit. I knew I was sick. Too sick to make a fire. So I lay down beside the stream.

"I slept sleep, and I slept a sleep that was not a sleep. I thought many thoughts, but there are no words for my thoughts. And strangely, when Morning Star rose, though I was cold and weak and ill, I felt good. I felt good because I knew help would come. It came. It was Palemon.

"This I say, with my face and my belly put out before you. And now my heart is empty."

Had they all fallen asleep—these rows of old men slumped against the walls, the whitewash rubbing off on their blankets, head down or arm upraised to shut out the last sputtering pulgado of candle? If so, they continued dozing. Only the Cacique sat upright in his chair, a rock jutting into the waves of sleep. Somebody threw another piñon knot on the fire. Somebody spat noisily into one of the little sand boxes. One of the sentinels opened the door and stood inside to get warm. When he went out, the two boys, Filadelphio and Jesús, followed him.

Well, here were the facts thrust down the maw of silence. You could hear them being digested. They fitted into the responsibilities of the Governor and Lieutenant-Governor of the pueblo, the "Outside Chief"—the War Captain, the Chiefs of the Kivas, all the officers, all the Council. And so one after another, with proper pause, the guttural Indian voices began to speak.

Let us move evenly together, brothers.

A young man went into the mountains. He killed a deer out

of season. He got arrested, and a knock on the head to boot. He will have to pay a fine, doubtless, for disobeying those Government laws we have sworn to uphold with our canes of office. A simple matter.

But wait. Was it so simple?

This young man was an Indian, born in our pueblo, belonging to our tribe. Or was he, properly speaking? There was the definition of an Indian by the Government—so much Indian blood, land ownership, all that. But there was the definition of an Indian by the Council according to his conformance to custom, tradition, his participation in ceremonials. Now this young man has been lax, very lax; we have warned him. He has disobeyed us; we have punished him. And now he has disobeyed the laws of the Government outside, likewise. What have we to do with this, that we should interfere?

Now there is this. There are good Indians among us, and there are those who look under their eyes. But we are all in one nest. No Indian is an individual. He is a piece of the pueblo, the tribe. Is it proper to consider that we have done wrong against the Government, our white father, betrayed our canes of office?

Yet there was this to consider. All this land was ours—the mountain, the valleys, the desert. Indian land. We have the papers to it from the Spanish King. The Mexicans came, the white people—the gringos. They built themselves a town on our land, Indian land. We got nothing for it. Now when the Spanish King opened his hand, Our Father at Washington closed his own hand upon the land. He told us, "You will be paid for it. The day will come with compensation." What did we want with money? We wanted land, our land, Indian land. But mostly we wanted the mountains. We wanted the mountains, our mother, between whose breasts lies the little blue eye of faith. The deep turquoise lake of life. Our lake, our church. Where we make our pilgrimages, hold our ceremonials . . . Now what is this? We have waited. The day of compensation has not come. The mountains are Government forests. Not ours. The Mexicans pasture their sheep and goats upon the slopes. Turistas scatter paper bags unseemly upon the ground. They throw old fish bait into our sacred lake. Government men, these rangers, ride through it at will. Is any man safe? Look at this one's broken head. Will our ceremonials long be inviolate from foreign eyes? Now then, is it we who are injured and must seek reparation, demand our rights, our mountains? This is what I say. God knows, will help us, will give us strength.

The voices kept creeping around the room . . .

In the Government office two hundred miles away there is that Indian lawyer, our mouth in many matters. There is the judge in town, a short walk. Are we to turn this young man alone over to the judge? Or are we to call this Indian lawyer? And what are we to tell him? We must move evenly together. We must be one mind, one heart, one body.

Silence spoke, and it spoke the loudest of all.

*There is no such thing as a simple thing. One drops a pebble into a pool, but the ripples travel far. One picks up a little stone in the mountains, one of the little stones called Lagrimas de Cristo—and look! It is shaped like a star; the sloping mountain is full of stars as the sloping sky. Or take a kernel of corn. Plant it in Our Mother Earth with the sweat of your body, with what you know of the times and seasons, with your proper prayers. And with your strength and manhood Our Father Sun multiplies and gives it back into your flesh. What then is this kernel of corn? It is not a simple thing.*

*Nothing is simple and alone. We are not separate and alone. The breathing mountains, the living stones, each blade of grass, the clouds, the rain, each star, the beasts, the birds and the invisible spirits of the air—we are all one, indivisible. Nothing that any of us does but affects us all.*

*So I would have you look upon this thing not as a separate simple thing, but as a stone which is a star in the firmament of earth, as a ripple in a pool, as a kernel of corn. I would have you consider how it fits into the pattern of the whole. How far its influence may spread. What it may grow into . . .*

*So there is something else to consider. The deer. It is dead. In the old days we all remember, we did not go out on a hunt lightly. We said to the deer we were going to kill, "We know your life is as precious as ours. We know that we are both children of the same Great True Ones. We know that we are all one life on the same Mother Earth, beneath the same plains of the sky. But we also know that one life must sometimes give way to another so that the one great life of all may continue unbroken. So we ask your permission, we obtain your consent to this killing."*

*Ceremonially we said this, and we sprinkled meal and corn pollen to Our Father Sun. And when we killed the deer we laid his head toward the East, and sprinkled him with meal and pollen. And we dropped drops of his blood and bits of his flesh on the ground for Our Mother Earth. It was proper so. For then when we too built its flesh into our flesh, when we walked in the moccasins of its skin, when we danced in its robe and antlers, we knew that the life of the deer was continued in our life, as it in turn was continued in the one life all around us, below us and above us.*

*We knew the deer knew this and was satisfied.*

*But this deer's permission was not obtained. What have we done to this deer, our brother? What have we done to ourselves? For we are all bound together, and our touch upon one travels through all to return to us again. Let us not forget the deer.*

The old Cacique spoke. It was true that the young men nowadays did not observe such proper steps. And it was true that the game was becoming scarce because of it. Was it true that next the water would fail them, the air become dull and tasteless, the life go out of the land?

"So I would have you consider whether it is not time to be more strict with our young men so corrupted with evil modern ways, lest we ourselves dwindle and vanish entirely. This I say," he ended. "Dios knows, will help us, will give us medicine."

Here they were then, all these things and shadows of things ensnared like flies in the web of silence. They fluttered their wings. They shook and distorted the whole vast web. But they did not break free. For it was the web which binds us each to the other, and all to the life of which we are an inseparable part—binds us to the invisible shapes that have gone and those to come, in the solidarity of one flowing whole.

So the night grew thin as the thinnest gray blanket around the walls. The embers heaped upon growing gray ashes. The little wooden sand boxes filled with cigarette stubs. The two sentinels came in a last time for warmth. In with them stalked daylight.

And now the old men rose and stretched their stiff, bent limbs. They gathered their blankets about their dark faces and bent shoulders. They hobbled out across the plaza in the dawn-dusk.

The meeting of the Council was over. They were one body, one mind, one heart. They moved evenly together.

## 2

Two mornings later when the sun was high a few Indians began to straggle out of the pueblo. A blanketed old man hobbling along with a stick between the wild plum hedges. Boys kicking by on small, quick-stepping burros. An old springless wagon with a boneless woman wrapped up in a turquoise shawl and shaking on the plank seat, and a man standing upright to the reins, his long hair braids wrapped in pink ribbon hanging down his back. A lone dark horseman jogging past a group of women waddling spread-legged in snowy boots and flowered shawls. All small blotches of color against the gray-green sage and the stainless blue mountains. And all bobbing slowly along in the narrow river of dust curving out of the reservation to the village below.

Its corona of mud huts appeared, thick-walled, flat-topped adobes squatting along ditch and arroyo. Shreds of yellow straw and flecks of mica in the adobe reflected the bright sunlight. The walls shimmered, and the shimmer seemed a shake. As if the sturdy walls were continually trembling from a volcanic stirring deep below, under the pulsing mountain. And the shimmer showed deep in the bright black eyes of their Mexican inhabitants. The scrawny little women in rusty black rebozos splitting wood in bare feet, and forever smearing more mud upon the rain-washed walls. And the squat muscular men in blue denim trousers sauntering out to loaf in the village plaza, their heavy inert bodies sullenly acclimated, curiously resilient, to the faint illusive shake and throb of the earth below.

Now a little square plaza lined with hitching racks and dusty Fords, rows of American stores, Mexican markets and Indian trading posts: La Oreja. It shimmered on the shelf midway between desert and mountain, in the center of that sage-brush triangle whose points were the pueblo above, the deep river gorge below, and the gunsight pass beyond which lay the railroad junction. To which of these points was attuned the unknown ear for which the town was named no one knew. The far-off whistle of the daily train blew faintly through the pass. The Rio Bravo roared through the gorge. But the Ear—people, plaza and town itself—seemed perpetually turned toward the soft indented breast lifted above the body of the Reservation. The high-keyed vibrant quality of the air, the shimmering illusion of shaking walls, the epileptic tension in the bright black eyes, and the sullen impacted flesh—all these seemed curiously attuned to the deep, soundless, pulse-beat of the mountain. This is Indian land, it all seemed to say, and the quality of its life penetrates the life of all.

Even on court day, at ten o'clock, when the courthouse doors were opened and the bell rang lazily over the flat-topped roofs. There was nothing of note on the docket; some Indian or other had shot a deer and got himself arrested. But slowly the big room filled. A nucleus of hard old-timers spitting tobacco juice in the aisles; some commercial whites in town—storekeepers and a rancher; a resident artist caught in the illusive folly of trying to ensnare in paint the vibrant quality of the air; groups of Mexicans straggled in from the bars; and a row of blanketed Indians.

A hammer rapped loudly; Court came to order.

Martiniano, the Indian sitting down front with a white bandage round his head, was accused of shooting a deer out of season and resisting arrest. Three rangers testified against him. Their superior summed up the charges. He was a Mexican dressed in high, polished riding boots, pressed whipcord trousers and a flannel uniform shirt. One of the descendants of an old aristocratic Spanish family. a shrewd local politician and a mechanically efficient Government employee, he reflected in his arrogant face and precise speech these qualities so clearly that no others seemed left. He was Teodor Sanchez, Chief of the U. S. Forestry Service of the district. His words packed weight.

"Spanish-Americans, Anglo-Americans, Indians: they're all the same to my boys if they break the laws. We have only the National Forest Reserve at heart for the good of all. We patrol the forest against fire. We watch the water shed and streams. As deputized game-wardens we protect the fish, fowl and game. We're sorry about that clip on the head, but the accused reached for a knife."

There was some talk about his attack and escape. Martiniano, the Indian, upon questioning, stood up and rather dully refuted the charge with a long explanation. The row of blanketed old men remained sitting there impersonal, silent and fixed. Nor were there any witnesses to be called to help him. The district Indian Superintendent rose. His talk was hazy with generalities, sprinkled with references to "the children of nature in my charge" and "the Government's wards." When he finished, a short pallid Anglo beside him spoke up crisply.

"We plead guilty, your Honor, and ask for the clemency of the Court."

The Judge nodded respectfully. The speaker was Mr. Emil Strophy, legal counsel from the district Indian Service office.

The Judge glanced round the room. It was clear that the accused was left high and dry by his people and their legal counsel—who had, in fact, delivered him to justice. It was not so clear that he had attacked his arresting officer with intent to kill. Did Señor Sanchez wish to waive the charge of attempted manslaughter?

Sanchez hummed and hawed with his rangers. Resisting arrest by Government officers, he said, was a precedent he could not allow to be set, consistent with his position of representing the United States Government. Still, he realized that the Indian Superintendent in charge of this district was also a Government representative. If in the Court's judgment . . .

The Judge terminated his indecision with a blow from his hammer. Martiniano, Indian, had been duly adjudged guilty of killing a deer out of season on the Forest Reserve, and of resisting arrest. He was sentenced to three months' confinement in jail, with the alternative of paying a fine of one hundred and fifty dollars.

The hearing was over. It had been very dull. The court room began to empty of whites going back to their stores and bars, and the Mexicans to sit in the sunny plaza. The accused still sat huddled miserably in his blanket, staring stoically at the wall. He was aroused by a sudden call. He turned his head.

In the corner talking with the Judge and the clerk stood

an odd squat man wearing a dirty buckskin jacket, sloppy corduroy trousers and a battered Stetson hat—the strange white man, the Indian trader, Rodolfo Byers. His face was red and angry.

Again the Judge called. Martiniano rose and walked forward. The trader had stopped talking when he reached the table. Without looking at him, the trader turned and walked swiftly out of the room.

Martiniano waited silently. Perhaps the policemen were coming now, already, to take him to jail before he could see his wife. Instead, the Judge spoke kindly.

"The trader has paid your fine, Martiniano. He says he has you on his books for three months' staple groceries already. Now you owe him one hundred and fifty dollars more—and me the promise that you will get into no more trouble. You will pay?" Martiniano assented and slowly walked out the door. It was very beautiful this fall. The cottonwoods beyond the plaza were clouds of butter yellow. Groves of high aspens splotched the mountains like huge marigolds among the pines. He was free as an eagle hanging in the turquoise sky. Martiniano adjusted the bandage around his head. He felt very good about this, about his friend the strange white trader. There was ten cents in his pocket. He thought it would be a fine thing to take a little bag of ginger-snaps, those little hard cookies, home to his wife.

The court room had emptied of spectators; Judge and clerk had retired. But still three men sat talking around the little table up front.

"Well, I guess that fixes us up!" said Sanchez, flicking dust off his boots. "I appreciate your letting the local court handle this as a mere routine case, Mr. Strophy. That's the way we look at it. Maintaining the law impartially for your people, my people, and yours." He nodded cheerfully at each of his companions.

Strophy looked up through his spectacles, then bent down to some papers he had taken out of his ever-present briefcase—his perpetual gesture.

The third man at the table came from a family so much older than the first, and was so much more conversant with the aspects of the case than the second, that he had no need for either appearances or papers. Dressed in a soiled pink shirt and old trousers, with a cotton blanket wrapped round his waist, he sat quietly relaxed, stroking his long hair braids.

"Now, Governor," said Sanchez, rising, "my boys don't hold any grudge. They just did their duty. I hope your people forget this too. But just remember, all those mountains belong to the Government now. You can't kill deer up there all the time like you used to."

The old man's dark and wrinkled face remained a rusty iron mask of impassive nobility. The naked eyes under his plucked eyebrows seemed closed by invisible shutters.

Sanchez hesitated. He had the feeling that this matter was not yet closed. Abruptly he shook hands and stalked out peevishly as though silently dismissed.

The two remained at the table. The Governor sitting silently with his hands in his lap, and Strophy noisily stuffing papers in his briefcase. His frown grew deeper. The devil take it! Just when things had settled down, this old controversy had popped up again.

"Now look here!" he said petulantly. "Why don't you forget this thing? This young man at the pueblo did wrong and you brought him in to be punished as was proper. That was a good thing; the Superintendent and myself are very proud of you. It is also a good thing the trader paid his fine, so now he can repay it without suffering. Let us forget this thing. Why should we cause trouble to the Government? Hasn't it given you a hospital, school, a new ditch so you can have water for your fields, a threshing machine?"

The old man answered patiently. "They schools, but mebbe soon no children. They hospital, but mebbe soon people they dead, no sick. They new acequia and máquina, but mebbe soon earth she die too. This Dawn Lake our church. From it come all the good things we get. The mountains our land, Indian land. The Government promised. We no forget. This we say."

His voice was the gentlest of all, but it was the one which carried the tone of finality. Strophy too felt dismissed.

"Well, I shall write a paper. To Washington. It is all I can promise." He rose, still frowning, locked his briefcase and left.

There was an odd coincidence here, as the Governor watched him hurry across the plaza to catch a stage. The Spaniards came, conquered and left. The whites came and conquered, and now Strophy had gone. But the old Indian still remained in the portals of an empty hall of justice.

He stood in the doorway scratching his dirty pink shirt. The old man was in no hurry. What was there ever to hurry about? Only the evanescent passions of men gave way to others.

The white man, the trader, walked slowly home through the fading afternoon. "What the Hell!" he always said. "I like to travel on feet, not wheels. If I ain't got a horse's, I got my own!"

There was a road. The scaly snake which crawled along the edge of the Reservation, wriggled through the sage brush beyond, and, spanning the river gorge, slid out into the desert. But no. He liked the rutty wagon tracks branching away to the pueblo. And he trudged along in the straggle of homeward bound Indians.

Three fat squaws in cerise, yellow and turquoise shawls, and waddling bow-legged in snowy buckskin boots. Two men on horseback, swathed in thin cotton blankets. The old grandfather, Indian Hat, past ninety, who hobbled with his stick the three miles and back daily lest his legs knot up in cramps. And down ahead two boys whacking a burro loaded with firewood.

Yes! The wide, open earth. The wide, open sky tinged green as sage, blue as cedar smoke. And the calm slow figures and dark somber faces which bridged both. This was the life he liked around him.

At a stream a mile ahead, he turned off upon a narrow trail. The wild plum thickets gave way to grassy vegas, tawny pastures, brittle corn fields. All tinged at twilight a light fawn-pink. So diagonally he reached his post, just back from the road he had first ignored, and on the edge of Indian land.

It was a low, sprawling adobe with a long portal in front and a few Indian women still squatting on the flagstones. Long braided strings of colored Indian corn half-eaten by birds hung down the carved, weathered posts. The windows were stripped with iron bars, the best protection against washing. He opened the door, peeked inside.

Into the enormous, shadowy room holding long glass cases of turquoise, coral and coin-silver jewelry; at the stacks of rugs, the beautiful old serapes and pelts covering floor and walls; the shelves of pottery; the limp yellow buckskins, buffalo robes, fox pelts, ceremonial sashes; the beaded moccasins and deerskin boots of a dozen tribes; the feathered war-bonnets, buckskin shirts and vests embroidered with colored porcupine quills, the old fringed leggings; at old Mexican Santos and Bultos, carved chests, and silver bridles; at oil paintings and water-colors, and Indian drawings—into that musty, dusky room which held with its symbols of America's vanishing past nearly forty years of his own life.

A group of Indian women were still pawing a glass case with greasy fingers, and keeping his wife from preparing supper.

"Angelina!" he shouted irascibly. "Tell 'em to come back in the morning. We don't work all night!"

He let the door slam, and leaned against a portal post staring fixedly at the crimson flushing the far western peaks.

When he was about ten years old, he had had something like a dream. He knew that he was lying in bed, able to move legs and arms, and feel the wooly blankets. But he was more conscious of, more part of the dream which closed about him. He saw himself clambering stiffly out of a rude, flat-bottomed boat, and climbing a narrow trail to the top of a sandy bluff. The desolate grassy plains spread out below him on all sides, cut only by the slow-curving, muddy red river, and dotted miles away by small dark clumps as of scrub cedar—a herd of browsing buffalo. Before him on the hill-top was a single rude adobe hut. And in it, as he entered, stood a single man behind a wooden counter on the right.

He was like no one the boy had ever seen before, middle-aged, rather squat and ungainly with wide shoulders and long powerful arms. On his massive head sat a peculiar, round fur cap. He was dressed in a tattered, greasy buck-skin jacket, limp as chamois, cloth trousers, and a colored sash round his waist.

He was neither German as his blue eyes and sturdy build; French as his little voyageur's fur cap; Spanish as the sash around his waist; nor American as his buckskin. He was a little of all. A man who in this immense solitude was something of all men, and of the wilderness around him. He stood there lazily making unintelligible entries in an old ledger.

There was no language in which the boy could speak to him. There was no need to speak. He felt that he had come here to keep an appointment so ineluctable that its necessity and purpose were known to both. He sensed too that this man was aware of every thought in his mind; that he himself knew every fiber of this man's being, though unable to fathom the strange pattern they formed.

So he stood there at home, at ease, in the little post lost and alone in the wilderness of a continent. Suddenly the man scribbled out a single word and held the paper up before him. And there flashed into the boy's mind this strange conviction: "This word I have never seen, but I must remember it always, for it is a symbol of my being whose memory I must carry with me always as a talisman."

He smiled back at the man's gentle, toothy smile. And suddenly it was all gone; the word itself was lost. He was lying in bed, conscious of the texture of the wooly blankets. But the slow red river curving into the sunset, the illimitable grassy plains and little adobe hut on the bluff, and the appearance of the man within remained in his memory timeless and unchanged.

It had been years since he had recalled it; he did not now. And as he stood there leaning against the portal post nearly fifty years later, it never occurred to him that his outlandish appearance was that of the strange man in his dream.

This was the white man, the Indian trader, Rodolfo Byers.

He had picked up somewhere what might have been the same buckskin jacket, adding to its soft whiteness his own wear and grime. He wore underneath it a rumpled shirt no necktie could ever set straight on, sloppy khaki or corduroy trousers, and a battered beaver hat. But in winter he pulled forth from a cowhide trunk a round fur cap, shaking out the moths. When he stalked round the pueblo in the snow drifts to watch the dances, he sported an overcoat. No one knew if it fit; he wore it like a blanket.

He had lost a few teeth, but when he smiled there still seemed too many. His blue eyes were cold and sharp. Yet sometimes they took on a dreamy vacuousness—as if deep in his subconsciousness he was still seeking the symbol of his being, that talisman he had lost, the word long forgotten in a dream.

No one saw these rare moments. Few in town liked him; he was a piece of life they did not understand. He had lived so long among Indians that for whites he took on their subtle elusiveness. But knowing them so well, he punctured their own with the analytical mind of the white. Mexicans feared his sharpness in buying, as whites feared his bluntness in selling. Indians cautiously respected both.

Rodolfo Byers was simply a character. Among three races the stories about him kept spreading.

Someone once offering to buy his trading post asked him what it was worth.

"Oh, five thousand dollars gold," he replied carelessly.

The man returned with money and papers. Byers read them through carefully, pushed them back unsigned.

"What's the matter? You said you'd sell for five thousand!"

"I will. But I got to have fifty thousand more for the view," Byers said drily. "You didn't ask about that."

The post was a mile or more from town, fronting road and desert. The few acres behind, his own garden vegetables, corn and squash, terminated in a long thicket of impenetrable wild plum trees. It was the boundary of Indian land which sloped gently, mile after mile, into sage, piñon and scrub cedar, and finally into the high pine mountains. Like him, it was a link connecting two natures, two lives; and he loved to look behind as well as around and before him.

A few years back he had married a gentle young Spanish-American who looked like his daughter: Angelina. Between them they had another. Byers named the girl baby Chipeta after the squaw of his favorite Ute Chief, and dressed her in tiny moccasins and buckskin like a doll. Angelina grew plumper, darker. She too dressed in wine, sky blue or dark green velveteen blouses with silver buttons and concho belt, Navajo fashion, long full skirts and Pawnee beaded moccasins.

So little by little the rambling adobe post grew from a small store and a sleeping room in back. It was shop, rug room, storeroom, studio and ample living quarters; and behind were tool shop, barn and corrals. As he made and carved the posts of his bridal bed and Chipeta's cradle, so for each successive room he square-hewed his own vigas and carved the doors. In the tierra-blanca which washed the adobe walls he mixed red or blue clay to faintly tinge the glaring white. Not the best Mexican woman in the valley was allowed to help him construct and shape the fireplaces in every room.

His picture gallery was screened off by a blanket at one end to conceal his own easel and paints. He rarely got around to using them; he was practical and shrewd enough to know that it merely developed his eye for the values of the best work offered him by others.

His books of ethnology, anthropology, Indian culture and history, were voluminous and well thumbed—and he was contemptuous of them all. He merely liked to observe in them the mistakes of others to confirm his own wider knowledge.

Yet of all these nothing mattered. It was the substance of life he loved, not form. And something of its elusive mystery forever held him enchanted.

So gradually he had given up to Angelina the tending of his post on all ordinary matters. To Concha, a scrawny Mexican girl, the kitchen and all chores. To any Indian the care of his few acres.

"He has time for all his puttering about," complained visitors and townspeople who never found him available. "He never does any work!"

It was true; Byers, one could say, was a little lazy. But steadily he grew more successful. For as he grew more irascible and sarcastic to friends, more stonily impassive to strangers, and drove tourists away to buy cheap geegaws elsewhere, his peculiar reputation increased.

Even Angelina sometimes dared to look at him bewildered. As now, when he leaned against the post watching the sun set—this strange white man, the trader!

Timidly she knocked on the window and beckoned him in to supper.

Byers heaved away from the post and walked round to the back, leaving Angelina to lock the front door with an iron key nearly a foot long—another of his foibles, this old Spanish lock.

Concha had fed Chipeta her milk and mush and put the child to bed. She was surly because an Indian woman had been called in to help cook up wild plums and chokecherries for butter and jam: a fat squaw still bent over a great kettle on the roaring wood-stove. Buffalo-Old-Woman had been there all day. The kitchen was an oven. Every pot and pan was dirty. When Byers entered, Concha was standing, hand on hip, scowling at the mess.

Immediately he kicked back the stove-draft. "All you do here is try and see how much wood you can burn!" he stormed at the squaw. "Nice little logs all split up just so and stacked outside big as a mountain! Yes, burn it all up, by God! But when you have to chop and carry your own a mile home, you do just as well with two sticks!"

A thin bitter smile slashed the Mexican girl's face. Instantly it was healed over by the sullen frown as she saw Buffalo-Old-Woman's two hundred pounds shaking with silent laughter. Angelina quietly yanked Byers by the coattail down into his chair at the kitchen table, and motioned sharply to the others.

The food was good and plentiful; Concha was silent, and Buffalo-Old-Woman's face beamed cheerfully as a full moon; Angelina was tactful. Byers relaxed and ate heartily. Broad-shouldered and sturdy, with a deeply tanned face darkened by a black stubble of beard, he had a nature sensitive as a delicate scale. Now, having compensated for what he regarded as a sentimental weakness in doing an unpremeditated good turn, by a furious tongue-lashing of a faithful old friend and helper, he felt again in balance.

Finishing supper and lighting a cigarette, he escaped with Angelina into the big living room leaving Concha and Buffalo-Old-Woman to clean up. He stretched out on a rug before the glowing fireplace and stared up at his wife.

"By God!" he said affably. "If that old girl's hips get any wider there won't be any room for her in the kitchen!"

Angelina giggled like a girl. Then fully mature, she answered quietly, "Yes. Two months ago I thought of course—"

"Sure. Of course!"

"Well, last month I asked her, she was getting so huge. You know how her big face breaks open in a grin, and how she sucks in her breath when she's surprised. Well, she just had no idea she was getting any bigger. No; she hadn't noticed any signs. And still today she hadn't felt anything. Why, you'd have thought she'd never had a baby before! Aren't they funny? Just secretiveness in front of inquisitive strangers, I suppose."

"The devil take her! You know what'll happen as well as I do. Any one of these days—and damned if it couldn't be tomorrow from the way she looks!—she'll lie down with a belly ache. And ten minutes later out she'll come grinning. 'Look what has happened! A baby! Imagine! There is another baby!' No! They just don't know any more than trees know why they sprout blossoms in spring and apples in the fall!"

Angelina, back to the fireplace, let down the skirts she had hoisted and strolled back to the kitchen. Byers continued his thought. It was extravagant perhaps, but not wholly exaggerated. Indians, the older ones anyway, didn't reason from the act of procreation to the birth of child, from cause to effect. Things just happened. There was something monstrous and frightening about this as an attitude of complacent servility to fate. There was also about it a magnificent and courageous affirmation of faith in the instinctive movements of nature to which they confided themselves.

Often during his lonely life he had cursed the chance which had made him an Indian trader. No man knew better these people who had drained his youth, shaped his life and thought, and stamped on him forever their racial traits. He knew their surface indolence and cunning, their dirt and filth and lice, their secretiveness, barbarity, ignorance and stubborn denial of change. And so no man could better refute the sickly sentimentalism of lady tourists, the pampering enthusiasm of museum collectors, the false idealism of escapists and the mock gravity of anthropologists, ethnologists and myth mongers toward them—all the whining, shouting voices that proclaimed the Indian as nature's pet, a darling of the gods, and the only true American. Sometimes he damned them all to hell, swore that he would close up his post and go off to live, in white collars and shined shoes, the life of "a respectable white man."

What held him he never knew, but it was always there. In the look of an eye, in a curious phrase, in the beat of a drum—in a thousand irrelevant incidents that slowly built up into a whole he could not see, but which he felt existed.

Something that welled up from the unplumbed recesses of their deeper beings, overflowing the crude crust of their lives, permeating them with a wonderful, indescribable, living awareness. Something that could never be put into words, even by an Indian. He kept his medicine inviolate from knowledge.

That, he decided, rolling closer to the fire, was the damned catch when you tried to think intelligently about Indians.

They couldn't be thought about intelligently. They had to be either dismissed or taken on their own ground. And their premises of life were based not on the rational, the reasoning, evaluating approach, but wholly on the instinctive and intuitive. Things came or they didn't; they didn't proceed logically from point to point. So you had to take them or leave them as they were in fact, not theory.

Byers scowled as he sat up and rolled a cigarette. Whatever he thought came back to the incident of the afternoon, that poor devil arrested for killing a deer. That Martiniano who had got himself in Dutch again with the Council. On the surface it was a simple matter. But nothing Indian was as simple as it looked on the surface.

Byers had heard of the matter at the pueblo. He had talked casually to one of the old men. Then by chance and even more casually he had mentioned it to Palemon whom he had long carried on his books. The man's free and easy acknowledgment without explanation was what still engrossed Byers.

The simple and ignored fact of how Palemon had known intuitively of trouble, and had gone without question or delay directly to Martiniano's aid.

It seemed at once the very core of the life and the wonder and the mystery which had ever held him.

# 3

EDGELESS and phantasmal, like figures seen in deep water, they glided into the ebb of twilight—all these dark shrouded women stepping out of low doorways, shuffling spread-legged across the plaza, past church and corrals, up along the low crumbling wall to the Campo de Santo. Heads down, unspeaking, with secrets bulging under their shawls, they filed like watery ghosts from the living mystery of one tomb to the everlasting mystery of another. It was the quality of all places Indian: the furtive, slow-pulsed life that flows, as if submerged, between deep caverns.

For as the miasmic blue mist of dusk seeped down the mountainside and rose between the pueblo walls, it all took on the dark, deep blueness of an ancient town long sunk under sea. Lines of cedar smoke undulated gently as seaweeds growing out of chimneys. Doors slowly opened and shut as if swinging on a current. And the women too seemed breasting a watery blue. A pale fish-shape floated past with gaping mouth—the protruding head of a white burro trotting along on the other side of the wall. A garden of kelp stung with phosphorescent glows appeared: the weedy graveyard.

The women kneeled down, lighted more candles, and from under their shawls took out wafer bread, loaves of long-bread, corn meal baked in corn husks, pans of panocha, even a cheap store sponge-cake to place on the sunken graves.

It was el Dia de los Muertos, and they had come with offerings for the dead.

*They who lie here were as alive as we who have not forgotten. We too will lie here and will not be forgotten. Are we all alive, or all dead, in this unceasing file from one mystery to another, through this watery blue veil of November dusk? Let no man say. Let him say only: I am the seed of the husk that lies here, my Corn Mother; and I am the seed of those husks which will follow after me; and this meal I now place here is the bond between us all; and may our Earth Mother, our Corn Mother, attest I have not forgotten . . .*

Planting her last feathers and drawing her shawl close, a young woman trudged back to the little adobe hut outside the pueblo walls. Martiniano was waiting supper.

"You did so—according to custom?" he asked quietly.

"According to the custom, as you said. There were many there," answered Flowers Playing.

"Look! I have cut off a piece of our deer. The corn is already roasting beside the coals it will cook on."

"And I brought back some of that bread. Because there were others who did also. Fiesta! We shall have fiesta!" Her face lighted up with a smile.

There were two rooms in the small hut, a scrubby little kitchen with an iron cook-stove, and a bigger room beyond. Here they ate on the dirt floor before the fireplace, on a thick Navajo rug.

Martiniano watched his wife munching corn. How nimble her long fingers with the hot ear! How beautiful she was, even in her dirty gingham dress! "Here!" She held up in her fingers a piece of venison dripping fat. "Catch these drops on your corn. It is sweet. It has the taste of the mountains. There is nothing better!"

"There is little left of our deer. We will save the rest," she added quietly.

It was true. There was the haunch given to Palemon; the friends and relatives coming for a piece, stroking the deer and saying "Thank you"; the old people with chest sickness coming to ask for blood to warm and drink.

"It is strange. They did not ask for my deer, there at the Court, there at the Council. Perhaps the Court forgot—though they made me pay a hundred and fifty dollars for it! But not the Council . . . I have thought about this."

Flowers Playing was a good woman; she kept silent.

"I should have kept those insides," continued Martiniano. "Scraped clean and dried they would have made good sinew, good thread for your moccasins . . . But before you make them, be sure to bury the bones and the hair in the big ash pile; it is the custom. But it was a long way home. I expected to walk with it on my back, as you know . . . Then too," he continued as if to himself, "perhaps if I had brought it home whole I could have left it lying overnight, head to the east, with prayer-feathers on it according to custom."

"You do not worry? Palemon is a good man, he obeys all the old ways. He was glad to get the meat."

"That is true. What is, is! It is behind me . . . But, you know, I have been thinking about that deer. It strays into my dreams like a gentle doe into a moonlit glade. It bounds into my thoughts like a rutting buck breaking from the thickets . . . Maybe it is this Day of the Dead, of my father's spirit, the spirits of my father's fathers and all those that surrounded them, which made me think of the dead, of all dead."

He sat moodily staring into the coals, drawing frugally on his cigarette stub, while Flowers Playing emptied the coffee grounds to use with fresh in the morning, stacked the few dishes in the kitchen. The sound of her washing in the tin basin behind in the corner aroused him. He listened to her undressing, to the rustle of blankets as she turned down the bed.

In a cheap muslin nightdress she came and sat beside him. Through it the flamelight outlined her long, ripe body. He pulled her back to lean against him, slowly drew aside the clinging cloth, gently stroking her bare body. How warm and soft it was. The color of October oak leaves in the afternoon sun.

"The root of that mountain plant with yellow berries, boiled and drunk at the menstrual period as a contraceptive—has no woman falsely induced you to use it?" he asked.

She leaned back her head, kissed him, stared into his with dark, shining eyes. "Well do you know I could not so betray the truth between us," she answered lowly. "It is late, but it will come. Are we not one, complete in faith?"

Again she murmured. "Of child-grass I have learned. It looks like asparagus, and has a small red bloom. To chew it aids conception. That is what they say."

"It springs up after rain," answered Martiniano. "Now it is too late."

"It will come—it will come," she answered confidently. "Are you afraid that in one year my desire, my passion, my body, has lost its life?" She laughed, low and deep; the laugh of a loved woman who loves.

After a time she rose, shook down the loose, wrinkled muslin, and got into the hand-made wooden bed piled with blankets.

"I will just sit here awhile and mend my old harness," said Martiniano. "Then it will be all ready by morning."

He was part Apache—those tall broad-shouldered men with great, black, high-crowned Stetsons who came from their western range to gorge mutton at ceremonial time. Only the wildness showed sometimes in his eyes, but their indomitable stubbornness was bred into his spirit.

This wary freshness implanted in his gentle Pueblo strain had made him a very sharp boy. Smart, said the Government agent who had picked him out for away-school.

Martiniano did not want to go. His father did not want him to go, nor the Chief of the Kiva he was soon to enter for the long initiation period. The Council did not want him, or any of the boys, to be taken away.

But there was a "kwota" to fill—something for which the Great Father at Washington had to have smart boys from among all his obedient red children. The Council agreed. So did Martiniano's father, under the threat of a public whipping. The boy left with a little buckskin bag, fringed, beaded, and tinkling with tiny bells.

Six years later he returned with a paper suitcase full of American clothes, the craft of carpentry and eighty dollars he had earned by it. He seemed at first the great gainer by this exchange. Later he began to wonder if he hadn't lost more.

His mother had long been dead. His father had died while he was away. There was little sleeping room for him in the crowded pueblo quarters of his many "Uncles," none whose hospitality and authority he cared to accept. The stuffy rooms, the patches of cracked linoleum and the few cracked cups and saucers of which they were so proud—it all really seemed a bit shabby. Besides, he was due his father's land outside the pueblo walls: even a good piece was left after his shrewd Uncles had appropriated part of it for their care and "taxes." On this Martiniano moved. He built a small adobe hut, bought a horse. Money he earned by riding into town daily and working as a carpenter.

Work was sporadic and soon ran out; La Oreja was a sleepy little town and the coarse work of native Mexicans was cheaper. His few friendships with the whites he went through faster. To them Indians were a part of the scenery, picturesque portraits to photograph and paint when properly dressed in feathers, servants or merely bad business risks on which to palm off stale meat and old staples.

Martiniano returned to his land and bought a few farming implements. He discovered that he had a green hand; things grew under it; he had enough to eat. But little by little the reproaches and displeasure of the old men began to press him.

"It is true you have kept your hair long to be worn in braids as is proper," they would say. "But these American shoes, they are not the custom. They must be got rid of."

"They are good strong shoes. Why should I ruin them by cutting off the heels? How is it that would make them Indian shoes? I will wear them as they are."

"You are fined two dollars," they answered him. "It is the order of the Governor. The Lieutenant-Governor will collect."

After every Catholic Mass, the old men would preach to the people on dress. They came to Martiniano and said, "My son, your father has told you what we wore in the old days. Long leggings up to the thigh, held up by a cord around the waist, which also held up a breech-clout, narrow but hanging down to the knees in front and behind. Now these American trousers. They are not the custom. You must fix them as ours."

Martiniano laughed. "Why should I cut the seat out of my pants, to convert them into imitation leggings, and wear a blanket wrapped round my middle to hide my naked behind? That is very funny. I will not ruin my good pants."

"You are fined two dollars," they told him sternly. "The Lieutenant-Governor will collect without fail."

Spring came, the tender corn shoots, a little rain but not enough. Martiniano one evening heard his name called out sonorously from the high roof-tops for the Green Corn Dance next day. He did not heed the summons, but spent the day cleaning out his acequia for water for his land.

Late next afternoon four men came to him. "You heard your name called, yet you did not take part in the dance as bidden," said one.

"That is so, Grandfather," Martiniano answered calmly. "I am poor. I could not hire help. I had to spend the day cleaning out my ditches to be ready for water for my thirsty fields."

"You are fined five dollars. We will collect them at your house tomorrow morning."

They came: the Governor, the Lieutenant-Governor, and two assistants. Martiniano met them with a set, stubborn face. "I am poor. I do not have five dollars to give you for nothing," he announced calmly.

"The alternative, according to custom, is five lashes. It will be a disgrace. But I have said it."

"I am ready," answered Martiniano stubbornly, with dark gleaming eyes.

They took him instead into the plaza, in front of the old men, in front of the people. There they held him, they whipped him. Five strong, deliberate lashes counted out slowly by the old men. And then they released him to his shame.

Martiniano stood up in his Apache shell. Deliberately before them he unbuckled his brass studded belt, let down his trousers, and pulled out the sheepskin which he had wrapped around his middle, underneath. Flinging it over his shoulder, and doing up his pants, he walked slowly, contemptuously away.

But in his hut he threw on the bed his proud and stubborn Apache shell with the gentle sensitive Pueblo spirit within it. He did not go out into his thirsty fields all day. He lay face down, his arms outstretched above his head, his fists clenched.

At dawn he wrapped his braids in his brightest ribbons, put on necktie and coat, and strode jauntily into La Oreja. He walked slowly out on the highway. A truck came and gave him a ride. Then he walked. A car full of tourists took him farther. He walked some more. By night he was in the city.

In the morning, after two hours' wait in the outer office of the District Indian Superintendent, he was ushered into Mr. Strophy's suave presence. Martiniano talked an hour.

"Was I not obedient, industrious, smart, in this Indian school? For six years? Did I not learn good English, a trade, to wash my ears, to wear American clothes. Look! My necktie is tied better than yours!"

Strophy nervously straightened his own, and began to rattle the papers on his desk.

"Why?" demanded Martiniano. "You taught me all this, and when I return to my people I am punished, I am shamed for doing what you taught. Why?

"My father, the old men, my people did not want me to go. It was you who took me, this Indian Service. Now this I say: Let you, the Superintendent, this Indian Service, go to my pueblo, my people, and punish them for the wrongs they have committed upon me. Let me return these five lashes as is proper . . . Or else let you go there and explain that it is your will I do as you taught, as you taught me for six years against my will!"

Strophy rattled his papers, put on his glasses.

"Well, now I'll tell you, Martiniano, maybe you're right in point of logic. But I think you're wrong in point of fact. Here's the way it is. The Indian Service doesn't try to govern the Indians. It only tries to help them govern themselves. Now the officers of your pueblo, your Council, govern the pueblo just like the officers and the council here govern this city. I can't go up there, the Superintendent can't go up there, and mix in their affairs. They're boss. You live there, you've got to obey their laws. See, boy?"

"I see!" broke out Martiniano hotly. "You grab us boys out of our houses and send us away to school and teach us all this nonsense, all these lies about becoming good citizens, about being like white men. And then you kick us out, and send us back home, and tell us, 'Now be good Indians again! Don't wash your ears any more! Wear a blanket. Cut the heels off your shoes. Cut the seat out of your Montgomery-Ward pants! We've had our fun. Now you go back and pay for it!' "

Strophy's dignity was disturbed. To regain it, he leaned back and put the fat tips of his fingers together.

"Is that what you want?" Martiniano bent forward accusingly.

"No boy. I—"

A long, shrill whistle sounded. The Indian turned, looked out the window. A long, streamlined train, gleaming silver, was slipping swiftly out of town.

Martiniano smiled contemptuously. " 'The Chief!' " he said pointing. "The modern, up-to-the-minute, Indian Chief riding by in all his platinum feathers. Listen. If you could ride on a train like that, would you wait and take a slow, dirty, old coal-burner? Would you climb into an old springless wagon to jolt over the ruts?"

Strophy smiled. He brought his hand down with a bang on the table-top. "No, by God, I wouldn't!"

"Well, I won't either!" answered Martiniano stubbornly. "I won't cut off the heels of my shoes. I won't cut the seat out of my pants. I'll use good clean dishes. I'll irrigate my land instead of dancing for rain. And if I don't get any help from you, I'll do it myself."

He rose with his peculiar set face.

"Now don't take it like that, Martiniano," remonstrated Strophy, rising. "Just remember there's a big, big gulf between you Indians and us—between the old men and you, rather," he amended hurriedly. "There's got to be a bridge. You young fellows are the ones to make it. Remember it takes time and patience. Let's don't have any trouble up there. Why, we're just all settled down, comfortable. . . . And if there's any help we can give you, why—"

Martiniano gave him a straight look from his hard black eyes, and stalked out.

A bridge: between the old and the new, red and white, blind intuition and blinding rationalization; and below him, in the profundity of immeasurable depths, the hidden, haunting mystery of his deeper self.

He returned to the pueblo, an outcast in his shabby little hut outside the walls. Two friends were left him, Palemon and Byers. Between them he plodded, taciturn and bitter, disillusioned, without faith. Slowly loneliness ate into him and it was the worst of all.

He quit going to the little adobe church within its low wall. The plum-red and black-and-yellow piebald horses had been erased from the façade; the whole front had been whitewashed. The old altar with its panels of crudely painted corn stalks had been replaced with regulation Catholic paraphernalia of cheap gilt and dusty lace. Nor did he like the fat, sly Mexican priest from town who demanded all his fees days in advance and who rode away so quickly from Mass.

But sometimes in the idle hot afternoons he came in to the pueblo to watch the summer Corn Dances. A dozen men and a dozen women facing each other in two lines dancing to the belly drum and song of a group of old men standing at the end. Lounging against a wall, cigarette in mouth, visitors pushing around him, Martiniano saw the bright, dyed feathers, the gaudy silk dress stuff alternating the old ceremonial mantas of black embroidered with red, even the colored chemises protruding from the bare shoulders. The young boys giggled at the girls self-conscious in front of whites. Gourd rattles shook half-heartedly; hands holding sprigs of evergreen waved off flies, then dropped limply to their sides. They bumped each other in the turns, stumbled out of step.

Only the chorus of old men sang raptly, soughing like wind through pines, eyes half closed, impervious to swarms of flies, the stifling heat reflected from the walls, and the rising dust.

The kiva chief, the dance master, strolled through the throng. He stood off, impassively watching without word or gesture. His appearance was enough. The giggles stopped. Eyes lowered. The dancers straightened, turned, wheeled in stylized patterns while the old men's voices soughed louder, deeper, faster. Only in obedience to outward compulsion. Nothing from deep within spontaneously gushing out.

Martiniano slunk back to his field. . . .

It was that hot, second afternoon of September he saw her. A small group of Plains Indians had stopped to visit on their way home—Arapahoes, Kiowas, two or three Cheyennes, and a few mountain Utes who had come down to see them off. A gift dance was given them up the cañon. Martiniano, hearing the drum, wandered up.

Beside the stream, in a little glade under the great cottonwoods, all sat in a circle: the visitors knotted in front, surrounded by Pueblos. A few old men sat back against the bare, gray trunk of a tree older and more brittle than their own. Another shorter length of cottonwood stood before them. It was older than the living men, older than the dying tree, and more enduring, having won through life and death alike to an immortal impersonality. It was hollowed out, painted yellow and turquoise, both ends covered with taut rawhide, and lashed with thongs.

One of the men, on his haunches, lifted the drumstick. Slowly, rhythmically, he began to beat. The glade, like a well, filled with sound. It was the heart-beat of the great, ancient cottonwood, and the heart-beat of the old men at its foot; of all the primeval forests and all the vanished tribes before them, but whose pulse still echoed unbroken and unchanged.

One after another, three women got up and began dancing. Then three men joined them within the squatting circle. They were Pueblo men with bare bodies and faces painted red, breech-clouts of green or purple velveteen, straps of bells around their legs, beaded moccasins on their feet. At their backs flashed great round feather suns. Shooting rays of more feathers made a halo round their heads.

Round and round the three women they whirled. Heads down, knees up, the straps of bells jingling, the feet thudding in a quick and powerful stamp, their bodies bent and unsprung like bows. Faces uplifted ecstatically to the skies and crying queer cries, bent over with the great feather suns outspread, they danced like splendid birds.

But the women in the center seemed to move only to the slow, deep throbbing voice of the drum. Seldom moving from one spot save to turn slowly about, hardly lifting their feet, arms hanging limply at their sides, eyes modestly lowered: thus they danced as women dance, with only the rhythm of muscle, nerve and blood.

They were visitors, Plains women. Each wore simply a long soft buckskin gown loosely belted at the waist, beaded moccasins, and a narrow band of beadwork across the forehead. Their long black hair was parted in the middle, oiled back in smooth wings, and hanging to the waist in two long braids. Each of their lowered faces was passive and somber, lighting suddenly and briefly into a strangely human smile—a flash of lightning across a cloudy sky. So they shuffled, hips and knees, their whole bodies under the soft buckskin trembling in one steady rhythm.

The difference between them was not their appearance, but the indefinable quality of their dancing. The mature, buxom woman had borne many children, danced many years. Her heavy shoulders and buttocks quivered with ease and mastery to the difficult rhythm—a body and spirit which had plumbed deeply the mysterious flow of life. The little scrawny girl, a bit pock-marked, was fresh and alive as a young mare held with tight rein. The third was a tall, slim young woman with the great brown eyes and gentleness of a deer. This graceful timidity, with all its dream-like quality, at first belied the wildness and the strength so perfectly restrained. Then little by little it broke through to remain the jutting characteristic.

How beautiful she was! How wild, how strong! Martiniano could not tear his glance away from her.

Abruptly the drum quit beating. The dancers stopped, the women walking demurely back to sit on the grass, the men flinging themselves down to rest and laugh.

There was no applause, no comments. But from the circle of watchers a big handsome man stepped forth in polished riding boots and a beautiful double-thickness Chief blanket of pure bayeta, wine red on one side, dark blue on the other. Martiniano recognized him as Manuel Rena, a rich man, the Pueblo host. Beside him was a man carrying presents.

He walked to each of the men dancers and handed them a dollar bill, folded lengthwise and tied with a piece of red yarn. But to the women he paid no such tribute of approach. He merely stood imperiously in the clearing, and pointed a long dark hand at each woman in turn. She rose, walked quietly to stand before him. From the arms of his attendant, he took a piece of calico and handed it to her. She walked quietly back, sat down and laid it on the ground beside her, courteously refraining from looking at it too closely. And after a pause the drum began again.

So it kept up all afternoon. The men leaping and prancing wildly, ecstatically as great birds; the women, like demure hens, treading softly but dancing with their bodies. The grass trod down. Dust began to rise like tufts of smoke under the moccasins. Shafts of sunlight struck through the canopy of trees, lighting up the brilliant feather suns. And at each pause, presents. Dollar bills, tobacco, store cigarettes and plain work moccasins for the men. To each of the women strips of silk, lengths of gingham and calico, a bracelet, moccasins, a blanket, shawl, necklaces of corn or dyed squash and melon seeds.

Not only Rena, the host, gave them, but the people. A woman, remembering her own youth, darting out with a new shiny pot. A man, well pleased, stalking out into the clearing and pointing to a woman to come for a silver dollar. What beautiful dancers these women were! And during the pauses how modestly they sat beside the growing heaps of presents, leaving the women behind them to finger the cloth and chatter at the generosity of the givers.

Martiniano had vanished. In a half-hour he returned. He had come at first muddy from the fields, a dirty cotton blanket wrapped round his head like a turban. Now he had on a fresh shirt, and a clean blanket wrapped round his waist. At the next pause he too stalked into the clearing, and impersonally pointed to the tall slim young woman. When she came up to him demurely, he laid over her arm a Navajo saddle blanket. At the unexpected weight she looked up swiftly into his face, with silent thanks, and walked back to lay it negligently on her heap of presents.

An hour later he got up again and gave her an old silver bracelet set with chunk turquoise. She smiled and walked back without speaking.

Martiniano hid somberly in the throng, unable to keep his eyes off her. Quietly, beautifully, untiring, she kept dancing. But three times she met his eyes in the crowd. And in a little while, though she no longer looked at him, he saw that she had unobtrusively slipped out his bracelet from her heap of presents and was wearing it under her long loose buckskin sleeve.

At sunset people began to leave; the dance was coming to an end; the visitors were to be given a feast that night.

Martiniano waited until the old man put up his drum stick. In the press of people he rode up on his horse beside her. When she turned to him, he handed down his most prized possession—an old bridle mounted with hand-hammered silver. For a long moment their eyes met. Then swiftly he rode away.

He was hungry and happy that night, and restless too. He heard the feast in the pueblo going on until nearly ten o'clock. A half moon came up. The young men in pale clumps among the willow thickets began to sing. "Hi-yah! Ai! Hi-yah!" welled their deep, strong voices. And from far away, up the stream above the pueblo, a single voice carried back the haunting, happy echo of their song. It was Martiniano, hands empty, giving his heart to the night.

At sunrise he was there, in the little glade under the cottonwoods where the grass had been trod down by dancing.

She was already there.

Look! Have you ever seen an Arapahoe maiden down in the willows beside the stream? The fresh, cool dew clinging like Navajo-silver buttons to her plain brown moccasins, the first arrows of sunlight glancing off the shining wings of her blue-black hair, the flush of dawn still in her smooth brown cheeks? Is she a long, slim willow in her dark green dress, bending over the water? Or only what a man sees once in the morning of his life, is never forgotten, but continues to grow upon him with the lush maturity of noon?

He only stood soundless on the grass, leaning against the tree, holding his blanket slightly opened toward her.

She turned and saw the eyes of his longing upon her, then walked to stand almost within the folds of his blanket.

"You are a rich man to give me such fine presents."

"I am a poor man. I gave you all I had," he answered quietly.

And then after a moment he said again, "I have but two things more to give you."

"And they?"

"My little hut among my fields."

"I will take it," she answered simply.

Still unsmiling, with dark calm eyes, she stood before him like a queen accepting her rightful homage.

"Once you are there," he said again steadily, "I have but my life to give you."

"I will take that too."

Martiniano straightened. He felt a little dizzy, as if he were standing on the edge of a fathomless chasm into which he might plunge at any instant. This was his sensitive, gentle Pueblo spirit, weak with longing. The stern, proud and arrogant Apache shell did not betray it. It stood there on that crumbling brink, erect, impassive, with one thumb hooked under his wide brass-studded belt and the other hand still holding open his blanket.

This was the woman's moment. Throughout her life others would see the fence of pride, sense the wildness and feel the strength that was her protective characteristic. But never again Martiniano. Her great brown eyes softened. With graceful timidity, and all its dream-like quality, she gently stepped up against him.

"I have said it," she said softly. "And what is your name?"

Then with a sudden ringing peal of laughter she whirled away before he could speak or move. Martiniano looked down at his outstretched blanket, then plunged wildly into the willows after her. . . .

They lay on the grass talking above the giggling stream.

"Yes," she said. "When the aspens change I will leave. When the willows change I will be here. We will be together."

For a long time there was silence. With it ebbed the dream-moment and the mood. When next she spoke, it was in boarding-school American slang. "And won't my old Aunts and Uncles raise the devil!" She laughed mirthlessly, yet neither voice nor words altered her tone of sweet gentleness. They only gave it an edge. And Martiniano felt in her practical talk the same stubborn wildness and wiry strength he had felt in her dancing.

"Arapahoe?" he questioned. "And you are not with them who return today to the Plains?"

Flowers Playing explained swiftly. She was part Arapahoe—from the old days when her grandmother as a young girl was made captive by the Utes. She had visited them many times in these days when all Indians were friends and brothers in adversity, and knew their dances well. But she lived north in the Colorado Rockies among her father's people, the White River and Uncompaghgre Utes. She also had been to away-school.

"They taught me to cook bacon on gas, and to use ice in the summer time," she said smiling. "But we are too poor to have bacon. I have not seen gas for these years I have returned. And what Indian has a refrigerator in his hut! Imagine!"

These visitors, the Arapahoes, Kiowas and Cheyennes, had been to visit her people. They would return to their Plains homes today. But she would return to the mountains with the few Utes who had come this far to see them off—as soon as the Big Talk was over; it had started last night.

"How did you know I would be here this morning?" she asked suddenly, laying her head on his breast.

Martiniano stroked her face with his forefinger. "How does one know these things that one knows?" he queried. "I only know there has always been a power in me which sometimes knows what I do not know. It is strange, but it is true. Perhaps it is wise not to question it."

This was their courtship, an hour among the willows beside the stream, in the little cottonwood glade where the grass was trodden down by dancing.

The sun rose high and warm. Men and wagons were going into the fields. The stream no longer giggled. It murmured solemnly, sadly, in the low tones of farewell, then sang joyfully with the promise of her return.

Martiniano left her in the plaza. He did not show her her hut in her fields; there was little there to eat. The Big Talk was over. The open door of Rena's house showed a big table crowded with visitors. Flowers Playing would have here a bigger breakfast.

Just after noon he glimpsed her, over the low pueblo wall, driving away. She was sitting demurely in the back of an old Ford truck on a pile of blankets. It was crowded with pots and pans, with the heavy figures and dark somber faces of Utes in their tall sombreros, their hair braids hanging down the backs of their wrinkled store coats. . . .

He could have written to her during that month of waiting. Every week he trudged to the little Post Office in town to find without disappointment there was no letter for him. "This thing," he thought, "is too inevitable and too simple to require words. When the high aspens change she will leave. When the willows change she will be here." So he waited.

Perhaps he should have told all his Uncles, the old men

and the Governor. They would have gone, as was proper, in a small group to formally request of the Ute Chief the adoption of a member of his tribe into their pueblo, to ask in marriage Flowers Playing of her family. With them he should have gone with an old wooden chest or a shiny new trunk full of presents to be opened at the betrothal ceremony by all her women friends, the worth of each article volubly discussed while she looked on helplessly from a corner, and he waited sweating outside for his prestige to be ascertained. . . . Or did her people, the Utes, have a still more foolish custom?

But Martiniano had no money for the trip. The families of his Uncles would have given him no presents. The Governor and the old men did not approve of him. So he told only a few. They listened quietly, then impassively stalked away: he was an improvident, impulsive young man. All this unseemly haste, this undignified American way of taking a wife with less concern and deliberation than one chose a blanket!

"Does he think she will really return? Having seen him but once? To a poor man, without standing? To an outcast?"

But Martiniano was untroubled. There was that within him which spoke with faith.

*It is a strange thing, this. All they say is true. But it is the little truth which does not matter. It is the big truth that fills me. Who can say the words that belong to it? I only look at myself alone in my hut, alone in my field, and see myself a child. Then I see her with me and I am a man. I have grown already. A new strength fills my body. My mind clears like a muddy pool which receives and empties a running stream. My spirit is no longer tied to the earth; it soars like an eagle; it sees how vast the world is and how alone we are in it, alone.*

And only to Palemon he emptied his heart.

Palemon nodded. "Is it not an old saying that one becomes a man only when he is married?" He looked at his wife sewing in the corner. He looked at his two children playing silently on the floor. Gently he smiled at Martiniano. "No doubt you will grow even more, my friend. Peace."

Martiniano walked away, refreshed. Palemon was a good man. Though he belonged to the old ways, he believed in the substance of life more than in the form.

Martiniano grew, and in peace. He was not over-eager nor too anxious. His faith was whole. He kept to himself. And lying alone at night, feeling the world rushing with him through space and time, he knew how necessary and precious was this time of waiting for the thing that was to come upon him. Had not he heard that young men in the old days fasted and slept alone under the stars before assuming manhood, warriors before taking the trail, priests before taking their vows? There was a great deal of all of these in marriage, he thought. There was the body, the mind, the spirit—and this was what troubled him the most. "With her, with the world, I must be all one. It is strange, I did not think of these things until I met her, so I know that it is a good thing. I will not be troubled with what people say or do not say." Peacefully he fell asleep.

The high aspen groves on the mountainside grew orange among the pines; the leaves fell with the first snow upon the peaks; the mountains were green again. Yet the color, like slow fire, ate down the cañon. The great cottonwoods flamed yellow against the blue sky. Along stream and road scrub oak and barberry glowed like cooling coals. Slowly they became thin, brittle pieces of brass, then copper. The willows changed color, drooped.

They were still yellow, but limp and curled with frost when she came—a slim young woman in a shabby long coat who had walked from town carrying a scuffed paper suitcase.

"See? There are still leaves on the willows, though few," she said, looking tired and worn.

"I was not anxious, but eager," he said quietly.

"There is an old tin trunk waiting at the junction when we have five dollars to have it brought here."

"I have a wagon. We will carry meat to cook in the mountains when we go after it. And bring back a load of wood," answered Martiniano. It was Spring in his heart, not Fall. Flowers Playing!

They had no great wedding feast gorged by Pueblo and Ute friends. The fat, sly Mexican priest from town rode out grumblingly to marry them in the little church—after his fees had been paid three days in advance. A few of Martiniano's Uncles came with fewer presents. But the good white man, the strange trader, sent word of a box of trade-goods waiting for them. And Palemon and his wife helped arrange a little feast.

How was this? Flowers Playing, a beautiful Arapahoe maiden, had come on a short visit to dance. She was respected, honored, her presents had heaped up waist high, she was invited to a great feast. Now she had returned to stay, but these people who were to be her people did not come into her open heart.

"Because you are my wife I have brought this shame upon you," said Martiniano. "Like me, you are not Indian. You are a good American citizen! In my selfishness, I did not warn you."

Flowers Playing laughed. "How dull are your ears, my husband. Do you not hear what the old women cackle under their breath as I walk by? Do you not know my new name? Listen. Because we are one, you must know what I know. My people, the Utes, call your people in derision Piñon Jays because the birds calling 'a-a-a-a' sound just like your old men officers calling from the house-tops! Thus the old women mock me.

"See, you have married a Ute. You have shamed yourself. You have brought disgrace upon your people. In my selfishness, I did not warn you."

They smiled together.

It was a good year, their first. In joy, in misery, they were one.

So thought Martiniano at the end of it, as he sat by the fire mending his old harness.

Flowers Playing was already dozing in bed; she would be up at dawn. He quietly put up his tools and walked outside for a last look at his animals. The night was frosty, the peak shone white in the clear air. Returning, Martiniano undressed and got into bed beside her.

He lay staring into the coals across the room. Turning over, he stared up through the little square window high up under the vigas. The Night People smiled. Wind Old Woman brushed her skirts along the walls. Life was good. With her beside him, Martiniano was content.

But suddenly, just as he flung his arm around his wife, a few brittle leaves pattered on the portal. They sounded like the light hoofs of a scampering deer, a frightened, an angry deer, a spirit deer. Martiniano straightened out stiffly, and removed the arm flung around his wife. Resolutely he tried to put sound and thought from him. He could not. He lay sleepless.

# 4

SO A COLDNESS grew up between them. Flowers Playing no longer lounged beside him of an evening in front of the fire while he caressed her. As if ashamed of her body which had failed their desire, she went to bed and huddled close against the wall, back to him, knees up, staring open-eyed into the darkness. Martiniano crawled in late beside her. His hand no longer gently stroked her long thigh or drew her against him for warmth. His breath did not bathe her cheek and throat in sleep. He lay apart. And between them always lay this new strange coldness that was like a pain for which neither had a remedy.

Martiniano felt betrayed. He remembered how barren a waste had been his life before she had come, an oasis of love and faith in a desert of unbelief. It was nothing but a mirage! And the bitterness, the corrosive loneliness, filled him as before.

The chokecherries had been gathered. Wagon loads of wild plums had been spread out to dry upon the flat roof tops. The corn had come in. Great heaps everywhere, holding women like hens in their nests, shucking and laying aside the brightest colored and most perfect ears to be braided together and kept for ceremonial, seed and ornament. Scarlet necklaces of chile from the lowlands hung along the walls turning blood-red, black. Between walls, like long lines of flags and pennants, hung drying pelts and intestines of butchered sheep. The corrals had been lined with branches of pine and spruce to keep out the wind. Hundreds of burros staggered down the trails with loads of piñon and cedar.

Then slowly a warm hush ate into the cold afternoon like a bad spot in a sound apple. Out of the low gray sky fluttered a speck of white. It looked like a loose feather dropped from the breast of a solitary wild goose. It twisted and turned buoyantly against the blue mountain wall, fluttered down lazily past the brown adobe wall, settled lightly on the hard reddish earth. Another. Others. They came! They came! The mystery, the miracle, the beauty of the first snow.

By morning it was all gone. The sun was bright, the air warm. But the message of a new mystery, new miracle and new beauty remained. A sonorous voice proclaimed it from the high house-tops. It was time when all must move in from their summer houses out in the fields, from their little huts in the cañon. It was time when all must move into the pueblo, into one nest together.

Martiniano went to the Governor for the assignment of a vacant room or two. The price was too high, and he walked back to his little adobe outside the walls with his stubbornness and pride unspent.

Flowers Playing assumed a consoling cheerfulness. "We have a home. Look. In that old trunk of mine I found it. This pretty cloth which makes us curtains for our windows. When the snow flies past we shall just reach out our hands and pick these red raspberries!"

Martiniano's sullen look rent the curtain of her smiling consolation. He had seen that cloth printed with red raspberries in her old trunk; it was one of her old school dresses. Scowling at her foolish attempt to obscure the tawdry truth between them, he strode in to sit gloomily in front of the fire.

A quick fright leapt into Flowers Playing's eyes. Her lips trembled. She went on with her work.

So the coldness grew between them.

Martiniano began to ignore her. She was merely a woman, a wife. He began to go to Palemon.

There was a great difference between them as they sat together, so much alike in appearance. One was vivid, sharp-witted, personal. The other sat with drooping head, relaxed, impersonal, silent. Martiniano felt the gulf between them. But because he also felt the dark, upwelling stream of compassion, he gave way to the repressed pain and bitterness within him.

"They fined me because I did not cut off the heels of my shoes and cut out the seat of my pants. They whipped me because I did not dance. My use of the thresher they forbade. They ignore me, they shame my wife. We are outcasts.

They will not let us move within the walls. No! All winter we must plod through snow to our little adobe. We must break trail to the road for our wagon. . . . What have we done to deserve all this? What is good about these old ways of yours which you uphold—this cruelty, this injustice to a blood-brother?"

The older man sucked slowly on his cigarette. He was not unaware of certain superficial injustices which had caused the younger one's sufferings, but he was amazed at the persistent, stubborn individuality which prevented him from seeing the real trouble. Perhaps it reflected the one's away-time in school, when he had lost the precious instruction at home. Palemon did his best to reveal his understanding. "There are no words for talk, for all my feelings, friend. Heart, mind, body. They are all together. All is one, everything. You are separate, alone. It must not be, my friend."

*You see, it is like this. I am mortal body and I am immortal spirit; they are one. Now on this earth I am imprisoned for a little while in my mortal body. This gives me no discomfort; I have learned its needs and limitations and how to supersede them.*

*Now I, in this mortal body, am imprisoned also in a form of life—that of my tribe, my pueblo, my people. Nor does this give me discomfort; I have learned its needs and limitations also and how to supersede them. For as my body blends into my tribe, my pueblo, so this greater form blends into the world without—the earth, the skies, the sun, moon, stars, and the spirits of all.*

*I have faith in my body. I have faith also in this form of life which is my greater body. How then can I object to its demands also? So I feed it with faith; I am obedient to its coarser needs; I lighten its burden by prayer-dance and ceremonial.*

*Now if I quarreled with my body, my spirit would not be free. Now if I quarreled with my greater body, my spirit would not be free. But by existing harmoniously in each, I am free to escape them for my greatest need—to become one, formless and without bounds, inseparable from the one flowing stream of all life.*

Palemon rolled another corn-husk cigarette.

*Now you, my friend, have your mortal body also, and are at peace with it. You too have a greater body, your form of life. It is not mine, for our old ways you reject; nor is it the Government's, the white man's, for you reject it also; but one you must have. Who knows which is best? They are all the same. All are merely shells of life. But they must be lived within harmoniously to be free. For only when there is no sense of imprisonment in form is the substance of spirit able to overflow and become one with the flowing stream of all life, everlasting, formless and without bounds.*

*Forgive me, my friend. Do you see what you lack? Not a form of life, for there are three for you to choose from: our old ways, the white man's new ways, or your own which may be part of both or newer still. You lack only a faith in one of them. The faith that will set you free from bitterness and envy and worry. That will free your spirit into a formless life without bounds, which will overflow and taste of all life.*

Palemon's feelings continued to gush out from him in waves of silent compassion. Martiniano's conscience illuminated his terse words quickly enough. He broke out into another tirade.

"Faith! What can a man have faith in nowadays? The Government betrayed me. My own people reject me. You remember how empty I was until my wife came. Then I was a new man. She was my faith. And now? That has gone too. Perhaps I should not have married her—not yet. She is as miserable as I. Why?

"Why?" he repeated stubbornly. "That deer!" he exclaimed suddenly. "That's what they are holding against me most of all. That cursed deer which I killed! That is what has destroyed my wife's love and faith!"

"Perhaps that is so," agreed Palemon calmly. "Perhaps there is something else about that deer you killed which you have forgotten. *I remember how clearly your spirit called. It was as if it left your mortal, wounded body, as if it broke the boundaries of this form of life of yours. It seemed that it stood beside me, whispered in my ear, pulled at my heart until I answered. That is how it seemed. I have not mentioned it to you. I do not know how you awakened this sleeping power. I do not ask. There is something about this thing that lies beyond words. We do wrong to question it.* But I would think about this thing when I think about faith. Listen not only to your body. Listen not only to your mind. Listen to your heart which holds the feelings of all."

Martiniano went away comforted. Always afterward he

felt enriched by Palemon's silent awareness. But in his presence he was also tortured by this same silence, as if in front of him he was no longer Indian but a talkative white.

He went to see the strange white man, the trader, and to thank him for paying his fine. And immediately, once there, he felt a curious barrier between them. He felt himself sink down deep within himself, in a heavy, Indian stolidity.

Byers looked up a little sharply; it was the first time he had seen Martiniano since the court hearing.

"That fine. One hundred and fifty dollars. I don't know when I can pay it," Martiniano heard himself saying coldly.

"I'm not asking you for it. It's on the books," growled Byers. "You know my wife tends to that kind of business!"

Martiniano stared at him a moment from a dark, impassive face, then turned and stalked out. Byers flung a look after him and noisily rasped a match across the counter. Never a word of thanks! Well, what did he expect—a speech?

On his way to the trading post Martiniano had passed the little Catholic church in the pueblo. Here the Indians went to Mass on Saint Days—and the instant it was over began their own ceremonial dance. The fat, sly Mexican priest so greedy for fees locked the door and rode quickly back to town; he was forbidden to countenance pagan rites, and so saved himself trouble by ignoring their existence. So the church meant nothing at all. It was merely an empty form by which the Indians were dutifully baptized and buried, though they lived by their own. A tall pointed steeple with a cross, the phallic symbol of the male lustful to conquer. Everywhere this was the white's form of faith.

On his way through the pueblo to Palemon's house Martiniano always passed a kiva. The circular, soft adobe walls sinking like a womb into the dark resistless earth, with a ladder sticking out for men to enter by. The female symbol of fertility imbedded in Our Mother Earth. The Kiva. This was the Indian church. A form of life whose substance was passivity, not action, and which had no will to conquer, to even oppose. A creed of supplication and appeasement. And so when water was needed the people merely danced for rain instead of digging more ditches.

Martiniano looked at neither in passing. They were the two opposite poles of his own being, and he was polarized to neither. He remained miserable between them.

There is this about words. Put feelings into words and the feelings are gone, scattered like chaff before the wind.

But there is something else about words. Some of them are like the few, carefully selected seeds of a whole crop. They grow and keep growing into the full stalks of new feelings. Such were Palemon's few words. Martiniano felt them maturing with meaning.

Deep within him he had felt always a strange, quiescent power. It was like the beat of a far-off drum, sometimes faint, sometimes throbbing powerfully through his blood, but never quite still. But a faith he lacked; he knew it now. And scarce is the faith without a church to lend it form.

The spirit of the deer he had killed worried him, but the kivas were closed to him and the old men steeped in such matters would not talk outside. He was bothered about his wife, but there was no comfort at dreary Mass. So he began to hunger for a faith, a form to give allegiance to.

The Corn Depositing Moon which shone upon the corn contributions to the dead slowly waned. Martiniano was surprised to see Manuel Rena talking to Flowers Playing in the plaza. Observed, he walked over to join them.

"This is a good woman you have taken for a wife," said Rena. "I have seen her dance. And I have just been to the Plains of her people, the Arapahoes. I visited Cheyennes, Kiowas, Osages, Pawnees and Cherokees, besides. They are good people. They have taught me much. Now I will walk to your home. I will tell you about it. Your wife will want to know some things and you others."

Martiniano nodded gravely. There were things he had heard about this rich man whose wine-red and dark blue blanket of pure bayeta brought up from Mexico was the finest in the pueblo. It was said his power did not alone come from his rich land, good horses and many sheep. And he remembered that it was from his land whence came so often at night the sound of a little water drum across the pastures. He also observed when they got home that the heels of his polished riding boots were not cut off, and that there was a leather seat in his riding breeches.

Manuel talked: about Flowers Playing's people, the Arapahoes: about the Plains people, the Cheyennes, Osages, Pawnees, Cherokees.

"The buffalo are gone," he said somberly. "And they were

meat-eaters, these tribes of the plains. So they dwindled. They almost vanished. But not quite. Something came which gave them new strength." He sat looking out of his big black eyes, intently, at nothing. "It is of this I would tell you," he said at length.

Flowers Playing rose quietly and went about that woman's business in the kitchen which has no beginning and no end.

"It has made twenty years and more that I first went to the Plains, to Oklahoma," continued Manuel. "With some boys from our pueblo. With that good white man, the strange trader, who has learned to keep his eyes and heart open, his mouth closed. It was a strange trip. Strange with mystery and power. I went a boy. I came back a man. Enough! Listen!

"We got there. We visited the Cheyennes and the Arapahoes. They spread robes for us. We delivered presents, we received presents. We ate, we smoked. We were all one.

"Now this is what happened. Me one night they took into a tepee. They sat me on a robe. With them I ate a certain plant, a strange herb of mystery and power. They beat their drums and sang their songs and made their prayers. My turn came to me with the drum. I sang my songs and made my prayer. And we ate again of this certain plant, this strange herb of mystery and power. And this we did all night.

"I saw them sitting in the tepee, passing the drum around the circle, each singing in turn. I saw myself there among them. This I saw because my spirit was no longer imprisoned within my body. It wandered outside. It saw herds of buffalo that covered the plains, men on horseback dressed the old way, with shaven heads. It saw war and the long hunger, peace and plenty of fat meat, and behind them both the thing that makes all men brothers. It saw money. They all were as dreams, and yet not dreams. It was this certain plant, this strange herb we ate that gave me this mystery.

"Its power it gave me too. The sun came up. We walked out of the tepee. You have drunk whiskey all night, felt the taste of its scum on your tongue, the fire which has scorched your insides? This herb but left my body clean and my mind whole. Would you know how my spirit felt? Look at this little silver pin fastened to my shirt."

He pulled back his blanket. A little silver goose hung on his breast, wings outspread, feet drooping, the long straight neck stretched upward—a wild goose shooting upward, ecstatically, into the higher skies. Martiniano nodded.

"So we rested and had a great feast. I felt happy and free. I was not tired. I was stronger," continued Manuel. "I said nothing, but before we came home they told me about this certain plant, this strange herb of mystery and power.

"It made a long time ago. A war party was on the trail. They were travelling light. It was necessary they leave behind them a sick warrior. You know how it was: meat for three days and a poor pony. If it was his fate, he regained his strength and returned to his lodge. If it was not so, it was war; there was only a poor pony lost. So he lay there, this sick warrior. Maybe it was day, maybe it was night; he could not tell them apart. A voice began to sing. There was nobody, nothing around. Then the voice stopped singing, and said, 'Come.' It came from this plant which grew near him. It blossomed. The blossom opened. He crawled down into it.

"He was in a great round room in the root of this plant. A kiva. Many men sat around him, dressed in buckskin. They rebuked him and his people for riding over the plains, killing, always on the warpath. They reproached him and his people for living like animals, with no thought for the lives of their spirits. Then they gave him some of this plant to eat which made him well. And they gave him some of this plant to take home to his people, telling him to rebuke and reproach them also, and to teach them how to use it. 'Believe in it like God,' they said. 'It will save them as it saved you.'

"So he rode home. The war-party had returned to the lodges of his people saying that he was dead. They had cut their hair and killed his horses. He called them all together, rebuked and reproached them as he had been bidden, and taught them the use of this cactus plant.

"This I learned from the Cheyennes and Arapahoes," stated Manuel, "and they learned it from the Kiowas. Now when I came home I brought some of this certain plant, this strange herb of mystery and power, to teach my people likewise how to use it. The day comes when it will be taken to the desert Apaches, the Navajos, the mountain Utes. We will all use it as do the tribes of the Plains. We will all be one people with one thought for the lives of our spirits. Peyote will be our Chief, our God. Peyote will save us."

Martiniano rolled a bit of tobacco in corn husk. Manuel delicately refused makings for himself.

"This I say. I have told you about Our Father Peyote," he said. "Now I have come again from the plains of the

Cheyennes and the Arapahoes, and brought more of this peyote plant. We will have church again, many times. The Peyote Road lies before you. My tepee is open to you. There is a place for your blanket to be spread."

Martiniano puffed in silence. "My thanks, friend," he said at last. "It is too great a matter to answer hastily. But I will consider it."

Manuel rose, shook hands, and went out.

There was much to consider as Martiniano learned more about it. The cactus plant was a drug, and like marihuana its use was forbidden in the State. The Plains Indians had taken it up instead of whiskey. It produced visions, it made the people crazy. Thus the sly and secret talk in town.

When questioned, Flowers Playing remembered something about it. "The Cheyennes and my people, the Arapahoes, learned of it from the Kiowas as Rena said. That is true. But the Kiowas learned of it from the tribes of Mexico—the Yaquis perhaps, and they from the Tarahumares and Coras. The Huicholes in the Sierra Madres use it too. But this I heard also: it was an old woman to whom Peyote spoke in a vision. Does not all mystery originate with woman? But does not power belong to man? So they gave it over to the men. Now that is what I have heard, my husband. It is very old, that is certain. Some were for it, some against it. It is all I remember."

Each Saturday night, in the deep cold silence, Martiniano heard again the throbbing of a little water-drum across the pastures. Two weeks he pondered. But he needed a faith, and new power. So on the next Saturday, at dusk, he took the Peyote Road.

It led up along the crumbling town wall, along the bare plum thickets, across the corn field palely splotched with snow. It led across the pastures to Rena's adobe house, and into the circle of trees behind. There he saw it: conical and pale gray in the deep dusk, its protruding lodge poles stark against the violet sky. A skin tepee, Arapahoe style, with the door facing east. The flap drew back. He ducked and entered.

Some thirty men in a circle were squatting around the wall. In the center was a small crescent moon of clean yellow sand. On it lay a button of peyote nearly as large as an onion. Between it and the door flickered a fire of seven sticks touching at the points.

Martiniano took his seat in the circle. An impenetrable silence filled the tepee. It was broken only by the entrance of a man who squatted down to tend the fire. Half-way round the circle, directly behind the moon-mound of sand, a brown hand lifted for an instant a red blanket from a brown face. It was the Peyote Chief's greeting to Martiniano. It was Manuel Rena.

Two men came in, closing the flap and passing around the circle clockwise to sit beside the Peyote Chief. One of them carried a small kettle drum filled with water, the other an armful of cedar and sage. After a time the Peyote Chief drew out tobacco and corn husks, rolled a cigarette, then passed them to the left. The Fire Chief rose with a brand, lit it for him, and passed round the circle to the left. When all had finished smoking, the Peyote Chief prayed and each in turn after him.

The guttural sing-song Indian voices joined together like beads on a string. "Our Father Peyote, Our Father God, this boy she asking for prayer this night this house is put up with this cigarette to help me my prayer good, to give me without getting tired. Our Father Peyote, our Father God, this poor one asking to help him good, to go right with his prayer, to give good living for his family house, because his right living . . ."

At its end a sack of small peyote buttons were passed around to the left. Each man took four, placing them on the ground before him. Martiniano did as those around him: one at a time he cleaned with his knife, chewed it up into a fine paste, spat it into his hands, rolled it into a ball and then swallowed.

The Peyote Chief with his left hand raised a cane, one end resting on the ground for the strength of life. In his right hand he shook a small gourd rattle. With the Drum Chief on his right beating the little water drum, he sang four songs. Then he passed cane and rattle to Cedar Man on his left, and the drummer passed along his drum. He too, and each in turn, sang four songs.

Martiniano slumped down on his blanket. He listened to the songs, and the drum beat was his own pulse, the voices the song of his blood. He felt the warmth of the little fire, and it was the warmth growing in his belly like a great tree whose branches reached up into his chest. He stared at the

Father Peyote—the big button lying on the crescent moon of clean yellow sand before him. Why, it was no longer round! It was conical. It was a tepee. He entered. Why, it was not small and crowded! It was huge. It was a whole world. Herds of buffalo drifted past over the yellow grassy plains. A band of wild horses raced by, snorting. They were bright red stallions. Their manes were saw-tooths of fire. Behind them stood mountains of blue. It was a beautiful world, blue crinkled mountains, flat yellow plains, dashing red horses. He wanted to stay, but someone was calling him back.

It was Cedar Man who had passed him some sage, and was helping him to rub it over his hands and face "to keep the smell of it upon you so you won't feel weak and dizzy."

Again he lay down on one arm, and the tepee closed about him. What a strange tepee! From the lodge poles at the top dangled a string of yellow and white corn. The string lengthened. The ears of corn grew. The kernels grew. The white ones were silver pesos, the yellow ones were gold coins. They rattled, they rattled, rattled . . .

It was the rattling of the gourd beside him. When it stopped, and gourd, cane and drum were handed past him to the man on his left, Martiniano sat up.

"I have just come back from where I have been," he said quietly. "From the far blue mountains beyond the yellow plains over which the red horses race. From that strange tepee whose lodge poles dangle white corn of silver pesos and yellow corn whose kernels are gold coins. Now since I have come back in time, why is it I should not sing also? . . . I shall sing my songs!"

The drum came back to the man beside him. Quietly Martiniano was handed cane and gourd. He was not a good singer, but those two songs he knew rose out of him as geese from out of the marshes. Then he sang a little Arapahoe lullaby he had heard Flowers Playing singing among her pots and pans. When his memory failed him, he began a verse of a Mexican drinking song.

"Borrachita, me voy . . ."

The cane and gourd were politely taken from his hands; the drum was handed on.

At midnight water was passed to drink. He went outside a moment. The world had stopped whirling through space. The singing had stopped it. It was neither night nor day. He stood in the calm, cold blueness that forever holds between the stars, and the star-dust lay sparsely on the ground between the dead trees. He was at the heart of time. He could hear its slow, measured beat.

Martiniano went back inside. Cedar Man smoked him with a burning branch of cedar as he passed to his seat. The sack of peyote buttons was handed around again. The beat of the drum, the rattle of the gourd, the singing resumed.

A young man in the circle became ill. The Fire Chief removed the vomit with a shovel. Now Cedar Man lighted a small branch of the sharp, clean-smelling, sacred cedar. He smoked the ill man and the Fire Chief when he returned, fanning the smoke towards the squatting circle with a beautiful fan of turkey wing feathers. And all the men fanned it slowly past their dark, somber faces, past their half closed eyes and rhythmically chewing lips, and into the folds of their blankets with their own fans.

Martiniano lay staring at the fans. There were black and white ones of the long, slender tail-feathers of a magpie; speckled brown ones of the feathers of a hawk; of the striped cloud tail of grandfather turkey, the eagle's thin cloud tail, the striped cloud wings and massed cloud tails of all the birds of summer, of all the water birds. The quills of each were wrapped into a handle of soft buckskin with a small tuft of white eagle-down and with a pendant of iridescent parrot feathers, or set in buckskin richly embroidered with colored beads. All waved gently back and forth from their pivots of brown hands.

The blanketed figures receded into the smoky dusk of the skin tepee. But the bright colored fans kept gently moving. All the brown hands held at the breast became one long hand, one long horizon, and it was the long level horizon of the rich brown earth. All the bright-colored fans became one fan, and it was the long, rainbow dawn breaking over the horizon. To it, into the dawn, Martiniano followed the Peyote Road.

*It led into the corn fields where grew the white corn of silver pesos and the yellow corn whose kernels were gold pieces. Here he lingered, wandering among the tall corn, fondling the heavy ears, listening to them rattle and jingle in the wind. I will stuff my pockets with this corn, he thought. No one will know that it is not corn; they will think it silver and gold. I will be rich.*

*Then suddenly, as if someone had spoken the thought into his head, he asked himself, "But what will I buy when all I seek is a faith?" and he knew he was lost and wandered on.*

*He came to the yellow plains over which the red stallions raced. Here he lingered, watching the sparks leap from their hoofs, the lightning jumping from their flowing manes, the fires in their nostrils. This is power, he thought. What power! With these horses, I would have the old men, my persecutors, bending to my will!*

*Then suddenly someone spoke the thought into his head, "Power is persecution: you yourself have said it. It does not lead to peace. You have lost the Road again."*

*He wandered farther. He came to the great blue mountains. The tall ancient pines stood with their feet on earth, their heads in heaven. They were rooted in peace, dreaming in solitude, meditating in tranquil aloneness. Streams flowed softly by. Tall columbines grew beside them. Great birds flapped sleepily overhead. An animal stirred in the thickets. Martiniano paused. The blue mountains of peace opened their blankets to him, but he would not stay and deliberate with the tall ancient pines upon the meaning of this strange peace. He was restless; he wanted more. He wanted to look over the deep blue horizon into the fan-like rainbow dawn.*

*Then suddenly, as he struggled upward, the thickets broke before him with a crash. A deer stood in the clearing, the deer he had killed.*

*Martiniano reached for his gun; he had forgotten it. The deer stood looking at him. It was strong and beautiful, but its sad brown eyes began to glitter. It raised one forefoot, snorted and tossed its horns.*

*Martiniano was suddenly afraid. He looked around him quickly for a club, and noticed that the tall pines were sadly nodding. But not at him. At the deer. And he knew that he was an intruding stranger who had not stopped to consider what constituted this strange peace, this universal brotherhood between deer and pines and birds. He turned swiftly and fled.*

*The deer raced after him. Its hot breath burnt the back of his head, its pointed forefeet struck at and thundered behind him. The great birds whistled, the tall pines moaned.*

*He was hot and panting when he reached the yellow plains where the red stallions raced, spent and weary as he flung himself back through the silver and gold corn. And when he burst back into the tepee he lay quivering from a haunting terror. Outside, the deer kept racing around the pegged skin walls. Martiniano could hear the drum-thunder of its hoofs furiously pawing the hard earth. He covered his sweaty head with his blanket and lay shaking.*

The sounds ceased. He could feel sage being rubbed upon his hands and face, the gentle breath of feather fans wafting cedar smoke around him. He quieted. The whole earth quieted. After a time the darkness lifted from it and from his heart. Against the smoky walls of the tepee loomed bright colored blankets, brown faces, features. It was dawn. The sun was looking into the tepee to see the moon. The singing stopped. All returned from the Road.

Cold water was again brought in to drink. Then Rena's wife and another woman brought stewed fruit and hominy and raw beef ground together and sweetened. Martiniano ate, and rested. In a little while he got up and went outside. The air was clear and sharp. A horse neighed. He could smell sage and cedar in the breeze.

How good he felt! How strong and clean! Sleep did not pull at his eyes, nor the dream at his memory. He strode lively up the cañon trail.

When he came back from his walk the ground around Rena's house was littered with his night's companions. They were lounging in the sun, talking and laughing, and pointing at the busy women hurrying in and out of the house preparing a big feast. Martiniano recognized many, young Jesús and Filadelphio among them. All spoke to him, laughed and joked. It was good: they had travelled the Road together.

It was Rena who drew him off for awhile.

"A place was kept for you. You came. That is good," he said kindly.

"It is true. I feel good," answered Martiniano. "As you told me, my heart feels lighter. There is no bad taste in my mouth. Sleep does not drag at my eyes."

Rena touched his silver pin lightly, and smiled.

"You travelled the Road?" he asked seriously.

Martiniano frowned: he remembered something about that deer he had killed. "I travelled the Road. I saw, it seems . . ."

"Illusions," answered Rena abruptly. "It is not necessary you tell me or any man. We each have our illusions; they mean nothing to any other man. The Peyote Road is long and difficult. It is beset with the weaknesses and evils lurking in each traveller. It calls for personal discipline and self-examination. Who can run lightly over the Road? You were lost in your own weaknesses, your own evils, your own illusions. But Peyote, the compassionate, brought you back safely. He is always there to help and guide the traveller. Next time you will go farther."

"The Road—"

'The Road is long and painful, but the rewards are great. It returns man to his pristine goodness, and brings him back to his original nature from the lust for selfish ends he has left far behind. The Peyote Road leads to a true understanding of the world, and to a proper understanding of the passions. The Road leads to spiritual unity with the Great Father Peyote who in Himself contains all.

"Now let us talk no further. You will understand more later. Besides, look at my wife beckoning! The ribs are brown. That is the last bread her sister takes from the oven. The feast is ready!"

"How good I feel!" Martiniano told Flowers Playing complacently when he arrived home that afternoon. "Not tired or anything. Besides, we had a great feast. The next time perhaps you shall eat too—you can help serve. This peyote faith is not a bad thing."

But near midnight Rodolfo Byers was aroused by a noisy battering at his door and window. With a curse, he swung his legs out of bed, threw a blanket over his long nightgown, and scuffed across the cold floor to the window.

A coatless Indian, blanket dragging on the ground, was shivering outside. Byers lit a candle and opened the door a few inches. In the flickering light he could see the fright in Martiniano's wild eyes.

"What the Goddam hell! This time of night!" he growled.

"That deer I killed! The skin of that deer I killed!" pleaded Martiniano. "To you I gave it for pawn only. You have not sold it? You have not cut it up for use? You are saving it for me? I could not sleep. It kept me awake, this deer. I—"

Byers snorted and disappeared with the candle into the darkness behind him. In a few moments he returned, threw a deerskin outside in the snow, and slammed the door.

Back in his room he looked out the window before going to bed. Martiniano, with the deerskin wrapped under his arm, was running wildly back across the snowy fields.

# 5

THE INDENTATION on the breast of the mountain began to overflow, and the viscous white crept down the cañon trails. Below, under the great cottonwoods, the deep still pools ringed with white. Rime covered the withered squash vines each morning. The roads rang hard and dry. Under a flurry of snow the desert beyond spread out bleak and illimitable as the sky overhead; one could scarcely distinguish where they met. The tone of land, sky and people was a somber gray. Its mood was a frosty silence. Even the voice of the white-blanketed figure on the house-tops seemed strangely muted.

Now had come the beginning of the time for staying still, it cried softly. There must be no digging within the pueblo walls, no plastering nor chopping of wood. No singing, no dancing, no hair cutting either. Women must clean their houses and do their noisy sweeping only after sundown, and then it was best to place a live coal near the door. No automobiles were allowed in the plaza. Wood could be brought in on burros only. It was the time of staying still. Our Mother Earth sleeps. The plaza is barred to iron-shod hoofs and wagon wheels. Step softly, brothers!

Martiniano frowned. When the first deep snow came two days later, his scowl was black as a crow against the soft whiteness. He hitched up his team to his loaded wagon. To drive across the snowy field was impossible. He lashed his horses through the still, deserted plaza, and drove to the village to deliver his wood as promised.

As he feared, they were waiting for him when he returned. To pay his fine it was necessary to give them almost all the money earned by his labor.

They knew I would have no way to get out with my wood, he thought bitterly, trudging back with no more than flour, sugar and salt. This persecution! How much can I bear? But proudly and stubbornly he hardened his heart to stand more . . .

It was the time of staying still; Our Mother Earth was

sleeping under her blanket of snow. This was the rest for renewal, a gathering of life for another period of gestation when she would again fling off her blanket and lay open to Our Father Sun, be fructified by the copious spring rain and bear abundantly—our enduring Mother Earth whose fertility was eternal.

But she, this human mother, would never bear again. Her task was finished, her body empty, her thoughts heavy. And the wife of Palemon looked at her little son and felt her heart cry out with anguish. *Napaita, my loved one, come once more to Takono, your mother, before you leave her. My little Hill Red Antelope, come to Antelope All Colors, your mother, before you lose her.*

But as Estefana, dutiful wife of Palemon, she only said to her little son known in school as Juan de Jesús, "Child, play more quietly with Batista, your sister! Your time approaches. You must prepare to be a man."

And as the small black-headed boy quieted on the kitchen floor, her heart cried out again. *I am a mother and I suffer as all mothers suffer who will never understand why they must lose their sons. He was mine from that first night in the womb. I saw his eyes open, his little limbs harden to play. He has been mine all these years. He is still mine! Why should he be taken from me? I am a mother. What mother can ever understand why her son should be taken from her?*

And she looked at his older sister with more love and more compassion, for now she understood. *Batista, my daughter, we are women together. And so my heart yearns toward you with new pity. Your first blood-letting comes; that hair braid down your back will then be changed to a double cue. You will be married. You will have a son only to lose him too. Then we will be mothers together, and weep for what we can never understand.*

But as Estefana, dutiful wife of Palemon, she only said to her daughter, "Batista! Do not irk your little brother. His time approaches. You must help him to prepare to be a man."

It was the time of staying still. It was the time when the work was done, when the old men gathered round the fires at night to talk of their youth, and youth to talk of their maturity, when the old stories were retold to children.

For these Martiniano and Flowers Playing trudged through the snow to Palemon's house during these cold winter nights. Thus they excused to themselves their frequent visits, both knowing it was the unbearable tension which drove them night after night out of their own home.

"Palemon belongs to the ignorant old ways although he has an iron stove, a bedstead and some 'white' dishes—all forbidden," said Martiniano. "Still, he is a good friend. I respect him."

"And Estefana is a dutiful wife and mother," said Flowers Playing. "Have you seen the tenderness in her fingers when she touches Juan de Jesús? Have you noticed lately the anguish in her eyes when she looks at her little son?"

"The boy is to be put into the kiva very soon," said Martiniano carelessly. "It is one of the old customs."

Flowers Playing looked at him wonderingly, and thought, "He is my husband for all the coldness between us. Yet he is a man, and so cannot understand what it means to a mother to lose her son." And she smiled at Estefena who smiled back. The smiles were one smile. It was the sad, secret smile of a woman from whom a son was withheld, and that of a woman from whom her son was being taken. It was the one sad secret smile of deprived motherhood.

The room was full. Piñon crackled in the fireplace. The pinkish light, reflected from the fire wall, outlined the rows of men smoking on the benches. Across from them squatted the women, and on the floor between sprawled all the children.

A woman was mumbling of those witches, the yiapana, the sleep makers who were abroad only in January, naked to the waist and with black breasts, and whose long hair hung down over their white painted faces.

The children's eyes grew round. Chills chased up their hot backs.

"Ah, but there is that flowerless weed, gray like sage, that may be burned in a room when these witches are abroad."

"I have heard it is best to carry in the belt a black stone —a night-stone," said another. "That will keep them away."

A man laughed. "Why should witches with cold naked breasts chase women on these winter nights? It is men they appear to. Now I—I am not afraid of these yiapana!"

The women giggled, noisily crackling piñon nuts between their teeth and spitting out the little brittle shells. A man, growing serious, remembered a medicine man whose power was so great that he could fly through the air like a bird to the four corners of the earth and return before daybreak. He himself had witnessed it once.

Who has forgotten the messages of the great Manitou, the lessons learned by the Old First Ones? Who has forgotten the legendary White Buffalo of the Pawnees, the Four Medicine-Arrows of the Cheyennes, the ancient fathers of the Navajos and their Raft of Whirling Logs, or the Grizzly Bear Who Married the Girl Created From an Aspen Staff to bring forth the mountain Utes? Who does not remember the Long White Hunger, the pranks of Old Man Coyote, the Winter of Many Snows?

They were all remembered, filtered through years and tribes, unaltered. After one, a slow voice added a moral.

"An Indian is a donkey. Only when he puts feathers on does he feel the spirit of his tribe, the spirit of life, within him."

After another, an expressive gesture of a wrinkled hand, the lifting of a hairless eyebrow, to punctuate the truth, "A man must learn to take and carry everything as it comes, like the water in a creek."

So the tales kept up, the tales told only in winter because "the snakes will bite you in punishment if you tell them in summer," the tales never told to strangers lest the teller's life be shortened. And at each pause the listeners responding with a loud "Ha!"; and at the end of each tale a narrator looking around the room, fixing his glance on one of those present and saying abruptly, "Now the tail is on you!" And to take it off the one designated began a story in turn.

Mrs. Wolf Red Belly Woman cleared her throat and spat noisily into the fire over the heads of her small listeners. She was more a shadow than a woman—a bodiless thin shadow of a skeleton wrapped in a rusty black rebozo, almost toothless, and with long gray hair. Her eyes were filmy gray smoke-stones set in pouches of wrinkled skins. Her voice, as she began, had the sound of two notched sticks rubbed together in a lonely aspen grove.

*Natö'ai.* There is this young man, Shell Boy, and this young woman, Blue Corn. And Shell Boy sings to Blue Corn among the red willows at night when she sleeps. And at day he meets her among the great cottonwoods where the grass is green, and the water white upon the stones. And Shell Boy and Blue Corn are married.

Now Shell Boy has a beautiful sister. Her long black hair sings. Her feet twinkle like stars. Her back is a tall, straight pine. Her heart is pure. But her eyes are sad. Now the beautiful sister will not marry. She dies.

So two moons fill and wane, and Shell Boy discovers that Blue Corn leaves him at night. When she comes back, he asks, "Why are your eyes so sleepless, your breath awake?"

And Blue Corn answers, "It is the wind. Cover me with your blanket."

Another night he asks her, "Blue Corn, why are your feet so cold and damp with dew?"

And Blue Corn says, "Because I have just gone outside. Cover me close with your blanket."

One night Shell Boy closes his eyes. He snores. He pretends he is asleep. Blue Corn bends over him. She sees his closed eyes. She hears him snore. She thinks he is asleep. So she rises and goes out.

Shell Boy follows Blue Corn. Across the stream where the water runs white upon the stones. Among the great cottonwoods where the grass is green. He follows her to the Witch Kiva.

There are many inside, but no one sees him as he hides outside in darkness. Now the Witch Chief gets up and says, "Let us have a feast." And each witch jumps through a willow hoop he holds out in his hand. And as each witch jumps through the willow hoop he holds out in his hand, he becomes a coyote, a crow, an animal or a bird.

Then Shell Boy sees his beautiful dead sister sitting against the wall as if asleep. And each witch goes up to her and says, "Now I take from her what I did," and each plucks from her body the stone, the stick or the porcupine quills they had shot into her to kill her with their bad medicine.

The beautiful dead sister opens her eyes. "I have been asleep," she says.

"No. You have been dead," says the Witch Chief. And he makes her jump through the willow hoop, too.

As she jumps through the willow hoop, too, she becomes a deer. Her eyes are still sad. Her feet twinkle like stars as she jumps up and runs outside. But all the witches run and fly after her, pounce upon her, and kill her. They bring her back, chop her up, and put her in a big black pot. But the meat won't cook.

The Witch Chief stands up. He looks around. He says, "Somebody is here who is not one of us!"

And then, just before daylight, Shell Boy runs home. He gets into bed. He pretends he is asleep.

Blue Corn comes in and lies down beside him. "Why are your eyes so sleepless, your breath awake?" she asks him.

"It is the wind. Cover me with my blanket," he answers.

In a little while Blue Corn says, "Why are your feet so cold and damp with dew?"

"Because I have just gone outside. Cover me closer with my blanket," he answers.

"But your whole body is cold and stiff," she says, and this time Shell Boy does not answer.

It is daylight; Blue Corn gets up and cooks him some panocha which she says had been given her.

"No! It is my beautiful sister's dried blood!" he cries, and throws it into the fire.

Now Blue Corn is frightened. She steals away with her fear to the Witch Chief.

"Tell your husband there is a big hunt tomorrow, and that he must go with all the other men," he instructs her. "Me, I shall make medicine to fix this Shell Boy."

So Shell Boy goes to the big hunt with all the other men. They hunt wide and long and well. Men this way. Men that way. In all directions. And the game in the center. Shell Boy crosses the river. He is tired.

"You have been a good hunter, Shell Boy," his companions tell him. "Lie down under this tree and rest. We will go a little way and see if the others return."

So Shell Boy lies down under the tree. He does not rest. He sleeps.

Now when Shell Boy awakes he is lying on top of a cliff. It is very high. Above the desert, above the fields, above the tall pines. He is in the clouds. The cliff is that high.

It is also very narrow. Shell Boy cannot move his head, his hands, his feet. There is room for him only to move his eyes. The cliff is that narrow.

It is also very steep. He knows that if he moves he will fall down out of the clouds, past the tall pines, and be crushed to death. And he knows that if he does not move, he will thirst, he will hunger, he will freeze. He knows he will die.

And so he lies and waits, and when the sun rises overhead, he calls out, "Father Sun, help me!" And he tells Our Father

Sun the story of his beautiful dead sister, Blue Corn and the Witch Chief who has made this medicine against him.

Now Our Father Sun takes pity on Shell Boy. But he calls down, "I can't stop for anybody. It is my work. Mother Earth needs me, and all her children, the corn, the trees, the animals, the birds, all that breathes and does not breathe, they need me. I have my work. But I shall send Morning Star to help you."

And soon Morning Star rises above Shell Boy.

"Morning Star Older Brother help me!" cries Shell Boy, and he tells Older Brother Morning Star the story of his beautiful dead sister, Blue Corn and the Witch Chief who has made this medicine against him.

Now Morning Star Older Brother takes pity on Shell Boy, and answers, "I can't come down to anybody. It is my work. I am not of day. I am not of night. I am of that which is greater than either, and so must stand between them both and cast my light for guidance to each. I have my work. But I shall send someone to help you."

And soon there comes to Shell Boy a tiny little blue bird. "I have come to help you," says the tiny little blue bird, and she makes him pick out all her feathers to lay around him.

Now Shell Boy can move his head, his arms, his legs. He can turn over.

"It is all I can do," says the naked little bird. "But I shall send someone else to help you further."

And soon there comes a little striped chipmunk to help Shell Boy. He plants a tiny seed at the foot of the high cliff. Then he races up and down the steep side of the high cliff.

The feathers of the tiny little blue bird enable Shell Boy to move and turn over as striped chipmunk races up and down the steep side of the high cliff. Father Sun gives striped chipmunk strength to race up and down the steep side of the high cliff. Morning Star divides the day from the night that he races up and down the steep side of the high cliff.

And as he keeps racing up and down the steep side of the high cliff, a tall pine tree grows out of the tiny seed below. It grows higher than the pine trees around it at the bottom of the cliff. It grows as high as the top of the high cliff, it grows higher, into the clouds. And when it grows high enough and strong enough, Shell Boy climbs down.

"Thank you, Father Sun. Thank you, Morning Star. Thank

you, tiny little blue bird. Thank you, striped chipmunk," says Shell Boy.

So striped chipmunk gives him a bow and five arrows, and tells him what to do.

Now Shell Boy goes home. Blue Corn is waiting for him. She gives him food, takes him to the river and washes his hair in amole—all as striped chipmunk said she would. And as his hair is washed in amole, and the life and strength comes up within him, Shell Boy does what striped chipmunk told him he should do.

He shoots an arrow toward the east, saying to Blue Corn, "See! This is how I shot a deer on the hunt!" And in the pine forest, the Witch Chief falls dead.

Now Shell Boy shoots an arrow each to the south, to the west, to the north, and all the witches of the Witch Kiva fall dead.

With the fifth arrow he shoots Blue Corn.

Then Shell Boy goes home. He finds his beautiful dead sister alive and well and happy again. Her long black hair sings. Her feet twinkle like stars. Her back is a tall and straight pine. Her heart is pure. But her eyes are no longer sad.

The visitors trudged home.

"A foolish, childish story," observed Martiniano angrily. "That a deer could be a woman or a witch! Imagine!"

"The day will come when I shall tell it to our son," murmured Flowers Playing gazing up at him with sad, appealing eyes.

Martiniano strode on without answering.

But as Estefana, behind, looked at her little sleeping son, she thought sadly, You will hear such pleasant stories no longer, Napaita. You will hear those with meanings only a man can understand. You leave me soon, my son.

All night, in a deep warm hush, it had snowed—great white flakes like great white moths fluttering gently down to cling to the rough adobe walls.

All morning, in a chill calm, it had snowed—an avalanche of feathers, as if the vast bare sky were the bare plucked breast of a wild goose.

All afternoon, in a bitter wind, it had snowed—a fine gritty spume whipped like sand into the face.

Now, near four o'clock, the storm cleared from a white

and freezing world. Fence post, bush and plaza lay smothered under soft snow covered with an icy crust. Women's hands turned blue as they plowed down to break the icy stream for water. Men shuddered in their blankets like cowled monks. Horses crowded close to the walls of evergreen-lined corrals. The breath of all rose and froze in the cold.

The old man squatting on the highest house-top did not look at the shrouded white breast of the mountain above, or at the pueblo blanketed like its people below. He only wrapped his own blanket closer and continued staring fixedly into frosty space. Over the far river gorge, across the desert, and to the last distant range where the sun's house was located: there his gaze remained fixed.

His old bent body was a cross of sticks covered by a tattered blanket, his face a mask of leather seamed and blackened by the sun and storms of a half-century of ceaseless watching. Only his eyes, black and timeless, held an indomitable fixity of purpose which nothing ever altered. He was the old Cacique who daily watched the sunset, making solar observations for his people.

The sun was a blurred red rider swimming through a milky mist over the jagged blue range. For six months the old Cacique had watched him sink in the west, a little farther south each night. Tonight the rider successfully breasted the mist and rode regally along the crest of mountains. He was tired and moved slowly, his bright red blanket about him, his brilliant feathers sticking up into the sky. For a moment he hesitated, then entered the doorway between two high peaks. The Cacique stood up to see him clearer. Wrinkles, like fingers, pulled his eyes into oblique slits. The red rider was gone. The sun had entered his house-mountain. From now on he would travel each night a little farther north.

A little while longer the Cacique remained in the bitter, winter dusk. Then slowly he walked back across the snowy roof-top and crawled down the ladder . . .

It was the winter solstice. The Night Fire Moon had risen overhead, and now, two nights later, a thousand more reflected it in the little village of La Oreja: brown paper bags rolled down at the top, and half filled with sand into which was stuck a lighted candle—the glowing luminarios lining wall and roof-top by which the villagers illumined this sacred eve, the Nacimiento de Nuestro Señor Jesu Cristo.

And now in the cold wintry dusk the pueblo too celebrated Him who was born on such a night.

In the crowded little church, the fat sly priest mumbled the end of a cold Mass. Guttering candles flared down at the blanketed figures rising with stiff knees from the cold bare floor. The Bocal, he who was known as the mouthpiece of the cura and served with a cornfield for pay, threw open the doors.

Out the people poured to stand in the snowfilled plaza, in the deep cold dusk, under the winter stars.

"Listen!" said Flowers Playing to Estefana who shivered beside her. "There are the bells! Christmas bells!"

Many bells. Christmas bells. The little straps of bells that hung on a dancer's legs. The deep-toned bell above the church. Then the first low murmur of rising voices soughing like wind in pines.

A little pink spark jumped through the still, dark plaza. The great bonfires of piñon, spruce and cedar burst into flame along the icy stream, in front of the two pueblo halves, in a great horseshoe curve of flame.

"He comes! He comes!" the people shouted as a great wooden arch of wood and evergreen burst into flame before them.

And they all came dancing out of the tiny church, through the great burning arch, around the icy plaza between the banks of snow. First the wooden Santo tottering on a litter carried on the shoulders of four men, with ocote torches burning around him. Then all the line of children dancing behind.

"Viva el Señor! Viva el Rey del Mundo! Viva Jesu Cristo!" shouted the Mexican visitors.

"Viva!" boomed the shotguns, the rifles, the old muskets. "He comes, He comes!"

"I see him not," muttered Estefana, crowded against a snow bank. "I prepared him so pretty too. In new moccasins lest his feet grow cold. In bright paint. With many feathers."

"He is but a little son," reminded Flowers Playing softly. "See? These are but the biggest children. Look! It is Batista."

They came—the bigger boys and girls brightly bedecked but with somber faces, dancing quietly between the snow banks. They passed—the smaller boys and girls staring wonderingly out of wide brown eyes as they danced in the flamelight to the blare and roar of guns.

It was he—Napaita! At the end of the line. Little, bright with feathers, shivering with cold and slipping on the ice, but still manfully trying to keep step.

They came, they passed—the long dancing line following the Santo on his litter. Past the crackling bonfires, between the pink-lit snowbanks. Around the blanketed throng, the pueblo, the plaza. The great burning arch crumpled and fell hissing. The fires burned low. The cold and dark returned, the stars, then silence.

"Beautiful! Beautiful!" murmured Flowers Playing, thinking, By next Christmas Eve perhaps I too shall have a son!

"It is a pleasant custom," replied Estefana quietly, but she thought, The next time I see it, it will not seem so beautiful, for in it I will no longer have a son.

Christmas came, and with it El Abuelo, El Toro and Malinche in the dance of the Matachines; taught the people, it was said, by the great Montezuma who once rode here in his litter bringing the flame to light the fire still kept burning these four hundred years.

Then King's Day, twelve days later, with the election and appointment of a new Governor and new officers, and the old Cacique handing over to them the canes of office.

What was this—that Palemon had an office?

"I am but an assistant. I am young. I am unworthy of honor, but I am called to serve," he replied simply to Martiniano. "Now to my house this night you must come and bring your wife lest I miss a good friend's presence."

How dark and somber it was at night: the empty, icy plaza greenish under the moon, and the two communal adobes standing black and lumpy like two mud cliffs. Like great, dark pyramids traversed by labyrinthine corridors, they seemed sealed to life and yet not quite dead. Who has ever penetrated the heart within the stone, through the hidden passage where men once ran carrying bows and arrows, water and corn, during siege, to the interior chamber where burns the sacred flame? It was all a legend, a fantasy in stone, yet not quite dead. A great mud sarcophagus full of mummies sleeping in the light of a tiny, flickering flame—and still visited by ghosts: groups of figures nebulous in the moonlight crossing the icy plaza and entering the pyramid to be swallowed by darkness and silence.

Palemon's room was crowded. Men in their best blankets filled the seating ledges and the small foot-high benches—

Palemon, Martiniano, the trader Rodolfo Byers, and a dozen others. The women sat on the floor and bed—Flowers Playing, Angelina, Mrs. Wolf Red Belly Woman, Estefana and all her friends. The fire crackled, piñon shells were cracked and spit out, jokes and laughter traded.

So they sat at home, the new Governor and each new officer with his friends. And to them each, one after another at long intervals throughout the night, came the ghosts of a life not quite dead, but reborn again. They were children coming in bands to give the dances of other tribes, complete to costume, gesture and song.

An opened door, the proper request and invitation. The old man with a drum standing unobtrusively in the corner, perhaps an old singer with him. And then, in the middle of the cleared floor, the dances. Sixteen-year-old youths and maidens brightly attired with feather suns giving a Round Dance borrowed from Cheyenne and Arapahoe. The Horse-Tail Dance from the Sioux, the Isleta Turtle Dance, the ornamental Chief Dance of the Arapahoes. Little devils came in; twelve-year-old boys wearing grotesque masks to do the Devil Dance of the Apaches. They glared around the room, stamped angrily, roared. But the bare little knees trembled with fright and cold; the frightening roars were thin, childish shouts. And the old men and women looked on without smiling their amusement. Two couples came in. The drum began.

"The Sun Dance of the White River Utes!" cried Flowers Playing. "How beautiful! How nice!" she clapped her hands in delight; and when, at its end, the old man came around with his basket for gifts, she dropped in her few, hoarded pennies.

They were followed an hour later by six youths wearing gray and black animal faces of buckskin with great round eyes, red and black kirtles with a fox tail dangling behind, carrying in their left hands a sprig of evergreen, and in their right a gourd rattle. One of them, without a mask, wearing huge black moustaches of charcoal. They faced east. The gourds rattled. Then suddenly the chant began:

"Ho-ho-ho-HOH,

"He-he-he-HEE-YAH . . ."

It was the Navajo Yei-bet-chai. The old men smiled broad grins of admiration. "Hai! Look at those moustaches! Listen at that song!"

And at the end of each dance, the old man in the corner picked up his drum. Basket or gunny sack was passed around for gifts of bread, pennies, cigarettes, a measure of meal. And the children filed out to continue their round.

Estefana still sat waiting. Batista had come and gone. Now the last group came. An old Pawnee dance it was at first. Then two couples, a twelve-year- and a five-year-old boy, with two small girls. They were beautifully attired. Long colored ribbons dangled from the boys and were held like reins by the girls who drove them around, all dancing. The little moccasins lifted and fell. The childish bodies twisted and turned.

A low murmur of approbation ran round the room. All glanced with new respect at Flowers Playing who had taught it to the children. They seemed to remember her for the first time as that fine dancer to whom they had given so many presents in the glade under the cottonwoods. She sat back, eyes shining, watching Martiniano stolidly sitting across the room. Does he know what I thought as I taught these children this dance? she wondered. That someday I shall teach our own son this dance also?

"The Ute Sariche!" grinned Byers. "I haven't seen that in twenty years!" And he dug out from his buckskin jacket store cigarettes and a handful of nickels and dimes.

Estefana's heart burned in her eyes as she watched her son dance. Her body was bent forward, her hands clasped. What presents filled the bag which the old man passed around! What a strange, fine dance these children had brought this night! And Estefana darted into the kitchen for great loaves of bread, one after another, to thrust into the gaping maw of the sack.

"Why, you will have no bread for yourselves, all this winter," chided a friend with Pueblo thriftiness.

"What!" indignantly answered Estefana. "With Palemon a new officer called to serve, is it not fitting that in his own house his own wife be generous to those who come to do him honor?" And she ran to wrap her son's little blanket closer about him as he stepped out into the night again.

Then suddenly it was all over, and Estefana was left in her lonely, breadless kitchen. Bread! Bread! she thought in pride and sadness. They chided me for giving bread. Why, I would give my life to keep my son!

So the days passed, each heavier with longing. The days passed, the time of staying still. And the daybreak came when everyone crept furtively out through the snow to break the ice in the stream and take a hasty, ceremonial bath. And the day came when Estefana was to lose her son.

It was the Man Moon. Napaita was to enter the kiva for a year and a half's instruction before initiation. Palemon prepared him. "You see, my son, it is your time. The time when you begin to learn to be a man as is your father. You are very proud, no doubt. And that is proper."

Estefana talked to him also. "You see, my son, your time comes. You must learn to be a man. You must no longer be a child who clings to a mother's skirts. That is very bad, and I would not have it so. Let us be happy about this thing together."

But when she told him he would not come home again, nor see her, his sister nor any other woman, and watched his little brown face quiver with wonder, her heart wept.

The day came—a day like any other. She did up a few things for him in a tiny bundle tied with cord. Palemon thrust it carelessly under one arm, took the boy by the hand and walked slowly and unconcernedly across the plaza.

A few strangers were strolling about. Two women, balancing pails of water on their heads, were coming back from the stream. The day was clear and bright. A bird sang. A burro brayed in the corrals.

Estefana stood in her doorway. It was unbelievable. She stifled the impulse to run inside, heap ashes on her head, gash face and breast with her fingernails, and run wailing round the plaza. For what? There were father and little son strolling carelessly up along the stream as they had always. No sign of emotion showed on her dark, moon face as she watched them stop at a circular wall of adobe some six feet high rising at the end of the plaza where the ceremonial race track began. An old weathered-gray ladder of cedar leaned against the kiva. She watched the boy turn around and look up at his father, then ascend patiently, with short arms and legs, the wide spaced rungs. Palemon followed behind. For a moment they were outlined on top against the dark blue mountains and the turquoise sky. Then suddenly they were gone.

Estefana turned and went back inside.

*"Father, Oh, father! I hear weeping. Is it my mother I leave in grief?"*

*"Have courage, son. You but leave the lesser mother for the greater."*

*"Father, my father! Where do I go? It is round and black and steep, this hole."*

*"Have no fear, son. It is an open womb you enter."*

*"But from the womb I came. Its lips thrust me out into sunlight. I saw the corn fields and the pine slopes. I saw the birds of the air, the beasts of the earth, the fish of its waters. I saw people. Like them, I was born to life. Why must I return to this black hole, this womb again, so soon?"*

*"You cry out like a frightened child. You cry out in ignorance. That is why you must enter. Go down the ladder, son."*

*"Oh, father! This chamber is deep and round and black. It is empty and stuffy. I cannot breathe. I see nothing but these embers and this little hole in the floor. Where am I, how long must I stay, why am I here, my father?"*

*"Hush, son! You are in the womb of Our Mother Earth. You will be here many, many months, a long, long time. You have entered a child. You will be reborn from here a man. Then you will know why it is you must stay. Let there be no more whimpering, no more questions, son. . . . You are in a womb: in it the eyes, the ears, the nose and babbling mouth do not function. The knowledge that will come to you is the intuitive truth of the spirit, the quiescent wisdom of the blood, transmitted through senses you do not use outside. The pulse of the earth throbs through these walls which inclose you; the embers there reflect the heat of its glowing heart; that little hole runs into the center of the world, into the lake of life itself. Remember you are in a womb, child.*

*"Listen, son. In your mother's womb you were conceived. From an individual human womb you were born to an individual human life. It was necessary, it was good. But individual human life is not sufficient to itself. It depends upon and is part of all life. So now another umbilical cord must be broken—that which binds you to your mother's affections, that which binds you to the individual human life she gave you. For twelve years you have belonged to your lesser mother. Now you belong to your greater mother. And you return to her womb to emerge once again, as a man with*

*no mother's hold upon him, as a man who knows himself not an individual but a unit of his tribe and a part of all life which ever surrounds him.*

*"Listen, son. You were born into the human-animal life of sense and nerve and will. But it is necessary that each man sometime be born again: into the consciousness of an even greater life.*

*"You have learned what in your ordinary animal-existence is necessary for your earthly body.*

*"Now you must have awakened in you the instinctive need for self-perfection in your inmost spiritual being.*

*"You must be taught the laws of world creation and world maintenance, the laws of all life whatever form it takes: the living stones, the breathing mountains, the tall walking rain, as well as those of bird and fish, beast and man.*

*"You must learn that each man has the debt of his arising and his individuality of existence to pay; that this debt must be discharged as early and quickly as possible so that you, as I, as all, may assist in turn the most rapid perfecting of other beings—those like ourselves, and those units of life advanced to the degree of self-individuality.*

*"For only in this way can life progress, can life exist.*

*"What is more fitting then, son, that to learn this you must return to the womb of the earth which is the mother of all life? That you be reborn from it into the greater spiritual life as you were born into the lesser life of the flesh?*

*"Peace, my son. And with it understanding. This period of your gestation will be long—twice as long as was the first, for the life it bears will be likewise longer. The lessons will be difficult, but they will be unceasing. Voices will speak them over and over until their meaning flows through your blood, though the words which must never be repeated be unintelligible to those who have no heart to understand.*

*"You will be taught the whole history of our people, of our tribe. How they had their last arising from the deep turquoise lake of life in the center of the world, the blue lake in whose depths gleams a tiny star, our Dawn Lake. How they emerged from a great cave whose lips opened into the world we see, from whose lips dripped water to congeal into perpetual flakes of ice white as eagle-down. You will understand then, son, why those of our clan are called the Deep Water people; why our kiva, this kiva, is called the Eagle-Down Kiva; the meaning of our masks, our dances,*

*our songs. You will see this cave. You will finally see this lake—our Dawn Lake.*

*"But behind all this you will learn of previous emergences. Of the significance of the four elements, corresponding to the four worlds from which man has successively risen. The fire world of rampant primordial forces; the world of air which separated from it; the third world of water which then came forth from the vaporous air; and the present world of earth. From your understanding that the body of man is itself a world derived from these four and hence composed of their elements and corresponding attributes, many things will be plain.*

*"You will perceive his kinship to all the living creatures of these four kingdoms of fire, air, water, earth. Not only his chieftainship over them, but his responsibility to them. For you will begin to understand that there is another world, a fifth world, to which we must all arise, and for the gaining of whose attributes this initiate is a preparation.*

*"Hence you will be taught, as those Old First Ones were taught, that the pine tree, the corn plant, have a life as we, but that they may be used and that they accede to their sacrifice for the maintenance of all life. You will be taught that the eagle, the trout, the deer, each has a life as we, but that they may be used and that they accede to their sacrifice for the need of progression of all life.*

*"But through all these truths will run the one great truth: the arising of all individual lives into one great life, and the necessary continuance of this one great life by the continual progression of the individual lives which form it.*

*"You will learn that this continuous progression seems to extend infinitely into time. But you will learn likewise that time also is an infinity.*

*"And that is life. Life must be lived, not learned from. And that is why in full consciousness only there is freedom. And that is why you learn awareness. To live life, in full consciousness, in freedom. Unbound by possessiveness, the possessiveness of your mother, the possessiveness for your son.*

*"Now I can say no more. You will grind your own corn: it makes song come easier. You will make your own moccasins: busy hands free the mind to the spirit.*

*"Now I, the father, having deposited his seed, withdraw from this womb.*

*"Now I, the father, say good-bye to his child.*

*"We will meet again. But as brothers. As men together. As equal parts of one great life. No longer separated. But in that consciousness of our oneness which gives us our only freedom."*

# 6

ACROSS THE fields to Byers' trading post plodded a strange figure. It looked like a straw-stuffed scarecrow suddenly touched to life in the corn fields. On its feet were remnants of moccasins wrapped in burlap through whose rents protruded muddy, bloody toes. Its torn trousers were loosely upheld by a string; a grimy, buttonless shirt flapped open to reveal a dark brown belly. Over all was draped a thin, cotton, Montgomery-Ward blanket. The scarecrow stalked into the post, leaned over the counter with offensive familiarity, and demanded a half-dollar.

"Get the hell out of here!" answered Byers without looking up.

The scarecrow leered, chuckled, stalked imperiously out. It plodded up the road and stopped at an old, rambling adobe house set back in an unkempt garden. A cringing Mexican girl led the way into an artist's cluttered studio. Shelves and bookcases were full of basketware, pottery, artifacts. Peyote fans, old feather war-bonnets, buckskin leggings and beaded moccasins hung on every nail and hook. The walls were covered with unsold paintings and quick color sketches. Many of these were portraits of a large, handsome Pueblo Indian in different poses, and wearing the articles seen around the room.

Benson hurried in—a small man quick of movement and nervous of manner, and wearing now a look of apprehension on his sharp, pinched face. The scarecrow, huddling beside the pot-bellied stove, drew out from his grimy shirt four scrubby ears of colored corn braided together. These he passed, grinning, to Benson. The artist looked at the corn, and then at a dozen strings more beautiful hanging around the room. He looked at his portraits: the one handsome, hawk-like face with its glossy, well-combed hair, the clear sharp eyes, the taut rose-brown skin stretched over the high cheek bones, the full but resolute mouth and muscular neck giving way to a broad smooth chest. He looked at the poetic gestures and beautiful body reproduced in color calendar prints for all of America to admire. Then he looked at the shabby limp body huddling beside the stove; at the puffy, muddy face with its sagging mouth and bloodshot eyes. He sighed, then tossed the scarecrow a quarter.

"I'm busy," he said tersely, kicking the corn under an easel.

The scarecrow grabbed the coin and stalked out. Drunken Panchilo was making his rounds.

He trudged into La Oreja, begging a cigarette on the plaza. In the back of a little bar he managed to wheedle a drink out of the pock-marked Mexican bartender when no one was looking. This made him feel better. He went into the lobby of the little hotel and slouched down beside two tourists. Out from the sloppy trousers came a little piece of greasy red rock. This he rubbed on his cheeks and open patch of belly.

"Look! This red rock. She Indian paint. What she use for big dance." He held it out in a dirty palm. "You buy? Fifty cents? Then I tell story where it come from. About the big giant turned to stone. To this red rock. This Indian paint. Heh?"

As the tourists alternated between the desire to hear more and to flinch from the teller's grimy, tattered body, the hotel manager appeared. Panchilo grabbed his rock and rapidly stalked out.

For a long time he squatted against a sunny wall in the plaza. Horses and wagons drew away from the hitching racks, and were replaced by others. Indians, Mexicans and whites trudged by. Panchilo did not look up. He sat as if alone on a mountain-top, nursing his secret devil under his tattered blanket.

It spoke. He got up, and went to a new curio store. Wile and shrewdness lent him a certain dignity. "These fine moccasins," he said carelessly, pointing out a pair. "I need them for our dance today. I am too poor to buy. I take them anyway. People will say, 'Where do these fine moccasins come from?' Panchilo will say, 'From my friend there at the corner of the plaza. There you may buy them. The very moccasins you have seen this Indian dance in.' Now! I will have these moccasins this afternoon. And you will sell them soon. We will both be pleased. We will be friends."

The woman, a comparative stranger in town, was impressed. Panchilo went out with the moccasins. He made the round of the plaza. Finally he was able to trade the pair for a pint of cheap whiskey. This was good! It was better when in back of a toilet on the outskirts of La Oreja he took his first swig. The raw liquor loosened his vocal cords, warmed his belly, raised his self-respect. Then turning into the upper road to the pueblo, he broke out into song.

Across the sage, along the stream, past the thickets of wild plum: here it was. A little rise beside the road. Panchilo settled down, spread out his legs. He took a puff at a cigarette butt he had saved, a gulp of whiskey. He sang. The stub he threw away when it began to burn his fingers, then the empty bottle. But still he sang, looking down across the fields, upon the desert . . .

At twilight Martiniano was riding home when his horse suddenly shied at a heap of rags lying beside the road. He dismounted. The thin cotton blanket had fallen off the scarecrow. Its torn trousers had slipped down a bit; the cold wind had blown open its grimy, buttonless shirt. The burlap-wrapped feet with the toes sticking out were lying in a puddle that would soon freeze over. Panchilo was drunk again.

Martiniano, throwing him across his horse, went on to the pueblo. In front of the church he let the limp, snoring body down and rode on home. Poor, drunken, childless, friendless—famous Panchilo. Was this the end of that beautiful, entrancing road, the Peyote Road?

It had begun to worry him; he did not know why. He had such beautiful dreams there in the tepee, and afterwards felt so high, so strong. There were great feasts too. Rena was a good man. It was a fine church. Yet something about it did not satisfy him. Something about it, indefinable and unseen, scratched like hoofs at the back of his mind.

Martiniano ignored it, and continued taking the Peyote Road.

One Saturday evening, a little early, for he was to help with the preparations, Martiniano started off to the meeting. He felt fine, really very cheerful. The sky was a light green turquoise, the mountains deep blue. The snow was melting. The soggy earth smelled rich and fresh. The edge of the wind was dull; winter had lost its temper. A bird sang in the thickets.

Suddenly the bushes crackled. A shape moved out of the dusk to stand before him—a deer.

Martiniano stopped in his tracks. One swift, helpless glance counted the five points of the horns. Another roved quickly over the skin he knew so well—hanging on the wall at home. There was the same-toned gray, the marking of black, and the little splotch of white under the left shoulder, down toward the belly.

It was the deer he had killed.

Martiniano was too astounded to question the unbelievable. He lacked the fright to flee, and the courage to move forward. He simply stood there, as a man stands before a miracle, with a calm acceptance of the mysterious made commonplace.

The deer did likewise. One forefoot was raised, but not in flight. The black nose was up without sniffing, the petals of its ears standing naturally. There was neither anger nor reproach in its great round eyes. It was as if two old acquaintances had met after a long separation, and accepted the meeting calmly.

*What shall I say to this deer I have killed? thought Martiniano. I cannot apologize, for what is done is done. Peculiarly, he knew the deer knew what he thought.*

*The fault is not all mine, he thought again. This deer has given me miserable nights. When I would have enjoyed my love and my sleep in Flowers Playing's arms it stamped round the house and upon the roof. I took the Peyote Road to find peace, yet this deer chased me back. Strangely, he knew what the deer thought, for what is done is done. We must all live in the full consciousness of the moment, and not in the one behind or before.*

So Martiniano kept quiet, and the deer. Both immobile in the dusk.

*Well! thought Martiniano. There is something between this deer and myself which I cannot understand. Perhaps it will come, now that we no longer fear or would harm the other. But now I must go on to the tepee.*

The deer's forefoot came down.

Martiniano looked to either side. The trail was narrow;

the thickets on each side were high and heavy. There was no room to pass.

The deer's head lifted. Its antlers swayed. Martiniano could see the flank muscles bunching.

*What is wrong with this deer? he thought angrily, facing its stern dark eyes. Why doesn't this deer I have killed go about its business and let me go about mine?*

And suddenly the deer was gone. Without a movement, without a crackling of the brush.

There was only the dusk, the clear green sky above the blue mountains, and the quick song of a bird unbroken for breath. Not a full moment had passed.

Martiniano blinked his usually still and steady eyes. Am I dreaming while still awake? he questioned himself. Am I drunk, or is it true what people have said about this peyote making a man mad?

He walked swiftly home, threw open the door.

"What is the trouble? You will be late," greeted Flowers Playing.

"I have forgotten something," he answered, striding quickly past her. There it was, hanging on the wall. The skin of the deer he had killed—yet faced a moment ago. The soft-toned gray marked with black, and with a little splotch of white at the left front edge, down toward the belly he had slit open.

Martiniano stared at it a moment in deep silence, then strode back out and swiftly up the trail again. He came to where he had met the deer. He stopped. The deer was gone, but the memory remained to confront him.

"I am a crazy Indian!" he muttered.

But he knew he could not pass.

He turned back again and slowly walked home.

"What is the matter with you?" asked Flowers Playing. "You are already late."

"This Peyote Meeting tonight. I am not going. I have changed my mind."

He went in and sat before the fire, smoking a cigarette and staring at the skin above him. After awhile he took off his clothes and went to bed. Flowers Playing continued her work in the kitchen. She ground corn, put beans to soak overnight. When she finished and came in, she stopped in surprise.

"In bed already? Are you ill, Martiniano? Is it your head, pains in the belly, or those fingers you froze?"

Martiniano did not answer. She undressed quickly and got into bed beside him.

"What is the trouble, husband? Why did you not go to the meeting tonight, but came home?"

Martiniano smiled in the darkness; in an instant his heart had become strangely, joyously light. "Why should a man take the long Road to peace, when one leads to his own door? It is not my head, pains in the belly or those fingers I froze. It is my heart which is again warm for you." And he took her great soft breasts and spread them apart, and sank his face between them.

Flowers Playing pressed it closer. She murmured, "It has been a long, long time. I felt that something was wrong. I felt that coldness which had come between us. Now it is no longer so. We are one together."

Martiniano slightly lifted his head and listened. There was no sound of hoofs overhead, around the house; no sound at all but Flowers Playing's quick breaths. He lay in her arms in love, and then in sleep, untroubled.

Late the next morning when he walked into the plaza Martiniano was conscious of a subdued excitement. He asked no questions and waited for a friend to casually draw him away, out in the open fields.

"You were not there last night, Martiniano. In the tepee. At the meeting. Now that is very strange. It is as if you had known . . ."

Martiniano maintained silence and a calm face.

"Yes. As if Our Father Peyote had told you before that we would be interrupted on the Road. Just after midnight when the Deer are up. I had just eaten my twelfth button. We were in the midst of our songs, our prayers, our dreams."

"Ah!" said Martiniano, and calmly rolled a cigarette. He waited for the teller to do likewise. A puff. Another. The news came out.

Just after midnight a crowd of men had broken up Rena's peyote meeting. They had burst into the tepee, grabbed all blankets and shawls, drum, fans and peyote. They had arrested Rena, the Drum Chief, Fire Chief and Cedar Man, and taken some of the rest. Then they had jerked up the stakes, collapsing the tepee.

The man's face, while talking, had turned into a sullen mask burnt through by two black holes.

"It was these new officers of ours who take this means of showing their authority! Burros! Every one!" He spat. "That new Governor most of all, who hates peyote knowing nothing about it. The Lieutenant-Governor, the War Captain and his assistants, the assistant to the Fiscal. They were all there! Even that Palemon! It was he who took your blanket."

"Ah," said Martiniano calmly.

"There will be the Devil to pay—perhaps many. No doubt there will be a Council meeting to start with. Who knows what after? Well, what is done is done. Only I cannot understand why you were so lucky to escape this terrible night. I feel, myself, as if I had been trampled by buffalo. My mouth tastes like a magpie's nest. I am worried, besides. No, I cannot understand why you were so lucky."

Later in the day Martiniano met Manuel Rena. The Peyote Chief was friendly.

"You were not at the meeting last night, my friend. The first that you have missed since you took the Road. Well, perhaps that was good. We had a little trouble about which you have no doubt heard."

Martiniano nodded assent. "No. I did not come. I started. I turned back. I cannot say why."

"A man does as that within him bids him do," Rena said simply. "But this I say. These Mexican Penitentes, our neighbors, who lash themselves with cactus whips until their backs run blood—a foolish custom, mortifying the body, the slave, for the weakness of the master, the spirit; their Church condemns them. Their laws, their neighbors persecute them. Yet they have faith and never falter. And that is right. For it is not the object, but the faith in it that redeems us.

"Now we are Indians, not Mexicans; Peyote Eaters, not Panocha Eaters." He smiled. "We too are ridiculed, persecuted. In the eyes of the ignorant world we are crazy as they. It does not matter. For we have faith, and faith is something the faithless will never understand.

"So there will be trouble. We will meet it. In faith. Our Father Peyote will save us."

And still later in the day Martiniano met Palemon. No word of the one's blanket which the other had confiscated passed between them. But their friendship held.

Martiniano walked home. To Flowers Playing he told all.

"Trouble comes. But I will meet it. I do not know what I am, what I want, where I go. But something has happened to me which makes me unafraid; I do not know what."

Trouble came. It came to Council and filled the room like a black storm cloud. All night the members talked. Their voices were slow, polite, measured. But the words were sharp forked tongues of lightning. The storm rolled this way, then that.

There were the old men who sing but do not dance, the old men with snow in their hair and moss on their faces. And there were the young men, those with cut hair and American clothes.

There were the Kiva Chiefs and the members of the Kivas, with their belief in ceremonialism and dance; the Fiscal, Sacristan and the Bocal, the mouthpiece of the Cura, who trembled for God and the Catholic Church at the encroaching steps of this new heresy, the Peyote Cult. And there were the Peyote Chief, the Fire Chief, Drum Chief and Cedar Man and those who believed in their Road.

There was the new Governor who hated this growing power of Peyote, and the rich Manuel Rena who upheld it. Was it true, as some believed, that each lusted for power, was jealous and afraid of the other's growing strength, and but used his leadership for personal ends?

There was faith and doubt, orthodoxy and heresy, wisdom and folly, the conservatism of age and the impetuousness of youth. There was trouble.

"This peyote! Will we never learn? The white men came and there was whiskey to drink. Thirst for it took away our land, our horses, our wives, the respect of our friends. We lay ragged in the ditches along the road to town. Then the laws came. We could not sell our land. No Indian could buy whiskey. We were saved.

"The Mexicans came and there was marihuana to smoke. Our eyes rolled, our thoughts rattled in our heads like seeds in a gourd, they buzzed around like angry bees. We drew knives. We used them. We were mad. Then the laws came. It was forbidden to sell or buy or use this dreadful marihuana.

"What now, brothers? We were saved from the white man's whiskey. We were saved from the Mexican's marihuana.

We returned from the illusions of drinking and smoking to the reality of living. To our own good ways.

"We were saved. For what? To be destroyed by our own evil, peyote? In the name of this foolishness they call Indian religion?

"Listen! What is this foolish religion? Think and then answer. Then listen to the beat of your heart and the beat of the heart within our mountain: they are the same. Nothing separates them. Neither are they bound together by idle dreams, by talk, by fancies. Thus you will see the difference. This I say."

After a long silence, a head raised, a voice spoke out. "What man among us has been destroyed by this dreadful thing, this peyote?"

"Panchilo! Drunken Panchilo! Is the one unfamiliar? Is he unknown in the town, in every ditch along the way? What is this you ask? He is not the only one. He is but one of many who have gone before."

Almost respectfully and sympathetically the voice answered him. "Drunken Panchilo? Your very words betray you. It is true he took the Peyote Road. But for a time only. As he took whiskey, as he took marihuana also. For the sensations of the body. It did not work. For Peyote is a thing of the spirit. It is a road to peace, to understanding. This I say."

Now Manuel Rena spoke. Kindly and deferentially. He craved the indulgence of those present, but there were things about this Peyote all should know. How it was revealed to the Cheyennes and Arapahoes, the Kiowas, to save them. How all the Plains Indians used it. How the Indians of Old Mexico used it also. Did that not show its strength and wisdom? And now it was spreading even more. To the Pueblos. And soon, no doubt, to the desert Navajos, the Apaches, the mountain Utes.

"Thus we shall be one people together," he said. "One strength, one wisdom, one faith. It will come. Now it has come to us. Let us accept it."

The men spoke who were for God and the Catholic Church.

The Kiva Chiefs spoke, and they spoke the longest of all.

And now at last the old men spoke: they spoke alike.

*Let us take this into our body, our mind, our heart. Let*

*us move evenly together. Now it seems that this peyote is not the work given us to do.*

*It is worse than the thirst for whiskey, the craving for the fumes of marihuana—this hunger for peyote. For these others are but physical indulgences and as such must be dismissed, for the desires of the flesh are but temporal things. But peyote has associated with it a certain faith, this foolishness called Indian religion.*

*As a faith then let us consider it.*

*There are three understandings: of the body, of the head, of the heart. What endures must be understood by all. Now God, the Father, we so understand. He is the Great Spirit with many names. Who would quarrel with names? We also understand His Son, the Señor Jesu Cristo, who died and was reborn as we ourselves, the earth itself, is ever reborn. And so the church exists among us: we accept it.*

*Now our dances, our races, our kiva ceremonials—how can we speak of these that are a part of us? That is all we can say. The corn plants sway in the summer wind, stretching out their arms for rain; thus we dance. The young men hurtle down the race-track, one after another, giving life back to Our Father Sun for his race, so that it will be returned to them, and both endure. And in our kivas we strive to perpetuate the wisdom of those Old First Ones who had their arising as we. Will the day come when on Our Mother Earth the corn no longer grows, when Our Father Sun no longer has strength to make his journey overhead, when men forget their arisings? Then we will have no need for our dances, our races, our kiva ceremonials. We can say no more about this thing which we are.*

*But this peyote. It too creates a faith. That is good, that which creates a faith. But what is this faith? It is a road that leads to a better world: this you say. The Peyote Road. Is this the road we should take, travellers dressed in American clothes? How is it we can forsake the four-fold world of which we are a part?*

*From the fire element of the first world we hold the heat of animal beings. That of air gave us the breath of life. That of water produced our life-stream, our blood. And from that of the earth we derived the solid substance of our physical forms. From each of these worlds we have had our successive emergences. We are all that we have been.*

*So we ask: what kind of religion is it which would refute*

*that which we are; that falsely subjugates the body, inflames the mind with dreams and leads away the spirit?*

*Now something else. What is this better world to which the Peyote Road would entice us?*

*Through all our previous arisings we have slowly emerged from formlessness to separateness. Now we must return again to the formless, to the boundless, to the undivided. From the worlds of the physical to the world of the spirit which transcends them. But with the consciousness of their non-separateness. . . . That is our new emergence. We are all that we shall be.*

*But this Peyote Road to a new and better world. It is not an arising. It leaves one world behind. It returns a traveller to it once again. How is this? Can we cast away part of ourselves, either going or coming? It is an illusionary journey, a dream.*

*There is only one world of which we are all a part: Our Father Sun, Our Mother Earth, the birds of the air, the trout in the waters, the corn plant and the living stones, ourselves . . . all the life that is formless, that is separate, that in the essence of spirit will be formless once again.*

*We are all that we have been. We are all that we shall be. Shall we leave reality for illusion? Shall we strive for what we already have?*

*No. We already have our road. It is the road to where the life-giving road of our Sun Father comes out.*

*No. Let us forget this peyote. It is not the work given us to do.*

Thus they thought and spoke, and they all moved evenly together.

Manuel Rena, being rich and the leader of this Peyote business, was fined a thousand dollars. Three members were ousted from their kivas. Two young boys, Jesús and Filadelphio, were given five lashes each for having participated.

None of those arrested, fined and punished revealed the names of the others. But all the escaped ones' blankets had been confiscated and were kept: good Navajo weaves, Two Grey Hills, yellow Chin Lees, striped Chiefs, old Chimayo blankets, and the old soft Hopi blankets long obtained in trade. No owner dared demand his lest he be identified and punished too.

Martiniano thought about this. He thought about the

Peyote Road—around it, before and behind it, all ways. He thought of the deer he had killed. . . .

Then he went to Manuel Rena and said simply, "Friend, you are a fine man. I respect you. I respect the Peyote Road. But I have come to think that it is not my road. I do not know why, but it is so. And so I leave it.

"Now there is trouble. You will call me a coward for leaving it now. But I would have you know I had a sign before the trouble came. To ignore it I would have to call myself a coward, and that is worse.

"There is that blanket of mine. When the moment comes I shall claim it. I am not ashamed of having taken the Road as far as I can go. But I can go no farther."

"I understand," answered Rena. "I would have you obey the voice within you as I obey that within me. But the trouble is not yet over. So leave your blanket yet unclaimed."

Martiniano walked home. He had a great respect for the Peyote Chief. And to the old men who opposed him, he gave also a grudging admiration. They thought so simply and directly; they believed in life. But he was glad to be free of both.

This deer he had killed. This deer he had met on the trail. He did not know what it meant. It brought him evil and unhappiness. Then it saved him from evil and brought him happiness. Could it be true that real happiness comes only from real unhappiness conscientiously endured? Had he come upon a great truth which proclaimed that in the fruit of evil lies the seed of good?

Ah! How does one know the things that one knows? he queried. I only feel, as I have always felt, there is that power in me which knows what I do not know. But now, he thought darkly, as his bitterness returned, what am I to believe in? What faith can a man have, in these changing times?

The trouble grew worse; the Pueblo divided against itself as the Peyote Eaters retaliated against the new Governor and the old men.

Jesús and Filadelphio went round among all the young men and the new boys returned from away-school persuading them not to cut the heels off their shoes nor the seat out of their pants, not to wear blankets nor to let their hair grow long. "Look!" they said. "We do likewise. Times have changed. Shall we go back to being blanket Indians? Or shall we put to use what we have learned? I myself—I have ridden on a train. Some day I am going to buy a Ford. But tonight I am going to walk into La Oreja and see those moving pictures again. I have learned how to live."

The men ousted from their kivas surlily proclaimed against the stringent old ceremonialism, the old dances. They enlisted new members for the Peyote Church. "We are American citizens," they said, "with freedom to worship as we will. Why should we be denied our own Indian church?"

Manuel Rena did more. He was a rich man, but not rich enough to pay a thousand dollars fine, so a piece of his land had been confiscated. He went into La Oreja, hired a lawyer, and brought suit in the American Court. The decision came: Manuel Rena was an Indian and thus under the jurisdiction of his Pueblo government. But at the same time he was an American citizen, a communal property holder, and had committed no crime. The punishment was too severe. He was to be given back most of his land.

The row brought the Superintendent and Emil Strophy running after him with his briefcase.

"God Almighty!" wailed the Superintendent. "Just when you were all settled down with all the good things the Government has given you! Then the trouble about that deer which was killed. And now this! This trouble about a bit of peyote. What has got into you? You fine peaceful people on your rich land?"

"What about the land you promised?" they were asked calmly, sternly. "What about that land which is ours but still withheld from us? The land in the mountains, around our sacred lake, our blue Dawn Lake?"

Strophy blinked his eyes. These Indians! Do they never forget?

"Why, of course, of course! Did I not say we would look into this matter? Have I not written letters, sent papers to our father at Washington? Patience. But what has that got to do with peyote—this dreadful peyote trouble?"

They met that night. The old men sitting around the walls in their blankets, and the Government men sitting at the little table in chairs brought in from outside. Flowing brown waves of soft living awareness beating steadily, hour after hour, against a cliff of cold reason.

"I think we ought to get this straight," said the Superintendent, stopping for the interpreter to translate, and then continuing. "Your good friend, the Commissioner, is displeased about this disgraceful way you have acted. The Commissioner, the Government, has accepted peyote for all Indians. For all Indians everywhere. Peyotism has been organized as the 'Native American Church.' It is the true Indian Church."

A deep silence followed the explosion. He looked round the room. The old men were sitting heads down or with blankets drawn over their faces. There, he thought, that'll put them in their places.

"We think it's a good thing," he went on, "for the Indians to have their own faith, their own religion—the Native American Church. The old ceremonial life is gone forever with the passing of the hunting and simple agricultural life. The old ceremonies are good; but it's getting so that they can't be held any longer on account of the cost, the length of time to prepare and perform them; and many of the ritualistic forms are being forgotten anyway. Is it better to die with these ancient ceremonies, or to preserve the life of your tribe in this new church? The Native American Church is the answer. We want to preserve the continuity of Indian culture and religion, so we give you this Native American Church. You want to preserve your way, the Indian way, so you will accept it. Yes?"

And still the silence, the stifling, heavy negation of Indian silence.

He explained still further. "This Peyotism is a new thing to all of you perhaps. But it is very old. The Indians of Mexico have it, the Coras, Huicholes and Tarahumares, and the Indians of the Plains, the Kiowas, Comanches, the Arapahoes and Cheyennes. It is spreading. Soon all will have it. It is all Indian. In it are fused many of the ancient religious experiences of the Indians and some phases of Christianity. So the Indian has become modern or universal in spirit. In fusing these two together he builds something new and original, all his own. For Peyotism is not only a religion, but a way of life that accommodates itself to the present and hopes for the future. The Indians are a great people. They will not die, they will become greater when they have their own new church. See what the Government does for you: it opens the gates for the genius of your race to express itself in modern life. It gives you this Native American Church."

A log popped. Silence swallowed the sound. The old men had been very respectful, very attentive. But this talk. The talk of culture, of religion. What did it all mean? So it was all explained again, more slowly. And then these explanations were elaborated. It all went down the maw of silence. Silence, silence, silence. It shouted, screamed. The visitors began to squirm.

At last the old men began to speak. This was worse. A steadily flowing ten-minute talk crisply translated into a dozen strange sentences; and then each of these sentences necessarily expanded into a half-hour's interpretation.

"Peyote. We are to look at, to speak of this thing as a church then? Then let us look at and speak of it as a church. An old church?—strange we have not heard of it before, from our fathers. An Indian Church?—strange that it must be given to us by white men, the Government. Yes. A strange church.

"Well, let us think of it as a church. Let us look at this Peyote Church, and at our blue Dawn Lake, our church. Thus we will see the difference.

"Peyote. It is a ripple on the one great blue lake of life. It will pass. But life endures. All roads lead from it. All roads lead back to it. It is the one reality. The great blue lake of life. That is our faith.

"Give us back our Dawn Lake if the Government would give us a church we want. Give us back our Dawn Lake as you have promised. So we say."

This is what the Superintendent and Strophy managed to make out.

Another spoke.

"Regarding churches. Why does the Government want to give us an Indian church? To preserve our way, the good old ways. That is good; it is proper. But we already have an Indian Church to preserve our good old ways. Would it not be easier for the Government to show its good heart by just allowing us to keep this old church instead of giving us a new one? It has been promised to us for these many years. Why promise us a new one instead of keeping the promise of the old? Does the Government not want to give us our Dawn Lake? We want our Dawn Lake."

The visitors were beginning to catch on, but still the talk continued.

"Let us speak of churches as churches are meant to be spoken of. Not as buildings, neither adobes with bells, nor tepees. Let us speak of churches as those edifices of the spirit from which come all the blessings of life.

"Now from the Peyote Church may come these blessings; we do not know. But we know that from our Dawn Lake flow all the blessings of our life, all the good things we get —the water for our corn fields, our springs, the water to keep the deer and trout alive and the mountains ever green, the waters of life which continually refresh the human spirit, these also. Can we forsake this church which gives us all these blessings for one which can give us no more? Our Dawn Lake. This is our church. Give us our Dawn Lake. This I say."

Others spoke. All spoke. And it was as if they spoke with one voice, one mind, one heart. Thus they moved evenly together.

The two visitors returned to La Oreja. They rode the old auto-stage through the gunsight pass where they took the train: the Superintendent to his city office, and Strophy to continue on later to Washington, his briefcase bulging.

Damn that fellow who killed the deer! Damn this peyote business! They had only awakened sleeping trouble. Both men knew what kind. It had the long memory and obstinacy of an elephant.

In the pueblo, the peyote members went around complacent and appeased. Manuel Rena had been given back most of his land. The Government approved of their Road. They were members of the Native American Church. But gradually they grew aware that their unblemished appeasement was tainted by a spot of Indian red. And as they heard the people begin to murmur, they knew they were but a ripple on the one great blue lake of life.

Give us back our blue Dawn Lake, beat the heart of the mountain and all the hearts below. Let everything be as it was, with the children ascending, singing and bedecked with flowers, and the tepees and the fires growing around the water's edge, and deep in the middle the blue star shining.

# 7

EASTER came late. The heavens wept, the people wailed with grief; and then to the peal of bells, from the ecstatic murmurs of mankind, He rose triumphant from the dead—Nuestro Señor Jesu Cristo, Our Savior, the Blessed Son, Our Lord.

But Easter came late. The earth of which He was a symbol was already resurrected. Ice-locked avalanches plunged down the cañons. The river roared through the gorge with the spring thaw. Over the new-plowed fields crows flew low, cawing. Ai. Our Mother Earth was awake again and crying for new seed, the little pinto stallions were fierce with love, men were clutched by strange longings.

Even the strange white man, the trader.

Martiniano had gone to see him; he was stamping around in his tool shop behind the post, and cursing the rats which had been gnawing at one of his pelts. Martiniano opened his jackknife and squatted down to make a mousetrap: a narrow gangplank of two sticks meeting over the top of a bucket of water in a loose notch covered by a piece of cheese.

As he whittled, he said quietly, "We have not discussed for many months the money I owe you—the fine you paid when I killed the deer. It is about this I have come."

"Let it go—let it go," Byers replied gruffly. "Pay when you can."

"There was that one-hundred and fifty dollars," Martiniano continued. "There was forty-two before that, and sixteen dollars after. That was two hundred and eight. But this winter I brought wood, chopped in little pieces for stove and cut in big logs for fireplace. Fifty-six dollars' worth. There still remains one hundred and fifty-two owing. That is a great deal of money. Perhaps from my small field I will not harvest that much money, and still it will be owed. Yet I must pay, and quickly. I feel it so."

"God damn it! Don't bother me about business. Talk to my wife."

"That is what I thought this spring. And so I worked as I have never worked before. On that far slope rising toward the mountain, along the Acequia Madre. I dug out the sage with its obstinate roots until my hands bled. I cleared this new land. I plowed. I harrowed. It is ready. But I am not. I have no seed for planting. I have no money for seed. So I have come to you with the debt between us.

"This I mean. I have cleared new land to show you, not knowing whether it would be planted. Now buy seed and the first harvest will be yours in payment for both debt and seed. . . . It is peaceful there up the cañon and over on the slope. There is an old sheepherder's hut there—of adobe. We will live there this summer; my wife, being Ute, likes the mountains. We are not well regarded in the pueblo, besides. And besides that, I have my old horse to ride down to my smaller field. Thus above I work for you and my debt, and below for ourselves. What do you say?"

"Lazy Indian! It will probably be a bad year besides!"

Martiniano stood up and threw back his pig-tails. "There. It is finished. This mousetrap. As my father used to make them."

"Mousetraps! God Almighty! On a day like this! I need a new room, not a mousetrap."

"Another room! Is it truly needed?"

"Hell, no! What more does a man need than one room with a stove to cook on and a bed to sleep in? I have too many already. It is this weather that makes me want to feel new walls rising, fresh adobe taking shape."

Martiniano drew up his blanket. "You will think about this seed? El Día de Santa Cruz approaches, the day for planting."

Byers turned around; he had been leaning against the doorway, listening to a meadow lark.

"No!" he said. "What I need is a little new dust on my shoes. A buying trip. Yes, by God! Look here. My wife and I are going down river; I have just decided. I will buy some new stuff. Pick up some clay at the bottom of those red cliffs for my new room. Get that seed too; it's cheaper down below. Three or four days, that's all. But I need someone along. I'll pay you for the work. You and your wife be ready at daybreak tomorrow. Bring along your own blankets."

So just past Easter at sun-up, in a muck-smeared automobile, they started out. Byers, unshaven, driving with Angelina in denim trousers beside him, and Martiniano and Flowers Playing squeezed by luggage and blankets behind. With them all, unseen, rode Spring.

It was not quite noon of the third day, and the drum was still beating as they knew it had been beating all morning—like an almost imperceptible echo of a pulse within the lifeless, lumpy mud hills.

The car ground through a sandy arroyo, lurched up a barren slope. "There," said Martiniano when they reached the crest. "That pueblo."

There on the sandy plain below, between the lumpy mud hills and curving brown river. A low mud town as if sliced out of a low mud hill. A few corn fields outside. A patch of ancient cottonwoods across the river. And beyond, the pale, cedar-splotched desert sloping up and away to a far blue rampart of mountains.

They could hear it clearer now. A deep, resonant beat that held against the wind.

Leaving the car near the little church within its low mud wall, they walked into the corona of filth and acrid odor of urine and ordure that edged the pueblo, past the lanes opening between rows of squat, flat-topped houses. Dust eddied in the empty streets. A dog sprawled in the sunlight, biting at his flees. A pig ran squealing out of a blue doorway. Only the drum, full-toned now, betrayed the lifeless negation.

Abruptly they came upon the long, wide street that served for plaza. A stinging blast of sand swept up and lifted. It revealed not only the pulsing heart, but the voice, the will, the blood-stream and the ligaments—the hidden and working anatomy of the body of the desolate town. Its function was the Spring Corn Dance.

At the near end of the plaza stood a high, circular, adobe kiva whose smooth wall was broken by a flight of terraced steps. On these stood resting a file of dusty painted Indians. In front had been erected a little green shelter facing the plaza. And in this, on a rude altar, sat a wooden Santo bedecked in bright cloths and silver ornaments.

The four visitors squatted on the ground against a wall, and stared down the arid street. At the far end rose another kiva. Out of it, to the beat of a drum, was filing a long line of dancers.

In front, up one side of the street, came straggling four rows of old men in their brightest colored shirts, tail out over gaudy, flowered, full-legged pajama pants, and carrying in each hand a sprig of evergreen. In their midst one beat a small drum tied round his waist.

Beside them, up the middle of the plaza, walked a man beating powerfully a great belly drum. With him walked the flag carrier. The long smooth pole carried on top a narrow hand-woven kirtle and a fox-skin, and was adorned with parrot feathers, shells and beads.

Behind them, in two files, slouched the dancers—perhaps a hundred and fifty men, women and children.

Little by little as they straggled forward, colors screamed against the dun gray walls, a life emerged into the monotone of sand and sky.

The men, naked to the waist, were painted a golden copper. Their freshly washed hair, now gray with dust, fell to their wide shoulders and held entwined a few green and blue parrot feathers. Each wore a white ceremonial kirtle embroidered in red and green, and tied with a red and black wool sash, the long fringe dangling from right knee to ankle. At the back, swaying between their legs, hung the everpresent fox-skin. On their legs tinkled straps of little bells, sea shells and hollow deer hoof rattles. Their ankle-high, fawn-colored moccasins were trimmed with a band of black and white skunk fur. They carried in the right hand a gourd rattle, in the left a sprig of evergreen.

The women, alternating with the men, shuffled along barefooted in the eddying dust. Their squat, heavy figures were covered by loose, black wool Mother Hubbards beautifully embroidered around the hem in red, leaving one shoulder free, and belted round the waist with a green and scarlet Hopi sash. Their waist-long hair, like that of the men, rippled free in the wind. Each carried on her head a turquoise-blue tablita held by a string passing under the chin—a thin wooden tiara, perhaps a foot high, shaped like a doorway, painted with cloud symbols and tipped with tufts of eagle-down. They wore heavy silver bracelets and rings, silver squash-blossom necklaces and strings of turquoise and coral, and carried in each hand a sprig of evergreen.

Everywhere evergreen, the symbol of everlasting life. It

was as if they had chopped down a spruce forest and brought it down to the mud flats.

The two files stopped, facing each other, the children on one end. Between them the flag carrier dipped his long pole over their heads, the drummer began to beat the great drum.

The outside ends of the four rows of old men halted, curving round and inward to form a four-deep semi-circle facing the two lines of waiting dancers, the small drum in the center.

Now in wind and dust the thing resumed.

The great belly drum throbbed hoarsely. The gaze of the forty old men turned inward, became fixed. They began to chant—a powerful soughing like wind among the pines. The pole dipped and rose. The sprigs of evergreen lifted and fell. Then came a tinkle of bells, the clatter of deer hoofs, a rattle of gourds. The lackadaisical dancers drew together like the segments of a chopped up snake.

They were dancing.

In two long rows, the stable, stolid women alternating with the leaping men. Then in four shorter rows as the women stepped back to face the turning men. And now in a great, slow moving circle, each woman a shadow at the heels of her man.

A powerful, down-sinking stamp, insistent and heavy from the men. Then faster, double-time, stamping to one beat and to the next marking time with bending knees. But from the old gray-headed crones, from all the subtle, submissive women, the barely lifted flat feet and the whole body shaking with the rhythm.

Occasionally an instant's pause. Then a shrill yell, a quickening rattle of gourds. The thunder-throb, the blood-beat of the great belly drum. The old men's rapt voices soughing through the green sprigs. A spruce forest moved down to the mud flats to shake and toss in the acrid stinging dust, under the hard, alkaline sky.

The group danced for a half-hour or more, then filed back to its kiva. But as the Summer People left, the Winter People came out from the opposite kiva. Thus alternating as winter follows summer, and summer yet again winter, the two groups kept dancing.

None of the four visitors moved from the lee of a protruding wall. Angelina had wrapped a handkerchief around her face to breathe through; Martiniano was shrouded in his blanket. Byers squatted patiently, legs crossed. Only Flowers Playing's eyes, uncovered, gleamed as she watched.

Gleamed at the insistent, down-pressing stamp; the same insistent, lifting chant. The stamp that sinks down deep into the earth, as the throb of the drum sinks deep into the bloodstream; and the rising chant that lifts, lifts up into the shaking spruce twigs, up to the rain-feathers on the pole, to the clouds in the turquoise sky.

It was all one: a mesmeric beat of the blood that closed the mind to sight and sound, to wind and dust. The beat of the blood through the flesh of the earth and the earth of the flesh, through the growing corn and the earth-flesh of the people who would envelop the ripened corn again for the strength and power to perpetuate both.

Late in the afternoon the wind increased. Swirls of dust blew down into the plaza from the bare mud hills. A choking gray mist through which the little children, too, still kept dancing. The boys in little kirtles and doll moccasins, and the girls wearing on their heads diminutive blue tablitas painted with tiny sunflowers. Two straggling rows of fresh-hatched chickens caught in a sand blizzard.

Easter had come to the mountains above with rushing spring torrents, the smell of fresh plowed fields. In the hot river lowlands below, the earth had been longer awake; the fruit trees were already in blossom, the bottomlands planted with chile and melons; the sun glared white and hot. But here on this dreary sandy plain no sign of resurrection appeared. And so the people called it forth, group after group, with rapt and unrelenting persistence. The people who were themselves the seeds of everlasting life planted between the mysterious depths and heights of the wide universe. They shook the earth awake to give forth the tiny shoots of new green corn in the scrubby patches. They stilled the serpentine clouds writhing overhead, they gathered the fat bellied clouds hovering there over the far buttes and mesas, above the desert. They called down rain, they called the tall walking rain out of the doorways of cloud with the fluttering tufts of eagle-down.

And all the while the Koshares pantomimed the insistent prayer as the people danced it, and as the old gray-haired chorus sang it. The eight loose Koshares, the most vigorous and alive of all.

Their ashy gray bodies, naked but for dark blue loin

cloths, were splotched with white and black spots, their faces weird masks of zigzag lines. Their hair was gathered up into a knot on top of the head, plastered with white clay, and tied with a dirty blue rag. From the tuft stuck up a thick cluster of corn-husks, dry, brittle corn leaves. Fantastic figures. Blackened ghosts of old cornstalks.

But beautiful of movement as they weaved continually through the unheeding dancers like alert, spotted leopards. Heads down, eyes lowered, they danced up and down, between and outside the lines. Their loose flexible arms with gentle motion drew up the deep power from the blackness of the earth with which they were painted, drew up the hidden juices into the roots, drew up the corn shoots. Then at a change of rhythm, their heads raised. They drew down the rain like threads, drew down from the sky its star-power and moon-glow, its pink-tipped arrows of fire, its waters.

But also they were very watchful to correct a child's step, to mark a change in timing, to hitch up a little boy's knee strap and tie on a girl's tablita blown off by the wind. For the dancers must not hesitate to the end. And when a tot squatted down exhausted, one picked her up, piggy-back, to carry off for rest.

And so it kept on all day. The tossing forest of spruce twigs and the deep soughing among it. The leaping, golden-copper bodies of the men amongst the forest. And the women, powerful and subtle, holding the green tablitas, the painted doorways, almost steady as they danced between the men. All in long lines, flexible as corn, straight as rain.

Till finally, towards sunset, the two groups merged. A hundred singing old men, three hundred dancers, two dipping poles, two great drums.

It was over.

Angelina looked suddenly a little sick. She held a hand against her belly.

"Here. Take this," said Martiniano, passing her a crust of bread. "It is that empty-sickness when the drums stop beating. I have seen it many times."

The dancers, spitting dust, were beginning to line up in front of the little shelter, each in turn to kneel and cross himself before the wooden Santo.

The visitors walked slowly past.

"I feel that I could fly!" said Flowers Playing simply.

Byers strode on without speaking.

They camped that night in the grove along the river. With dark the wind had died. Only the massive cottonwoods creaked above them like old, unstable pillars of an abandoned cathedral. They finished eating: thick steaks laid on the coals, potatoes charred in the ashes, coffee, bread, fruit. Martiniano threw on fresh wood. By its light he unloaded blankets from the car, and went down to wash the dishes at the river's edge.

Angelina and Flowers Playing sat talking, woman-like, of many things. It had been a good trip. Much had been bought: thick blankets from a Navajo trader, many pieces of silver and turquoise, a few old pieces of pottery. They had packed a bag of red clay for Byers to use as a wash for the walls of his new room, and had bought two bags of seed for Martiniano. And there had been this day-long, Easter, Green Corn Dance. There was something about it that made all these familiar trivialities seem very important, very precious. The day-long soughing of the old men's voices had swept the cobwebs from their cluttered winter minds. The dancing had shaken loose their own stiff ligaments. The continuous pound of the great drum had shattered the corpuscles of their blood into a new pulse pattern. It all had been a great purge, a resurrection, that made life new, quick, immediate.

Byers, his own chemical make-up rejuvenated, felt this keenly. He lay outspread before the fire, unheeding the light patter. This is the life, he thought. Foot-loose and fancy free, with women not too far away to worry about nor too close to bother one, and an Indian to do the work! Such trips were his one indulgence. They reminded him of the old days, his trading days.

Well, those were all over—and soon these would be too. He himself belonged to the vanishing past. But he was no sentimentalist, he reminded himself again sternly. No sickly nostalgia! There is no going back. There is no standing still. There is only that everpresent change which keeps life fresh and ever new.

But he wondered less about the changing form than the enduring substance. These pueblos all looked alike. The same church, kivas, mud floor adobes spread out or in tiers, a few head of stock, some scrubby corn patches. A mountain behind, the desert in front. Even the people seemed alike. The squat powerful men, the squat shapeless women, all with their proud, simple, rosebrown faces and quick, poetic hands. But still there was a difference.

Here in this pueblo was a passive inertia to change more formidable than any barrier, and an old rich ceremonialism that seemed at once sufficient and indestructible. A people, like the dough of their own bread, heavy and down-sinking, unassimilative. Wary, self-sufficient, remote in these dreary mud flats, they still resisted every advance.

Two years ago there had been a quarrel over the dancing between the white priest and the old men. The priest had left, the church was closed. No more Masses, marriages or baptisms for these ungrateful, sinning people. The Indians kept dancing. A year later the Church sent back another priest. The Pope, the Father, had relented and forgiven, he said. The people accepted him calmly—and went on dancing.

"Good!" grinned Byers. "Let 'em stick to their guns."

But the pueblo at home was not so remote. It had always been a link between the mountain and pueblo Indians, and the Plains tribes. And so the people, as a dough with all the heavy, close-knit solidarity of the settled Pueblo stock, seemed leavened with the restless, arrogant individuality of the roving Plains tribes. Like this Martiniano, shell and kernel.

Was it this infiltration of new stock which had made it the only pueblo yet susceptible to peyote? Or was it because their racial faith itself was gradually disintegrating? Byers did not believe in peyote. No people, no sect in possession of the awareness of spiritual power within themselves requires an outside stimulus or depends wholly upon sacerdotal paraphernalia. And the majority of Indians still believed in life with only their own natural symbolism, ceremonials and great myth and dance dramas expressing their wordless faith.

That, he decided, was the trouble in a nut-shell. These great forms, whose meanings to most whites were intelligible only by an imperfect translation of their values, were gradually being lost to the Indians themselves. In many already only the empty movement persisted. And soon they too would pass forgotten, inarticulate in any other form.

It was still the content that plagued him. The instinctive, intuitive, non-reasoning approach to life; the magnificent surrender of self to those unseen forces whose instruments we are, and the fulfillment of whose purposes gives us our only meaning. By infallible instinct and undivided consciousness the Indian had proved the validity of his approach. And because he couldn't or wouldn't express it articulately the whole shebang was passing with him.

Well, let it go. Byers had had his fling. Only . . . only there were one or two things he'd like to know first. Not that he ever would, of course.

Like that rattlesnake business.

Indefinable and remote as the sensations of a dream remaining after its outlines had faded, it had hung for years at the back of his mind. Now as the moon rose, and down the nave of cottonwoods he could see Martiniano's solid shape faintly outlined against the river—the great slow-curving river which coiled like a snake around the quiet pueblo and ran on, unending, with a rippling glitter of scales—it all returned to him with the force of something not forgotten but only sleeping within him.

It had begun when he was a young man first come to La Oreja. He lived any way, in any adobe hut. But every day he put on his faded pink shirt and walked out to the pueblo. Byers was a little romantic then, though shrewd and hard. He did not admit to himself why he went. He told himself the lesser truth. The life appealed to him. He listened to the drums, the songs. He watched the people. And then, having spoken to no one, he walked back home to cook his simple supper.

One afternoon a group of Indians came up and led him into an empty house. "My people. We watch you," one told him sternly. "Young white man she want one of our young girls mebbe. No? No good. Huh?"

Byers sputtered and cursed in denial. But he was frightened away. He became a forest ranger of sorts in the mountains above. Between times he shot and trapped beaver and muskrat, bear, mountain lions, skunk and deer. Passing Indians stopped at his camps, became his friends. After a time he returned to town and set up a little shop for trading.

He became friends with an old Indian who warned him to be careful. Some of the old men at the pueblo still disliked him, and had cast a spell upon him.

They were sitting one day in his little shop when a young Indian came in to sell him some apples. Byers refused. The seller offered him one free. The old Indian shook his head warningly. Later he said that a spell had been cast on those apples; there was a worm in one that would have grown into a snake and devoured him.

"The devil!" laughed Byers. "Where did you get that nonsense?"

Well, that spring the old man had been up in the mountains cutting wood when he heard voices around him in the empty clearing. Soon he could distinguish their meaning: the rattlesnakes had been invoked to harm his white friend, the strange young trader. Now, and always, he must be very careful of snakes. They were his bad medicine, perhaps his fate.

Two or three years later, when he had established his post and was beginning to be well known, Byers had driven a wealthy white woman down river here in his buckboard. His client had given him a hundred dollars to buy for her a great belt of old, hand-beaten silver conchos—the oldest, heaviest and the best he could find. Here in this pueblo Byers had once seen one hanging from a rafter. He located the house, and they entered with small gifts. The belt was still there, dangling from a viga.

It was a beautiful old room. The walls were nearly four feet thick and plastered smooth, cream-white inside. The dirt floor had been trodden hard and level as cement by generations of naked feet. The cedar door posts were gray as moss. The great vigas overhead gleamed dark brown as old honey. In the corner was a large, old-style Santo Domingo fireplace, now seldom seen. While the woman remained to study it, Byers walked with his host into the back room to dicker for the concho belt.

There were no windows. A thin light filtered through the breathing shaft and revealed seated about a little fire of twigs several old women. As he entered, flinging back the blanket that hung in the doorway, the oldest of the wrinkled crones suddenly jumped up on her bare, twisted feet. Blind, clutching her flabby breast with a withered hand, she began to spit and scream invective.

Byers stepped back a pace from the sudden assault. His host, a man of fifty, stepped forward. The old woman could not be hushed. The stranger, this white man, she kept crying vituperatively, carried about him the slimy stench, the poison and curse of rattlesnakes.

He had almost forgotten this strange occurrence some two years later when he was invited to go fishing up La Jara

Creek. Benson had just got married and bought an automobile to celebrate—the first in town. Excited and voluble, he squawked the rubber bulb and brass tube horn, loaded the back with fishing paraphernalia, lunch basket, easel and water colors, and gallantly handed in his bride in a linen duster. Byers moodily climbed in the back. He hadn't wanted to go.

As the car rattled out of town his moroseness increased. Half-way up the rutty cañon road he had a sudden premonition of evil and danger, and begged to be let out to walk home.

Mrs. Benson giggled. Benson squawked his horn and roared with laughter. "That's a bachelor for you! Scared out by newlyweds! We're not going to make love in front of you, old boy. You can take her fishin' up the creek, and I'll make a couple of quick sketches. Then we'll eat. Peek in that basket! Fried chicken!"

Byers leaned back, frowning.

The cañon, usually so beautiful, seemed darkly foreboding. Byers did not see the clear running brook, halting in deep still trout pools like pauses in music, the green open clearings, the fresh leaved aspens, the banks of tall, wild columbines. He only felt the tall somber cliffs increasingly closing in upon him.

The car had begun to boil against the steep climb. Benson stopped. "This is as good a spot as any," he chuckled. "Fish and pictures are where you catch 'em. We'll just leave the car here in the road. Nobody ever comes up here anyway."

Clambering out, he suddenly stooped, picked up a rock and threw it in a bush. "Look out! Saw a rattler!" he warned.

Byers had already got out. Halted at the side of the road, legs apart and breathing hoarsely, he stood staring in a hypnosis of horror into the brush. As if obeying some deep inward compulsion that he dared not question, he suddenly strode forward, bent and plunged his hand into the bush.

Mrs. Benson screamed.

Byers had brought up a rattlesnake writhing as he choked and cast it from him. Now he stood there, sweat running down his face, stupidly staring at a small red mark on the end of his right thumb.

Immediately they started back to town. The ride up the steeply rising cañon had taken scarcely an hour. Now, downhill, with Benson driving like a man wild with fear, their return trip seemed beset by every possible, improbable obstacle. The hot brake bands froze and had to be loosened. A tire blew out which none of them knew how to replace. And when they at last reached the main road, it was only to find a Mexican wood wagon stalled crosswise before them.

Throughout this excruciating fantasy of strangely interrupted haste, Byers maintained the calm, deathly acquiescence of a hypnotic. His weathered brown face had turned sallow. He sat head down, his hands dangling between his knees, without any feeling of pain or fright. But the prickling in his thumb was spreading up into his fingers.

The car sputtered into the plaza. Benson jumped out. There were two doctors in La Oreja. One, a capable Anglo, had taken a hospital case to the city, a day's ride away. The other was a Mexican who was gradually displacing with his forceps the horde of native midwives with their herbs—and had just ridden away on his horse to a hut up one of the mountain cañons. But there was a new young dentist in town. His office was locked. To his home ran Benson.

A crowd of bystanders dragged Byers out of the car. One slashed open his thumb with a knife blade cauterized in the flame of a candle. Two others, taking his arms, began walking him round and round the little square plaza.

People poured from shops, markets, corrals and alleys. An old Mexican woman ran up with a squawking chicken, slit it down the middle, and clamped the bloody mess on Byer's hand. With this dripping, feathered appendage, he kept going round and round. He was staggering now, and the prickling in his hand had spread up into his wrist.

"Here, by God! Who ever heard of curin' a snake bite with anything but whiskey? Hold on, boys!" A long, emaciated old gambler with pale, watery blue eyes and walrus mustaches stopped them and poured a pint of Bourbon down Byers' throat.

Benson came running up with the dentist, and together they dragged him up to a dusty, cluttered office. The young dentist, a mere boy, was plainly perplexed. He could draw out teeth but not poison. But he had a bottle of grain alcohol into which he was mixing water and lemon juice.

"If whisky's good, this ought to be better," he said in a timid, cheerful voice. Byers, in a daze, finished the bottle.

He was now ill. A terrible drowsiness was beginning to choke him, as if he had taken a powerful sedative. The impact of whiskey and grain alcohol for a moment shook him awake. He leapt to his feet, knocking over a tray of instruments, and flung up the window. Clutched behind by the coat tails, he leaned out bellowing with pain and screaming his inarticulate convictions that he had met his fate, and demanding to be left alone.

The plaza by now was crowded with teams, buckboards, wagons and horses; the news had gone round. Indians, Mexicans and whites stood below the window shouting encouragement and advice, laughing at the ludicrous spectacle bellowing above them, murmuring with patient pity, or maintaining the stolid silence of complete awareness. Among them crept Mrs. Benson weeping and nervously wringing her hands. Just as Byers was yanked back inside the room, his old Indian friend shuffled into the plaza in split moccasins and wearing a dirty, torn blanket. He listened patiently to the crowd, then unobtrusively shuffled up the stairs.

The door was ajar. Benson, the dentist and two companions had thrown Byers into the stuffed chair, let it down, and propped up his feet. Here he lay, stripped of coat, and sweating, with his throbbing hand laid across his chest. He was breathing hoarsely, eyes open but unseeing, his mind a maelstrom of fear and pain.

What he was first aware of, as he hazily recalled it later, was a sudden deathly silence and with it a peculiar sensation of extraordinary brightness which enveloped him. He turned his head. Benson, the dentist and their companions were gone, and the door was closed. The street window and blinds were drawn; but those on the south, opening upon a stunted apple orchard, had been opened to let the sun stream in. The old Indian was standing beside him. As if obeying a clear but unspoken command, Byers staggered to his feet. His companion swiftly and gently stripped off his clothes, led him into the immersing sunlight, and propped him up like a puppet against the wall. From somewhere under his blanket he brought out a small tuft of eagle feathers with which he began to stroke Byers' body while singing softly.

A great undulatory wave swept over Byers, caught him

up and carried him away, gently rising and falling. He could feel its drowsy warmth, the wash of its ripples against his skin, the dim and far-off music of its flow. In it he felt at once reassured and helpless, and gave himself to it wholly. His knees buckled, he slid down. For a moment he was hazily conscious of the sunlight pouring in the open window, and the old Indian crouched beside him, singing, and gently stroking his body with the feathers. The old man's eyes were upon him—large, black, steady, like deep pools from which ripples spread, kept spreading, to enclose him. And again the wave carried him off.

When next Byers was conscious of his surroundings, he was at home, alone, in his own bed. He was neither asleep nor wholly awake, but cast up on that shore which lies between—that shore to which he had been carried and deposited by some strange wave. For only a moment was he conscious. But in that moment was the strange conviction of a man long ill who had awakened after his first rest to know he had made the turning to recovery; the peculiar consciousness of a man, terribly drunk, who awakens in a stupor, but yet knowing his realization of it is the first sign of later clarity.

He was ill for days; it was two months before he really recovered. The Anglo doctor had returned to attend him, and now muttered jovially of a strong constitution, the rarity of fatalities by mere snake bites, and of the psychological fear that once removed . . .

"Get the hell out of here!" muttered Byers. "I want to sleep."

And so he had recovered, admitting the fear so slowly built up, unknown, which had suddenly leapt out at him from ambush. Perhaps the old Indian had given him some neutralizing herb he could not remember taking. But yet within the indistinct memory of that old man crouching beside him, singing and stroking his body with feathers, there lurked something invisible and unprobed, like the assurance of an indefinable faith, that had never left him.

Byers stirred and looked around. The two women had turned in. Angelina, close to the car, in a double sleeping bag laid on an air mattress, and Flowers Playing farther off in the brush on a pile of blankets. The moon had risen high above the great, still trees. He could see between them, on one side, a jaundiced vista of the desert sloping up and away past a far, flat-topped butte to the long line of mountains lying like the upturned edge of the horizon. On the other side, across the broad, flat river still flowing sluggishly as a snake with a tiny play of light on its scales where the current struck sand bar and snag, the pueblo rose black and solid. Mountains, mesa, mud hills and pueblo; they were all of a piece.

"Get me that bottle hidden in the side-pocket of the car," he said abruptly.

Martiniano, squatting silently across the fire, rose silently as he was bid. Returning, he handed the pint to Byers and squatted down again, drawing his pig-tails over his shoulders into his lap. The white man popped the cork out of the half-filled bottle and took a long swig.

"Here," he said, passing over the bottle. "Have a drink. There's just two apiece."

"Whiskey?" answered the Indian. "Here on pueblo land? It is against the law."

Byers could not restrain a flicker of astonishment across his face. This school-Indian, this Martiniano who had killed the deer, had been fined and beaten for wearing American clothes and refusing to dance—the most stubborn trouble-maker in the pueblo, now objecting to a drink of whiskey because it was against the law! He eyed him carefully.

Martiniano was sitting cross-legged, a thin blanket wrapped round his shirt and store pants, and slowly undoing his hair braids. The glow of the fire brought out the deep rose-red in his dark cheeks, chiselled sharper his clear-cut features. The hunch came to Byers as suddenly and clearly as if a voice had spoken in his ear: this school-Indian was going back to the blanket.

Martiniano finished unbraiding his hair, rolled up the colored cloth wrappings, and shook loose over his wide shoulders the long, coarse black hair. Then deliberately he picked up the bottle and took a long drink.

"Yes, there is a law. There are many laws," asserted Byers. "Little laws for little men, and big laws for big men. But the most difficult laws are a man's own. . . . So I have no fear of drinking when and where it suits me, taking care to make no trouble for any man." As if somewhat astounded by this platitudinous declaration of defiance, he added petulantly, "What the hell! Have I ever been known to sneak liquor into a reservation for sale or trouble? The devil take it! This is the time I like a drink!"

He leaned back against the bole of a tree, crossed his outflung legs, and stared upward at the stars tremulous and shiny hanging above them. He could not get that rattlesnake business out of his mind, nor something else which had long troubled him.

It was not in Byers to ask any Indian a direct question. What prevented him now was not only his own extreme sensitiveness to mood, his delicate tact and apperception of the truth that explanations are but poor substitutes for understanding—themselves qualities essentially Indian, but the appearance of the man across the fire. Martiniano, long hair down, seemed no longer the obstinate, open rebel he had known. There was about him a soft, pliable, yet resistant secrecy, a deep impenetrability that forbade probing.

Without realizing the devious evasiveness of his own nature, Byers considered insinuations and suggestions, means and approaches.

"That deer skin," he said abruptly, "the one you left with me for pawn and came after that night . . ." He lashed at the fire with his boot, sending up a shower of sparks. The words had jumped out of him against his will and nature.

"The skin of the deer I killed," assented Martiniano softly, without looking up.

"Yes. I have never asked. But I have been troubled for my friend. I could keep it no longer."

The Indian kept combing the long, streaming black hair with his fingers. He combed time as well. The river flowed by, the moon sliced through the clouds.

"That deer I killed. It troubled me. I thought: I cannot escape it. It is best not to try. So from you I got the skin. On my wall it is."

There it was, simply asked, simply answered, without evasiveness and explanation. And suddenly for Byers that barrier he had fancied between them, all mystery, was gone. It was as if from the darkness a long-legged antlered shape had stepped forth, touching both their lives, and then dissolving into light. It was no longer a deer, but an evanescent glimmer of the truth which appears once to each man and then is gone, not yet completely understood, but revealing a shape dimly sensed within its own outward shape.

"Boy, I too have had my deer," muttered the white man deeply, staring into the fire. "Believe me, son, it will pass."

"I believe," Martiniano answered shortly, without raising his head.

A great weight seemed to have lifted from Byers. He gulped down all but two fingers, and passed the bottle to Martiniano to finish. "Ah! A little drink at night in front of a fire before bed! That is life. A good drum, a dance, that is life too. Anything that warms the heart, the blood, the mind, and makes one feel alive. Not to refuse it. That is life. That is my law. . . . But to avoid causing trouble to others, I would just take that empty bottle back to the car. We will not leave it here to be found on the reservation."

Martiniano did as he was told. He came back with a small drum. Squatting down with it across his lap, he began to beat it gently. In a moment he began to sing. His dark face relaxed with a peculiar womanly softness. His white teeth gleamed. Perhaps, with just two drinks, he was a little drunk. Liquor gets these people so quickly, thought Byers. But his eyes were clear, his voice steady.

So they sat, watching the embers cool. A song. A pause. And then another. Very low, but very intense, and sounding through the glade.

And suddenly as Martiniano began again, a rich clear voice from behind joined his. It was Flowers Playing singing from her blankets. At its end came a low, joyful laugh. "The one we sang in the car yesterday, all afternoon, as we crossed the desert," she cried. "Now let us try that Corn Dance Song. How I would love to dance it! Now! We will see if it comes in song."

So they sang in the chill, dark spring night, parted but yet together. Angelina stirred drowsily in her warm bag. Byers sat with bowed head. For him this had always been and would be always—a fire, darkness, the low beat of a drum, and a shape of something unseen yet dimly sensed within the shape of things visible.

Each man has his deer, he thought, and I have had mine. And for the first time he admitted to himself the secret desire that had lay coiled so long within him. How beautiful she had seemed then, so young when he was young and lonely and alone. The gentle moon face and the long, blue-black hair, the slow tantalizing movement of her hips, and the quick brown hands shucking corn. Who would ever recognize her now, so toothless, pock-marked, fat and shapeless, shaking with mirth as he cursed her good-naturedly for messing up the kitchen—Buffalo Old Woman!

He looked over toward his wife waiting for him in the darkness. Loosening his boots, he stood up and jerked off hat and jacket.

"Up early tomorrow. Home at noon," he said gruffly, and strode away.

Flowers Playing had stopped singing. Martiniano sat thumping gently on the little drum. After a while he laid it away, secure from sparks and dew, and slipped away into the opposite darkness.

# 8

MARTINIANO ran his hand a last time through his seed, lashed tight the bag, and lifted it into the wagon at the door.

"What fine seed!" he boasted. "I cannot wait to plant it. In new ground, too. I tell you our luck has changed!"

It was late afternoon, and Flowers Playing looked tired and worn. Since daybreak they had been up packing. Dishes, pots and pans, a few pieces of furniture, all were lashed securely in the old wagon. Flowers Playing in the morning would drive it up to their new summer hut. But Martiniano was going now, with a half bag of seed, to avoid wasting a day behind the plodding team. He really couldn't wait.

"I shall have it all swept out when you come, the window unboarded. A fire too, to give it life and the clean smell of cedar. Then it will not seem so small, so shabby."

He saddled his old mare, took up a light supper and rode off.

How happy he was after this dreadful winter! The trader

had taken them on an automobile trip, had bought them seed. Up in the mountains, alone, on new land, they would start a fresh life. And in it he would find a new faith. It was a resurrection he experienced. The whole world sang with him as he rode along on his shabby, ill-breathed, stumbling mare.

The rough, rutty road curved upward and around the pueblo. The files of rheumatic old cottonwoods fell behind. Over the thickets of wild plum he could see men working in the stony fields, their thin cotton blankets or dirty white sheets wrapped round their heads like great turbans. Some were singing; deep male voices, in minor key, breaking against the jutting mountain slope. At the turn he paused. A small group was holding a simple ceremony to terminate their clearing out the ditch—the Mother Ditch, straight down from the mountains lifting Dawn Lake. Two old Mexicans watched them; it would be a good year, they knew.

Now, as Martiniano rode north beside the acequia, he was on the long virgin slope of sage rising steeply into piñon and scrub cedar, into pines. The whole valley lay below him. The pueblo at the base of the mountain, in the mouth of the cañon; La Oreja's scatter of adobes farther out; the deep, dark cleft that marked the river gorge; and beyond, the tawny, sunlit desert stretching away tight as a drum skin over the plateau.

"We shall be like eagles in our nest!" he thought with pride. "No man and his wife have a higher summer house. No man has broken land so high!" And he began to sing the Eagle Song, a little brokenly, for he did not know it well. And he glanced down with fiercer pride at his palms, still cracked and blistered from uprooting the stubborn sage.

Abruptly he reined his panting mare. The song stuck between his teeth. His face went dark and dead. There on the rolling sage slope lay the few acres he had cleared. Black, but splotched with sheep. Behind them, beside the one stunted cottonwood, stood the little adobe hut he had patched and prepared. Smoke was coming out of the chimney.

Martiniano sat staring. The mare had recovered her breath, but still sweating, began to stamp restlessly under the cold breeze. Martiniano jerked out of his daze to boot her viciously in the sides. She threw up her head, struck with surprise, and lunged forward.

Martiniano rode with a dark, set face and wary black eyes fixed on the tiny hut. In front of it he swung off, tossing the reins over his mount's head, and lassoed the hut with a tight look. The thin straight line of smoke still rose defiantly out of it into the twilight. Around it swirled a flock of sheep, and behind it, like water trickling between rocks and pines, flowed still more. They were polluting and trampling down the sides of the spring he had dug out last week.

Quietly he stepped to the doorway. The room was small and dusky save for a tiny blaze in the freshly plastered fireplace, and empty but for a dirty pack thrown against the wall. Between them on the bare earthen floor knelt a Mexican, back to him. He was unlashing the sheepskin covering the pack, and laying out supper. A rifle leaned against the wall. Martiniano appraised him quickly. The tattered boots, the muscular thighs bulging the threadbare Levi trousers, the wide shoulders, the large bullet head with its fell of long, tousled hair. He also judged both their paces to the rifle.

The sheepherder, suddenly conscious of the figure shutting off the light, turned around a coarse unshaven face. "Pase," he said in Spanish. "Come in."

Martiniano remained quietly standing in the doorway, weight balanced evenly on both feet, arms free, his thumbs hooked loosely in his wide, brass-studded belt.

The Mexican went on with his unpacking. A greasy frying pan, a blackened pot, coffee, a flour sack containing a few handfuls of beans. Then he unfolded a blanket upon the sheepskin. "My house is yours," he said, using the old phrase. "Someone has cleaned it up for me. It saves me the trouble."

The tone expressed not so much contempt for the specific as a general aversion to all dwellings, especially clean ones. It also marked, as nothing else could have, the irreconcilable difference between an Indian's love for his home, and a Mexican's regard for it as a place merely to keep him and his beasts out of the night. Martiniano felt this difference without being aware of it. What struck him was the simple, literal statement.

"It is my house. Get out!"

The flat, terse answer halted the sheepherder's hand in the air. He slowly set down the coffee pot, and turned around. What he saw lounging in the doorway was a stray Indian who had ridden by on his way home to the pueblo. His loose face drew together into an expression of indolent cunning. He had been herding sheep on these mountain uplands too long not to know the arrogant assumption of these Indians that all the land was theirs.

"Of course, of course!" he replied affably. "Have I passed here these many years not to know it well? This hut has served me well as I moved my flock back and forth from the mountains according to custom—and the permission of the officials, the Government men to whom I pay my due." He paused to let this reference to authority sink in. Then, in a conciliatory voice that did not mask his disregard of the Indian's demand, he added politely, "So come into your house, compadre—whenever you will. There is always room to spread your blanket, to boil your coffee, to keep dry."

He was a man resolute enough to know that to this polite ultimatum should be added the casual gesture of turning away and going about his business. But he could not. The deathly quiet of the Indian held him. And the look in his eyes. They had hardened like obsidian into a reptilian fixity. The sheepherder saw behind the look too late.

As he leapt to his feet, Martiniano lunged forward. A kick from his left foot sent the rifle clattering out of reach. As he turned, the Mexican struck him a blow which glanced off the side of the head. Martiniano dropped to his knees; and as the Mexican with a snarl of triumph reached to his belt, he came up with a swing of the frying pan which knocked the knife from the man's hand.

The sheepherder staggered back to swing his fist. The accuracy of the Indian's timing, the kicking of the rifle out of reach and the safe parry of his knife with the iron pan, tempered his anger with a spot of fear. There was a cold, murderous deliberation about this Indian's attack which froze him an instant too long. Before he could drive in a blow, Martiniano had dived into him. They went down in a heap. The Mexican flailing with his fists, the Indian reaching for his throat and trying to drive a knee into his groin.

The sheepherder was the bigger man, with long strong legs from perpetual climbing and walking. The Indian, a little bandy-legged like most, had the better arms and shoulders from working in the fields. On the floor, he clearly had the advantage. So the Mexican threshed about, driving home his fists to head and face, trying to knock his adversary free long enough to regain his feet. Martiniano sank his battered face on the man's breast. With incommensurate ferocity and appalling singleness of purpose, he clung like a panther, clawing toward the throat.

Over and over they rolled, scattering pot and pan, coffee and beans upon the clean swept floor, and fetched up with a bang against the far wall. There! But just as the Indian's thumbs sank into the deep muscular hollow below the Adam's apple, and his fingers slipped behind for a hold, there was a sudden and terrific explosion behind them. Both men lay as if stunned for an instant. Then the sheepherder, with a heave, broke loose and staggered to his feet. Martiniano raised to his knees.

The Mexican was standing before him with glazed, frightened eyes, staring at the blood dripping down his shirt sleeve. One of them had kicked loose the trigger of the rifle, and the shot had torn loose half his ear.

With a frantic howl of pain and fright, the Mexican turned and fled.

Martiniano rose slowly, panting. Like a man driven by an unconquerable obsession from which he was not yet freed, he mechanically gathered up blanket and sheepskin, pot and pan and handfuls of coffee and beans, and threw them out the door. Then he slumped down in front of the fire.

The little blaze burnt out like his own anger. Darkness crept in the door, and with it contrition and fear. He broke the gun and threw it outside after removing the shells. The sheep had scattered; he could see their pale splotches far down the slope, and hear them in the underbrush above. Swiftly he slid out, unsaddled and hobbled his mare, lit a new fire in the hut. But he crept up the slope to sleep in the thick brush lest the Mexican returned in the night to attack him.

He did not return, nor did Martiniano sleep. He sat huddled in his blanket, staring down at the empty slope in the jaundiced moonlight, thinking.

In the morning he went down to bathe in the trampled, muddy pool below the spring, and then returned to his post. Near noon they came as he expected. Not only Flowers Playing, but a group of horsemen with her.

It had happened again. Martiniano, the trouble-maker, had caused more trouble. The man who killed the deer had almost killed a sheepherder.

The Mexican's account was simple. In the early spring, till lambing time, he kept his sheep down below—across river. Then as the snow cleared from the mountains he led them up into the high mountain meadows among the pines. Pues! He was a poor, simple sheepherder having no family or friends. He slept under the stars, alone with his sheep. He preferred it. But every year on his way back and forth he stopped a few days in that little abandoned hut. He had done this for years. Why should it be different now?

Mother of God! Who would have suspected it! He was making supper when a strange Indian had come in. This Indian refused his hospitality. He spoke no word, but suddenly leapt upon him. And he—José Maria, poor sheepherder—was forced to defend himself. But Our Lady! The crazy Indian had grabbed the rifle he kept for coyotes and had shot his ear off. Mire! Look how it hangs!

This was the sheepherder's explanation to the Mexicans in La Oreja to whom he had fled for help. His employer added more, to Teodor Sanchez, head of the Government Forest Reserve, to whom he paid the necessary grazing fees for his sheep. Sanchez, in turn, added still more when he officially visited the Governor of the pueblo.

"I remember this Indian, Martiniano by name," he said sternly. "The man who killed the deer. He attacked likewise one of my boys. Now the same thing has happened. It is clear he has a murderous disposition. We dismissed the charges of assault against him last fall. This time, Señor Gobernador," he ended with excessive politeness, "we demand closer co-operation in the matter of punishment."

Again Martiniano was brought before the Superintendent and the old men. He told his story simply and wearily, without excuses. He offered the work on the old hut as evidence of his faith, the new land he had cleared of sage, the new spring he had dug out and banked. He showed his cracked and blistered palms, a bit of his new seed, the unpaid bill from the trader.

They listened gravely, withheld judgment and dismissed him. Martiniano rode slowly back up the slope to his hut. There seemed no place else to go.

"They are all against me," he said sadly. "Everything I do is wrong."

This time Flowers Playing did not smile encouragement. She was stern as a Ute. "You are seeking a faith. Well, look: there is your seed. Now I too have a faith. It also is in your seed—the seed of your loins. Let us still keep faith together. It is our darkest hour."

So he planted his seed, not knowing when he would be called away for punishment, not knowing if he would ever harvest his crop.

Meanwhile the old men talked. This Martiniano had killed a deer. He had been duly punished. But his action had been like a stone impacting the surface of a lake whose widening ripples eddied swiftly into the darkest corners of the shore. Now this same Martiniano had almost killed a sheepherder. It was another, larger stone thrown into their lake. Their Dawn Lake. The eddying ripples spread still farther. . . .

Strophy was summoned again. He was more quiet because more worried. He listened better.

First to Sanchez, the sheepherder and his employer. Then to the Governor and the old men of the Council.

The two stories merged into one incontrovertible fact. A Mexican and an Indian had had a fight in a lonely hut in the mountains. Each had his version, of course. But there were no witnesses. It might have been over a personal matter. Either side could bring legal action if desired. But the pueblo, the Indian Service, could not be a party to it. They could not punish this Martiniano or consider him as representing the pueblo, the tribe.

Sanchez roared disappointment—and a certain truth. This damned Indian might not legally be representing the pueblo, but that's what he was doing actually. He had killed a deer on Government range and had had a fight with a ranger. Now there was hard feeling between all Indians and his park employees who had to patrol the mountains. Next this Indian had had a fight with a sheepherder, and because of it every Spanish-American in the neighborhood would be afraid of trespassing in the mountains.

"God damn it, Strophy!" he howled with exasperation. "What is this, anyway? Government forest reserves my men are half afraid to patrol. Government range any man who pays me a dollar a head is entitled to pasture his stock in, but is afraid to enter. Because these damned Indian wards of yours have got it into their heads the land is still theirs! Now who the hell *does* this land belong to?"

Then Strophy listened to the old men of the Council.

"This Martiniano," they said quietly. "He has been an unruly, stubborn Indian, and we have punished him. That is our business, as you know. But this is a bigger business. Look. This land sloping up to the mountains. It belongs to this Martiniano who got it from his father, his share of tribal land. It has never been developed, yet it was his to claim when he would. It was not the Mexican's land. It has never been a Mexican's land. So he defended himself, his land, against a stranger. Let us then dismiss him. Let us talk about the greater things.

"Ai. The great thing which concerns us all. Our land. Indian land. The mountains around our sacred lake. Our Dawn Lake.

"Listen. That Mexican was taking his sheep into the mountains. The mountains around our Dawn Lake. But you promised us these our mountains, our Dawn Lake. Not once but many times. Now we say: what was this Mexican doing leading his sheep into our mountains to ruin the grass and defile our Dawn Lake? Will there be more sheepherders and more Martinianos to stop them? Will there be more Government rangers at deer-time and more Martinianos to cause trouble with them?

"Now let us talk no more. Let us have no more empty promises of restitution. Give us back our land. Do you understand this we say?"

Strophy frowned and sighed. He understood well enough; it was the same old controversy that had never quite died down. . . .

In 1551, a grant of land was given the Pueblo Indians by the Crown of Spain, under Charles V; and during all the time Spain was in possession of this section of what was now the United States, the pueblo had absolute title to this land.

In 1848, under the treaty between the United States and Mexico which had taken over the region from Spain, the United States recognized the ownership of this grant of land held by the Indians, and in 1859 the Congress of the United States confirmed their title.

In 1864 President Lincoln called the tribal head of the pueblo to Washington, with the Governors of all the other sixteen pueblos, and gave him patent to the original grant of land from the King of Spain, together with a silver-headed cane to be used as the insignia of office by each successive Governor of the pueblo.

This land included the mountains, the plateau, the valley. But little by little Mexican settlers had come in. They built their little adobes, established their ranchitos and planted corn milpas around the indefinite boundary lines. Then white settlers encroached still farther. All peacefully enough, on the whole. A Mexican liked a piece of Indian land, and the Indian was glad to sell it for a horse, a blanket, a few pesos, a jug of whiskey. And the whites gradually bought it from them for little more. The Government did nothing to protect the Indians from this encroachment until 1913. Then the Supreme Court decided that the Indians were wards of the Government and could not dispose of their property without the consent of the Government; the land was theirs individually under a fee simple title, but a communal title.

It was too late. A town had grown up not far from the pueblo—La Oreja. The Government, to protect the watershed, assumed control of the mountains.

What was left? A pueblo huddled at the mouth of a deep cañon at the base of the mountains, and in a shrunken reservation. What more did they need? The population had dwindled fearfully from a wild estimate of fifteen thousand in pre-Conquest days to some seven hundred.

Strophy remonstrated, quoting relative facts and figures. The old men shrugged blanketed shoulders.

"Give us back our land if you would avoid still more trouble," they demanded quietly. "Give us back our Dawn Lake."

"You have been badly treated as the world has moved onward," he admitted patiently, "and now the Government is helping you. But what can be done? Times have changed . . . Good God! Do you want the Government to move La Oreja—the whole damned town away, because it stands on your land?" Exasperated at their stubbornness, he still managed a fatuous grin.

The old men did not smile. Not a muscle of their faces moved.

"Give us back our land. Give us back our Dawn Lake. We have no more to say."

Strophy knew what he was in for; he telegraphed Washington. The Commissioner came. Representatives came. Land experts came, and these remained. They pored over dusty records in the courthouse and at the State Capitol. They read through voluminous documents sent them daily. They began investigating titles and deeds.

The news got out: the Government was going to make restitution to the Indians—and probably, like everything else, at the taxpayers' expense. It was all sentimental nonsense. Why, in La Oreja there was not a dwelling, a single business lot on the plaza, where the owner had a clear legal title. And now he was going to have to fork over payment to that scrubby bunch of illiterate Indians who claimed to own the town. What political chicanery was this? Why, the thing would amount to thousands, to tens of thousands of dollars!

Thus the whites understood it. They began to write and telegraph protests to their Congressmen.

The investigators began interviewing the Mexican villagers. They went from ranchito to hut, across the valley, up into the tributary cañons. Of each family they asked the same patient questions.

"Señor Alebardo y Mondregon? You will pardon this foolish question, but this is your land?"

Señor Alebardo rubbed a naked shin with a bare toe sticking out of his huaraches.

"Of course, of course. Mine. As it was my father's before me."

"You have papers?"

"Papers? Pues. Of a certainty . . . Now let me see. I saw them last spring, or was it the spring before that?" He turned his vistors toward the house. "Pase. Pase, amigos. I will ask my wife . . . Wife! Where are those papers? The papers to our land?"

Señora Alebardo y Mondregon, like a worn broom, brushed a debris of children out of the squalid little adobe. She pawed through the drawers of an old hand-carved comodo, looked among stacks of old daguerreotypes, rummaged behind the cracked dishes in the cupboard. Meanwhile the host sat entertaining his guests.

"It is fine land I have, Señores. True, it is a little marshy in spots. It is the water which sinks at the foot of the mountains, flows underground, and rises here a little to the south. But there is this to be said for it. One does not need to dig deep for a well. Look. It is good water, clear and sweet." He dipped out a gourdful from a stale bucket in the corner. "I regret that on this day I have no wine to offer my guests. But . . . Well, yes, it is fine land. You are thinking of buying, perhaps? Well, you will like this fine house too. It is large, true. Three rooms. But when my fifth child came it seemed necessary to add this new third room. Since two others have come to bless our union I have not regretted it. Now—"

"The papers!" announced the Señora breathlessly. "I found them. In this old leather trunk they were. All of them."

Señor Alebardo went through them with stubby, calloused fingers. He squinted in the dim light. He murmured. "Twelve pesos . . . Twelve pesos . . . Thirteen pesos and forty-nine centavos, this. That was when the taxes were raised for our having elected that thief of a Republicano! Pues. How expensive it is to own property nowadays."

One of the visitors calmly reached out a hand and took the packet from him.

"My friend, these are tax receipts. Nothing more."

"Certainly. Have we not paid our taxes? I cannot remember when we have not paid taxes."

"But have you no other papers? Papers that say this land is yours, from whom it was bought, a description of the land? A title, a deed?"

"Pues. Such things are unnecessary. Everyone knows. My father's father bought this land from one of those Indians at the pueblo. I remember hearing what he paid: a good horse and forty silver pesos, with a bridle thrown in. And here, on this same land, we Alebardo y Mondregons have always lived. My father's father, his son, I, and my own son, just married, who is building his house below—one room. If you buy, you can keep your carro in it. Do you have a car? Of course it is yours! I saw it outside. A new shiny one. Yes. We have always paid taxes to the Government on this our land."

The visitors were writing it all down, murmuring among themselves. Señor Alebardo became suspicious.

"You doubt that it is my land? That is why you do not want to buy?"

The answer came gently but firmly. "Did we not say, my friend, that we were making investigations for the Government?"

"Ah! then you are not rich Anglos who would buy! You have deceived me! You are those men who think to take away our land because we have no papers, and give it back to those lazy Indians! My poor, barren, marshy land, so water-logged that it gives a stand of corn no higher than my knees. Scrubby little ears on which we starve year after year. But yet on which we are compelled to pay taxes. For what? So you can rob us of our land because we have no papers. Papers! Mother of God! Deceivers! Now go. You are no longer my guests!"

So the Mexican villagers understood it, and still the rumors spread. Over the far slopes of the mountains and into the remote cañons. It was a wild, desolate region of tall, weathered cliffs pointing up at the backs of the snowy peaks, and falling away in a jumbled talus slope of great glacial boulders and tangled brush into the arid, empty desert. But at the mouth of a wide arroyo was a single little group of adobe huts and rocky corrals. Long ago a group of outlaws had fled here and still remained. Tending sheep and goats for the most part, but growing a few patches of stunted corn among the boulders for tortillas.

Here one night they gathered to discuss the rumor that they were to be dispossessed of their land. They were strong, simple men, with sharp, fierce faces burnt by wind and rain, and dressed in hand-sewn leather vests. Candlelight gleamed on their dark, unlined cheeks. After rolling cigarettes with stubby, calloused fingers, their sinewy hands fell naturally and easily to rest on the bone hafts of the knives stuck loosely in their belts. Their black eyes were sharper than the blades.

None acknowledged a leader; each was separate and inviolable. Each kept his silence untarnished among men, as he polished it alone among his crags. But one ventured to begin.

"It is those Indians who are taking back all the land with the help of the Government. That we have heard. They are on the other side of the mountain. What do you think? Will they come here too?"

Broad shoulders shrugged. Brown hands loosened knives in belts.

"Those Indians. They have the best land in the country. It is fat with grain. But ours is lean with longing. Who can imagine what they would want with it—those lazy, greedy Indians suckled like lambs at the breast of the Government?"

After a time another spoke. "This land of ours. It is

worthless but to us who need its freedom. But it also lies at the base of those tall white peaks which surround that little lake so venerated by the Indians. Who remembers how we secretly watched their secret ceremonies so long ago until they drove us away? Perhaps that is why they want it."

And still they sat in the crowded, candlelit darkness, staring warily at each other.

"Well, what do you think? What shall we do? Why have we come if not to talk about this thing?" the speaker asked in desperation. "Let the oldest among us answer."

The old man rudely pushed forward, turned and swung his massive head from side to side like a trapped beast. His own habitual silence and aloneness had trapped him. He had escaped to these ragged crags forty, fifty years ago, had lived in a wary silence and aloneness from which he suddenly lashed out with a knife and into which he fled back with a clatter of hoofs. Now he was too old to fight or flee, living meagerly, alone and broken, in a tiny hut, tending a few stalks of corn to feed his toothless hunger. Now he was called upon to break this silence, to speak, to establish a solidarity with those around him for protection, and he could not. The heavy down-pressing silence, the wary aloneness, bound his great stiff legs, his gnarled hands. It weighed down his eyelids, his sagging jaw. He could not throw off the fetters which bound his mind.

So he swung his head from side to side, glowering helplessly from beneath his white shaggy eyebrows. He got out his knife with shaking fingers.

"Quien sabe?" he muttered hoarsely—his only words.

Who knows? It was their only answer to life and death alike.

And slowly, after a time, they all filed out into the chill darkness, mounted their horses or trudged silently up the trails—men beset by a common fear and danger, yet still helplessly alone and separate.

So it went. The whites shouting across a continent to waken sleeping Congressmen and lawyers, the Mexican villagers muttering ominously among themselves, and their lonely, remote primos staring warily, with knives loosened, into silence.

Among them all the men at the pueblo drew closer together within its walls. They were one body, one mind, one heart. They moved evenly together.

Only the Indian who had innocently started all this trouble, the man who killed the deer, seemed to go on serenely about his work.

He harrowed his field, planted his new seed. Laboriously he dug a little ditch from the Acequia Madre to water it. He rebanked the trampled sides of the little spring. The small hut he made a home. There was a wooden bedstead, a deal table and a bench, a packing case for dishes. They had no stove; it was necessary to cook in the fireplace. The floor was dirt, hard and clean swept. The landscape seen out the open door was their only picture. But it was enough: it was peace, a peace scented sharp and clean with sage, and with the cedar Flowers Playing burned to erase the smell of cooking.

The Corn Planting Moon had passed, the Corn Tassel Coming Out Moon. Now came the Sun House Moon, the time of the summer solstice.

His corn came up, small but hardy and full formed. While he waited for it to ripen, Martiniano built a little log corral for his team and riding mare. Against the side of the hill behind the house to save the labor of one wall, and to blend unobtrusively into the background. When this was finished he shaped a great adobe, ant-hill oven outside in which Flowers Playing could bake bread.

The first brown loaves came out. It was mid-morning, but Martiniano broke open a huge loaf and sat down to eat it all with coffee.

"Bread!" he said, dipping a chunk into his cup. "How long has it been since we have had bread!"

There was still bitterness and anxiety in his tone. It betrayed his serene composure of the past few weeks. His work was finished. The mountains had done Flowers Playing good; her eyes were clear, her skin gleamed warmly rose-brown. He himself felt better. But still . . .

"Now if we just had that fine big Navajo blanket to put on the floor at daytime, and over us at night," said Flowers Playing carelessly, "I would miss nothing else."

Martiniano did not answer. She had struck the heart of his worry. That blanket was the one which had been confiscated at the Peyote meeting.

The new bread went sour in his mouth. He laid down the chunk beside his cup.

"Is it you do not like my bread—the first?" asked Flowers Playing. "Is there too much salt or not enough? Here! Let me get you some bacon grease for butter that I have been saving these many weeks."

"No!" answered Martiniano moodily. "The bread is good enough. But shall I be a pig? I have eaten enough. I am sick of work! I am going fishing. What is the use of having a summer home in the mountains and never going fishing? Well, I shall bring trout for supper!"

He strode off quickly lest his wife take it into her head to go with him. No hooks nor bait he took. He fished as he had been taught as a boy. Kneeling quietly in the shadow of a spruce beside a deep pool. Letting down slowly a little lasso of fine twisted horsehair. Waiting patiently—so patiently!—for the dimly visible, shadowy trout to wriggle past and around. And then, when one entered the noose, jerking suddenly upward and lunging for the slippery fish before it flopped back off the bank. Such fishing was not possible with a woman around. It required concentration, patience. . . . What he really wanted was to be alone.

And as the long lonesome hours passed, and he stared at the dimly visible shapes sliding in and out of the mirror of his thoughts, Martiniano saw what he must do. He could no longer face the thought of Palemon who had confiscated his blanket during the raid, knew whose it was, but had never told. Peyote was not his Road; he had told Rena, but he could no longer conceal it from all men. Nor could he face the skin of the deer he had killed. It hung on the wall of his new little hut, hung there day and night, not limp and bodiless, but as something which could in an instant take shape before him, tremble with life and power, and threaten his false security.

"No. I cannot escape it," he thought. "I have done what I have done, and I must face it before I put it behind me."

So the next day he rode down to the pueblo and claimed his confiscated blanket.

Martiniano who would not cut the heels off his shoes and the seat out of his trousers; who had refused to dance, had married a Ute girl still childless, and had driven his wagon across the plaza during the time of staying still. The man who had killed the deer and started the trouble about

Dawn Lake. This stubborn troublemaker who had now let it be known he was also eating peyote. Well, this would make up for his not having been punished for the trouble he caused about that sheepherder!

"Take this your blanket," said the new Governor. "And tomorrow morning in the plaza take fifteen lashes besides."

The late morning sun was bright and hot when he knelt in the plaza, at the far end against the pueblo wall. Men were irrigating their fields. The great cottonwoods were clouds of green. An eagle circled overhead.

The bitterness went out of Martiniano's heart as he knelt, still staring upward at the eagle. The sullen defiance left his face; the great bird had dropped lower, to circle directly above him. The long wings tilted. It banked, fell headlong. He could see for an instant the hard yellow eyes and sharp curved beak. Then it straightened, shooting levelly past him with the air whistling through its pinions like the sound of torn paper, only to glide upward into another circle, its talons drawn up, its tail spread out like a peyote fan.

This was strange, this great eagle which had come so close to watch him. He remembered his father had told him when he was a boy how certain wild birds and animals, with a strange affinity, warn and protect and help one another. And that was why, he had said, one must not let an eagle see you when you are hunting. He will tell the deer. They are great friends.

Martiniano, watching the eagle and thinking of the deer he had killed, paid little attention to the old men who had gathered around him. Nor did he notice a young woman who had walked swiftly out of the grove of cottonwoods, and had now stopped some way from him in the willows along the stream.

The new Governor, remembering the previous sheepskin the culprit had stuffed inside his pants, ordered his shirt stripped off.

"Are you ready?" he asked.

Martiniano turned his head around. Sudden compassion gushed from his heart. It was Palemon who had been chosen to whip him. Poor Palemon, he thought, how difficult this is for him! So, not to embarrass him, he set his face into an impassive mask as if he had not recognized his friend, and nodded calmly.

Palemon too was a man. No sign of recognition showed on his face as he lifted the lash.

The first blow fell on Martiniano like a pine tree. There was the impact of the heavy trunk and an instant later the lacerating sting of its branches and needles.

Jesús! he thought. This Palemon has an arm! And he braced himself for the second.

It struck him like a bolt of lightning. He could hear the reverberating thunder, the sharp crackle, the hiss of flame —all at once. The impact dazed him for an instant. To clear his swimming gaze, he looked up. The eagle was still soaring directly above him, slowly now, intent on what went on below. Martiniano could see its eyes, its slightly opened beak. It seemed to be smiling. But kindly, without derision.

The third blow fell. It was as if he had been in a sealed up cave when all the winds rushed in. His body felt no particular pain; there was only the sensation of an irresistible, bodiless force that hit him from all sides, a roaring in his ears.

The blow had bowled him forward upon his face. He rose to his knees, and said in a low calm voice, "Pardon. I slipped. It was on this loose stone." His ears cleared. He could hear behind him the sound of Palemon's breathing, and around him a growing murmur.

The fourth blow was the strangest of all. It seemed to catch him up and plunge him deep into a black and slimy pool. His head swelled with pressure, his eyes popped. He came up gasping as the lash uncoiled around him. A warm trickle was running down his side.

"Ai, ai, ai," sounded a rapid murmur. It came from the old men. The tones expressed admiration for the whipped and a warning to the whipper, this lusty new officer who obeyed so resolutely the Governor's demand for ample justice.

Five! they counted.

It was then that Martiniano became suddenly aware of the young woman watching from the willows in front of him. It was Flowers Playing. He had ridden off early this morning on the foolish pretext of an errand in town so that she would not learn of this new disgraceful punishment until it was over. And there she was, slightly bent forward, head raised, one hand at her breast, watching it.

Seven!

And this was the peculiar thing about his wife's face. There was on it no anger at Palemon and the old men, no shame for him, neither pity nor sympathy. It was relaxed and smiling.

Ten!

His anxious gaze plumbed the dark pools of her eyes. Martiniano could not believe them. They were deep with the greatest love he had ever seen, and turbulent as if stirred by leaping trout to the joyousness of springtime. They were triumphant with a strange exultation.

The blows still fell after proper, deliberate pauses and exclamations from the old men, but they lacked vigor. Palemon, after the fifth, had been holding back. Or perhaps it was the strange, kind smile of the eagle, and the strange look of exalting triumph in his wife's eyes that made the lashes easier to bear.

Fifteen! Ai, ai, ai! It was enough.

As he rose, the old men stepped forward. One of them held out Martiniano's blanket. Martiniano ignored the conciliatory gesture. He took it and flung it himself loosely around his shoulders. It was over.

The eagle gave a shrill scream overhead that stilled any comment. All stopped and stared curiously above them. The huge bird swooped upward out of its last circle, straightened and disappeared high in the clear blue.

Several of the old men remained staring after it with a strange wonder in their eyes. Martiniano gathered the blanket about him, nodded impassively and stepped away. Two men passed by. A group of women were coming, single file, over the bridge. An old springless wagon jolted across the plaza. With calm dignity Martiniano walked forward to his wife.

She met him as if nothing had happened. With a face relaxed and smiling. With shining eyes.

"I came after you the moment I knew. Perhaps it is not true, but it has never happened before!" she exclaimed with a low, curiously vibrant voice. "It is this same phase of the moon—my usual time. But nothing has happened. Martiniano, my husband! I—yes! It has come, that which we have waited for. I feel it. I know it. Something tells me it is so!"

Yes! To him as to her this whipping was an unreal dream

which soared away, forgotten. For the second time in his life the earth gave way before him. He was standing alone at the brink of a fathomless chasm, and the world lay far below him unheeded. He was high, high as an eagle lifted by the wind, an eagle who smiled with understanding and screamed with triumph. A new strength filled him.

Martiniano rolled and lit a cigarette, and walked quietly away with Flowers Playing.

Two old men swathed in blankets, still standing where he had been whipped, watched them go. They walked neither too demurely as if ashamed, nor too proudly in defiance, but slowly, in quiet dignity, as if nothing had happened.

In the glade under the cottonwoods they stopped. At the stream running between the willows the woman washed the man's back, sopping off the blood with handfuls of grass, and helped him put on his shirt. Then they rode home slowly.

And that night, in a strange new tenderness, they lay together and were conscious of a third who lay with them. And when she fell asleep, he raised and looked down upon her. A thin flicker of moonlight shone on her face. It wore a look of deep humility, and a look of rapturous triumph. He had always seen the mean before, and it was beautiful; but now between these two extremes he saw her whole, and she was more than beautiful. She was a part of that which held the deer he had killed and the eagle who had rushed away screaming to tell it what had happened.

There is but one true faith, the strange, quick thought came to him, and it is faith in the mystery of life. Faith in that life which will deliver to us a son. "That it may be so," he prayed. "That it may be so . . ."

# 9

So LITTLE by little the richness and the wonder and the mystery of life stole in upon him.

In the hush of high noon he flung himself down to rest. From the shadow of a pine he looked out upon his corn, their sturdy gold-green stalks marching down the slope like warriors to battle adversity for him, their tassels swaying like war feathers in the breeze. He smelled the water gurgling through his ditch, watched his wife raking out the hot ashes from the outdoor oven before putting in her bread to bake. In her and in his fields he had deposited his seed. There was another power which gave them life and made them both grow. He had partaken in the mystery of creation, yet he did not know what it was.

He lay beside Flowers Playing at night, already gently feeling her body to see if it had grown, and he wondered sleepily, Is it my wife's thighs I feel, or the long rounded thighs of the pine slope outflung upon this sage desert? Is this her breast, now flattened at the crest, really in-curved like an old buffalo bow, or is it the outline of the mountain above? Whose heart do I hear beating faintly but steadily like a muffled drum? And he thought of the little blue lake of life hidden deep within them both. We are all images of one great shape, obeying its same laws.

Occasionally he slept alone outside. He could hardly go to sleep sometimes, so exquisite was the feeling that possessed him. The yellow moon low over the desert, the stars twinkling above the tips of the high ridge pines, the fireflies, the far-off throb of a drum, the silence, the tragic, soundless rushing of the great world through time—it caught at his breath, his heart.

His resentment against injustice left him, his bitterness, his sullen anger. Life was more than what he saw, heard and sensed. It extended beyond the visible, the audible, the sensory limits. Whenever he went down to the pueblo he was very careful—and cautioned Flowers Playing to be, likewise—of looking with scorn at an old woman's harelip or twisted feet, a man's odd eye or anyone's physical defect lest as prospective parents their own child be born that way. He advised her never to use a knife in water lest her own child be cut in its prenatal lake. The moon in eclipse eats a child and so retards its growth, so he gave her a stone arrowhead to carry for protection.

Early one morning Martiniano rode down the slope alone. As he entered the plaza he knew something was wrong. The ovens were still smoking. Women in their big snowy boots waddled spread-legged to and from the stream carrying water jars and pails on their heads. Young men were busy at the corrals, old men sat smoking against the sunny walls. It was the old, old form which nothing ever altered—the open secrecy of Pueblo life. But the substance within had changed. It was tense. A dangerous lull had becalmed the place over night. Whispers spread. A word here, a phrase there. The lifting of a hairless eyebrow, the flip of a blanket over the shoulder, and a man walking swiftly, but not too swiftly, away from another.

Martiniano went about his errands. First to Byers' post. "Our crop is doing well. Very well. You will be both comforted and pleased to hear this, no doubt."

The trader grumbled a curt reply. He wore a frown and seemed out of temper.

Martiniano rode on to La Oreja and tethered his horse to the rail. The plaza as usual in midsummer was full of visiting whites, Mexicans and Indians wearing their brightest shirts and cleanest sheets. But the Indians kept to themselves in wary groups about their wagons or did their trading and rode somberly away.

Martiniano did not delay. He rode back to the pueblo with a sack of flour laid across his mare and a little paper bag of ginger-snaps tied in his sheet for Flowers Playing.

All afternoon he worked in his small field outside the walls; he had neglected it a little lately for the big one above. At dusk he went to see Palemon and stayed for supper. There was a strange touch of formality about the hospitality: he and Palemon ate first and alone at the little kitchen table, then Estefana and Batista who had served them. While the women ate, the men sat silent in the other room. Palemon's face was relaxed and inscrutable, but Martiniano could see that he was worried. Martiniano let it pass. When the women came out he gave them each a ginger-snap and carefully tied up the little sack again. Batista had grown up; her hair was banged in front and tied behind. She stood in the open doorway looking down into the dark plaza.

"You will hear them soon," Martiniano chided her as he rose to leave. "These foolish young men who sing all night among the willows. Well, I would join them too and sing to my friend's new-grown daughter if it were not for that Ute girl who captured me—and now waits, doubtless, with a stick!"

Batista smiled shyly, then giggled.

Palemon answered slowly, "I think there will be little

singing tonight. It draws white people from town to listen. We don't want them here any more. Perhaps we shall keep them out . . . Come, I shall walk with you to your horse."

It was as he said. As they walked across the plaza to the corrals the singing broke out, one voice after another to flood the night. But as Martiniano was saddling his mare, a car from town came down the road. The headlights shone down the lane between the corrals, across the plaza, and upon the white-sheeted singers grouped along the stream. The singers stopped. A shadowy figure stepped forth and halted the car. Martiniano could hear the conversation.

"What you do?"

"We just drove in to listen to the singing. We're not going to get out of the car. Just turn off the lights and sit awhile here."

"No good. You go."

"Why, we've always come down! We like your singing. You know us, Joe! We've always given you cigarettes for yourself and the singers."

"Governor she say no. She say this Indian land, this our pueblo. These our songs. That what *we* say. You go now."

"Why, of all things! You—"

"You go! You back up!"

The car backed out of the narrow lane, turned around reluctantly, then roared angrily away. The singing did not resume. Already pale splotches were walking across the bridge; there was a Council meeting that night.

When Martiniano mounted, Palemon took the bridle and led him up the trail away from all ears.

"Now I will tell you what you have wanted to ask," he said quietly. "About this grievous thing, this terrible book of paper." His voice lowered. "It tells all—all, all," he repeated tonelessly. "All about our pueblo, our customs, our beliefs. It gives our names!" He paused to let this dreadful fact sink in, and then in a voice that expressed the greatest horror and sadness possible, he said, "It has given, on paper, for all to read, even the names of our kivas!"

Martiniano saw him glance around in the darkness at the ears in the bushes, the eyes in the stones, at the desecrated earth on which he stood and at the stars reeling in their orbits above.

"I do not know what will happen," Palemon went on sadly. "Perhaps it is the end of our good life. I have heard how the snows laid four feet deep just outside the pueblo in the old days. Now there is scarcely enough to cover a man's foot. The great spring in the Big Pasture where our buffalo are kept no longer bubbles up with water. The grass is dry and brown since I was small. Why? Because we have not kept the faith. We have lost our medicine. So the life is going out of the earth. The skies are wrinkling dry as old skin. And now the last of all evils has overtaken us. Our secrets have been betrayed. . . . No, I do not know what is going to happen."

Without farewell he strode away into the darkness.

Martiniano rode on home.

Who knew how it came? These Indians did not read books, magazines, even newspapers. How could they have been aware of a thin, paper-backed booklet that appeared inconspicuously in a store or two in the city nearly two hundred miles away? No one in La Oreja, not even Benson or Byers, had heard of it. But there it was in the Governor's hands scarcely a week after it had been published.

The booklet, "A Preliminary Study of Pueblo Culture," contained a few photographs, a description of customs, and a short history with the usual discursive assumption that the American Indians were descendants of Mongolians who had migrated over the Bering Crossing.

But in it was something else. A sketch map of the pueblo showed the location of the kivas properly named, and the arrangement of communal fields and pastures. A long list of family names, both Indian and Mexican, was segregated into kiva groups, and reference was made to an extinct kiva. This Never-Covered-by-Flood kiva was described as being not only historically and culturally important, but dating back to mythical times. It had been established here at the mystical center of the world by the Old First Ones when they emerged to the surface of the earth—the writer ignoring the contradiction of her assumption that the Indians were of Mongolian descent. In it undoubtedly human sacrifice had been made, and Montezuma had been received when he was carried by litter to visit the northern tribes four hundred years ago—carrying the sacred flame still kept burning in its "unused" depths.

The Governor lifted his hand for the interpreter to stop. He could read no further. These things and conjectures of things looming suddenly before him from a printed book stiffened him into an attitude of unmitigated horror. His old face cracked. His composure would have suffered less had his seatless pants suddenly fallen down as he was receiving a group of tourist ladies come with a dollar apiece to take his photograph. He felt more naked and shamed. Resentment and anger came later, when he called the Council together.

All night for five nights they sat together wrapped to the eyes in their blankets. There was only one voice, that of the interpreter reading through the booklet, page by page. He was not interrupted. At dawn he stopped. The book was hidden away, and the old men filed out, without a word, to return again at dark.

On the fifth night, just after midnight, the interpreter came to the last chapter. "In August culminates the yearly ceremonial life of the pueblo," he translated slowly, "when the people in a great procession climb up the mountains to their sacred Dawn Lake." Tepees were pitched on the shore. Great fires shone upon the clear blue water and the leaping bodies of naked dancers. The throb of drums, the whine of singing voices echoed through the pines. The ceremonies were secret. No stranger had ever been allowed to witness them. The trails were carefully guarded. For even revealing what went on the penalty was death. Yet there were indications. Young unmarried men and women were forced to go, and virgin maidens who came back like wilted flowers. It seemed certain that all participated in a monstrous sex orgy.

The interpreter laid down the booklet and took his seat in the corner. The old men uncovered their faces. The talk began and continued for more nights.

It was not a question of how much or little of the contents of the book approximated the truth. They were a people who so identified their lives with the one great flow of all life that they showed no sense of individuality, and seemed at once impersonal and anonymous. They had attained the faculty of so obliterating themselves when gathered together in a group that even their faces lost individual expression, and looked blankly out with the one face of the tribe. To them spoken words robbed a thought of power, and printed words destroyed it entirely. They never looked at or pointed to an object or person being discussed; never spoke another's name;

and always referred to a man as "she" and a woman as "he" lest direct reference rob the one of his power.

And now this!—the unbelievable, the impossible, the unbearable. The fingers and the eyes of the world were pointed at them. Their names were spoken, they were printed. Their power was taken from them.

A cold fear beset them. A quiet fury possessed them. So cold, so quiet, that of all those nights of Council-talk only one pronouncement filtered out to waiting ears—the calm judgment of the oldest of the old:

"It would not be too much if a man would die for this."

Who had betrayed them? They began to probe about. This book of paper. It had been written by one Mrs. Blackstone. Even her name denoted evil. She had stayed in La Oreja last fall, a friend of that picture man who had painted so many faces of Panchilo that now he had no face left. Drunken Panchilo was brought. All could see how his life, his power had been taken from him.

"Now what did you give of *our* lives, *our* power, to this white woman for a bottle of whiskey?" they demanded.

"I took whiskey, but I gave nothing. I lied!" quaked Panchilo in his rags. "He said, 'Panchilo, you are poor and unfortunate and not understood. Now come and talk to me every afternoon where we will be alone, and I will give you money for new shoes, a new shirt.' So I went. I talked. And I bought whiskey with what he gave me. Can I help it because I am poor and unfortunate and not understood—and am possessed by this strange craving? But even drunken Panchilo was more crafty than he. I lied and he did not know the difference, this ignorant white woman who thought I would betray my people."

His courage was returning; a smirk crawled into his dissolute face. He mimicked and pantomimed his patroness. They could see it all.

"Panchilo, I would hear today the story of creation. How the Indians began. How the Great Spirit gave life to his Red Children."

He had scratched himself and begun. "Now God she make world. She make trees, flowers, birds, animals, fish. She make sky and stars too. This good. No good 'nough. Dios say, 'I make people.' So she make big oven. She make big oven hot. Now she take clay and make in fingers like man and put in big hot oven. Pretty soon take out of oven first man: she alive but all black; Dios leave in oven too long and she burnt. 'Ai!' Dios say. 'You black man. You go odder place live.'

"Now Dios she try again. She take clay out too soon. This man alive but too pale. 'Ai!' Dios say. 'You pale face. You go odder place live.'

"Now Dios she try once more. She leave clay in oven just right time. Man come out cooked just enough. Nice red brown. 'Ai!' say Dios. 'You Indian. Good! You live here.' "

Panchilo's smirk grew into a lewd grin. "This white woman he say, 'Panchilo, that good story, but I would know where this clay come from.' So I say, 'From those clay pits up Arroyo Blanco. Is not the name true? Now that why Indian she paint her skin with this white clay when she dance.' Then I do this."

He drew apart his tattered shirt to reveal his dirty belly, and poked his exposed navel.

"I say, 'Indian she have this hole in belly. Why? Because when Indian in big hot oven, Dios she open door and poke finger in this clay to see if cooked, and leave this hole. See? Now you show Panchilo if white people have this hole in belly too!' "

He leaned back on his heels and finished laughing. Panchilo was a drunken reprobate but still a "good" Indian. They let him stalk out in the only sober dignity he had assumed in months.

More information came. They sent for Manuel Rena; he too had been seen talking with the white woman one day at the trading post.

The Peyote Chief did not look from under his eyelids. He answered in good voice. "We have quarreled about this Native American Church. I still uphold it. I still believe in Our Father Peyote. That is our business; we are all Indians together. But what man accuses me of betraying my people, my tribe, my pueblo to those outside?"

Next brought before them was Buffalo Old Woman. "You work for the trader, Señor Byers," they told her sternly. "One day this white woman came of whom we speak: that was how you knew her. One day after, she went down to the river to cook meat and coffee, to listen to some of our boys beat the drum and sing songs. On a picnic. She paid you to go, to cook this meat and coffee, to wash those dishes afterwards in the river. Now! What did you give her of our lives for more money? Speak!"

Fat shook on the frightened woman. "I talked to her but I lied as is proper! What woman knows anything of the kiva, of solemn matters? Are we not all magpies who always talk—but of trivial things only? Listen! That was how it was. Of little things only I talked. And I lied.

"This white woman ask how the dead are buried, about the turkey feathers, about the Corn Mothers. He ask for our customs. For two silver dollars I give big Indian-woman secret! That when something is lost or stolen we burn on San Antonio Day a candle upside down so that the flame will point to the missing thing. Ai! It is but a Mexican custom, as you know! Such things only I tell him. So I lied, as is proper."

They were still unsatisfied; they would always be unsatisfied. Thirty years ago a fetish of white stone had vanished from one of the kivas. Several men since had been taken to Washington as delegates to see the Great Father, the Presidente. The first place each had asked to visit was the Indian museum. They were still hoping to find on display the missing figure and to trace who had stolen it.

So the probing went on, and over the face of the pueblo dropped the invisible and impenetrable mask of secrecy and aloofness. Old Mexican neighbors were avoided on road and trail. Thin threads of friendship between whites and Indians snapped. An Indian girl working for a family in town suddenly lost her tongue, became shy or sullen. A man in town approached by a tourist who desired a horse and guide merely hitched up his blanket and said quietly, "I have my work," and went back to sleep in the sunny plaza. Whenever a visitor came to the pueblo an Indian boy stepped out from the Governor's house and stuck at his heels like a shadow wherever he walked. All the faces seemed blank. No one seemed to understand English. Occasionally a horseback rider happened to get past the pueblo and upon a mountain trail. Immediately a thin line of smoke rose from a housetop. And soon an Indian stepped out from the brush, his arms outstretched to turn back the rider.

Even Byers became annoyed. He had brought tobacco leaves from Mexico for their Council meetings, and parrot feathers for their ceremonials—gifts whose acceptance showed how long and fully he had been trusted. Now this relationship seemed changed. They treated him respectfully but aloofly, like a shop-keeper.

He got hold of a copy of the booklet and read it through. Over parts he frowned, over pages he laughed. It was mostly all damned stuff and nonsense. But the reaction of the old men to it was not so simple.

They had begun to calm down. It was indeed much foolishness and many lies, this ignorant writing, though the sketch map showing the peculiar arrangement of their fields, and the list of names could have been taken from old Government records. But there in print, like letters of fire, like fingers pointing, like voices shouting, were the names of their kivas, their own names.

Lastly, there was that allusion to their secret Dawn Lake ceremonies. This was something that could not be ignored. Their Dawn Lake!

The District Superintendent had found out about the booklet. It was unfortunate—damned unfortunate!—it had come at such a time. He managed to have it withdrawn from sale in the State lest it provoke both Indians and whites still more, and wired the Commissioner.

Now he could put off a visit no longer, and came up to inquire why the old men had not sent a representative to the All-Pueblo-Council-Meeting.

"We have our lives, we have our own pueblo," he was answered coldly. "We see no need of talk, talk, talk when it brings us nothing. We are still waiting to see what the Government is going to do about our land, our Dawn Lake."

So was Strophy—and the Government too.

The investigators had sent in their findings. A Land Board of three men was created to examine the claims—one member each representing the President, the Department of Justice and the Department of the Interior. They seemed agreed that where the Indian had lost land to a white or Mexican, the Indian should be compensated. And where the whites and the Mexicans had been in possession of the land and paid taxes for many years, though without title, they too should be compensated. But what they looked at made their heads ache. To compensate the pueblo they would require over $84,000; and to compensate the white and Mexican claimants for land within the pueblo grant would require over $57,000. This was a total of over $141,000 for compensation on claims within the shrunken grant of some 18,000 acres.

But what about the whole town of La Oreja? That—the fantastic impossible—would require the proceeds of a Government mint!

While the deliberations went on, another telegram came from Strophy and the district Indian Office. All the pueblos had heard of the rumpus and were likewise demanding restitution of or compensation for their lands—their promised lands.

Strophy, called back to Washington, talked again with the stubborn Council. "I am going to see the Commissioner, the Great Father at Washington, the President himself—the great Government that rules all councils," he said. "I have come first to talk with you. To see what it is you wish. Do you want all your white friends, all your Mexican neighbors to move off their land and be homeless? Do you want all the people to leave La Oreja? Where then will you buy flour, salt, blankets, shoes—where then will you sell corn, trade a bag of wheat for groceries? Is that what you wish?" he asked wearily and ironically.

"We want our Dawn Lake!"

"Then let us talk about it, this Dawn Lake," he answered curtly.

"No. We will talk about it no more. Already we have talked about it. In three ways. Are there more?

"We talked about it when we talked about this peyote. We talked about it as a church. The Government said, 'We will give you this peyote church, this Native American Church.' And we said we do not want any other church. We already have a church—our Dawn Lake, from which comes all the good things we get. That is what *we* say.

"We talked about it when we talked about the compensation the Government promised for our lands. And we said, 'Give us back our land—the land in the mountains about our Dawn Lake. So that it will be our land. Not land full of American policemen and Mexicans with their sheep.' That is what *we* say.

"We talked about it another way. Side by side with this matter of the book of paper. White people come at night to visit our pueblo. They listen to our young men singing down by the willows. Now these young men do not sing to ignorant white people who do not understand their songs. They sing to their girls in the pueblo who stand in the darkness, hidden in their doorways. White people come all day to visit our pueblo. They poke noses in our doors like hungry dogs. They walk into our houses unasked. How is this? Does an Indian walk in a white man's house in town and say, 'Well! So this is how a white man lives! How funny!' Does he pick up a blanket, a pair of shoes, and ask, 'How much you want for this?' And still white people come all a time. They look at our dances. They picnic under our trees and leave paper bags to make the land unsightly. They dirty our streams. And then they write books of lies about us! So we say, 'Whose pueblo is this, whose dances and songs, whose houses, whose customs, whose lives?' And we say, 'It is not the Indian way to put out his belly before all people, to shout out his business, to empty his heart. We must have one place where we can go and sing and dance, live and worship as we will, free from the eyes of the world, without fingers pointing at us, where no voices shout out our names. Give us our Dawn Lake.' This *we* say.

"So we talked about it as a church, as land and business, as a matter of living our lives with due modesty and not naked and ashamed before the world. We talked from the heart, the mind, the body. How now would you have us talk?

"We are all one together. We want our Dawn Lake. This is all we say."

The Corn Ripe Moon rose above the ridge pines. The nights began to sharpen. A thin blue haze smoked the days.

Martiniano was cutting wood. He had taken off his blanket and tied his pig-tails together in back so they would not whip about him as he worked. His dirty denim trousers were tightened about his narrow waist with his wide, brass-studded belt. His faded red cotton shirt stuck to his broad sweaty shoulders. He was stripping a felled pine. The blows of his axe were precise and rhythmical. The chips spurted out evenly, one after another, like leaves being torn from a book. The sound rang sharp and clean in the silent glade. When he was through, he wiped his dark face and moved on to another.

Flowers Playing followed behind him in a turquoise blue shawl and old shoes laced with greased string. She kneeled and laid out a piece of rope. Crosswise on this she stacked the faggots she gathered. When the stack was nearly waist high she drew up and knotted the rope around it, laboriously hoisted it upon her back, and staggered off toward the wagon. Within a few steps she straightened, and when she came back her breath was even.

It is not the force of a blow with an axe that matters, but its preciseness and rhythm. So too have Indian women learned the secret of carrying heavy loads, how to compensate for the gravitational pull.

When the sun was high they built a fire and cooked meat and coffee. "Those lifeless sandwiches white people eat, they make my blood run cold," said Martiniano disdainfully. "A fire and something hot in the belly. That is the way to live like people, not dogs." He stretched out and rolled a cigarette.

Flowers Playing scrubbed off the sooty tin on which she had heated their corn cakes, and washed the dishes. A rabbit hopped across the pine-needled floor of the forest. The smoke had drawn blue-jays to squawk in the trees above. The stream below gushed musically over the stones. She lay back and stared at the clear blue sky, felt the sun eating through her clothes. Life was all one. How beautiful it was!

Only one thought marred her deep content. Last week they had driven down to the pueblo. Leaving team and wagon in the grove of cottonwoods, they cut across a field to the plaza. Like them all, this one was irregular in shape, conforming to natural contours and flanked by thickets of wild plum. Trudging noiselessly along the hedge they were suddenly arrested by sight of a strange figure crouched down before them in the thicket, her upraised hands parting the branches.

It was Palemon's wife, Estefana. The stealthy, secretive posture of her body, and a glimpse in profile of the hungry, agonized look on her face showed them a woman too raptly absorbed in something beyond her to have noticed their approach.

Before Flowers Playing could speak, Martiniano nudged her for silence and nodded toward an opening in the thicket. On the other side sauntered a small boy. Flowers Playing at the first glance did not recognize Napaita. His moccasins were coarse and ill-sewn. He had grown; and his blanket, discolored by smoke, flapped open to reveal a long thin body from which the outline of ribs protruded. It was the boy's face that held her attention. It was drawn and pale, and yet curiously enlivened. His mouth was open and gulping rapid lungfuls of air; his nostrils quivered with its wild, sharp scents; his gaze swung from side to side with less wariness of detection than delight in the open fields and hills before him. He walked with quick, springy steps, flexing his legs as if they had never before known freedom.

The woman kneeling in the thicket did not stir, and let him pass. Martiniano drew Flowers Playing back; they retraced their steps and crossed the field on the other side.

"Napaita. Her own son it was, and she . . . poor Estefana!" mumbled Flowers Playing. "Why did not—"

"He is still in the kiva according to custom, but just out for air. Would you have him speak to a woman, which is forbidden?" interrupted Martiniano curtly. "That much I know. But you understand less."

And now remembering the look on her face as she knelt hidden in the bushes, Flowers Playing was sad for her friend. Why, it might be Estefana and not herself waiting these months for a son to be born to her—a son secretly glimpsed striding in the sunlight, but one to whom she could not yet speak.

They quit early, not quite midafternoon, and drove down to the pueblo. The heavy, loaded wagon rumbled slowly past the clearings. In one a fat, husky woman got up from a log as they passed, pushed back her big brown breast inside her cerise dress, and handed the child she had been suckling to an old crone in rusty black beside her. Then taking up a double-bladed axe she resumed work. Two older children were gathering the branches she chopped, while a girl of four was picking up the chips. Farther along two men were felling pines and stripping off the shaggy bark. All winter the long, smooth yellow timbers would be left to season for vigas, and then snaked down to a new house. From down along the stream came the crackle and cackle of women picking choke-cherries and wild plums. On the slope above crawled shadows of stooped old women patiently filling bags with piñones. The road was full of quick-footed, fastidious-stepping little burros heaped with faggots and being beaten onward by small boys. Bright, sweaty shirts and flowered shawls flashed in the dark green glades. Colored head-bands gleamed against the sunny hillsides. Bursts of song jetted from the somber, rocky cañons.

For as the voice still delayed announcing from the house-tops that it was time to gather in the corn, the people, ever responsive to the change of weather, stirred through the smoky autumn haze about their new tasks.

"One more load to our little house down below," muttered Martiniano complacently, jogging on the seat. "Then I will feel we can face fall. It keeps a man busy when he has two houses, two fields to care for."

There was a strange new pride in his voice. Flowers Playing smiled to herself. Martiniano was preparing for a long, cold winter down below as if for a family of ten! This thing which had happened to them was giving him a new importance.

It showed in his eyes, his walk; and it remained for the little while they stayed in the pueblo before returning home. Suddenly, half-way back up the dusky slope, he gave it voice.

"Now I know what makes me feel so good! 'It would not be too much if a man died for this.' That was what they said, those foolish old men worrying about this book. Did you hear the quaver in Palemon's voice as he told me, see the fright in his eyes? Hah! Why not Martiniano? They have suspicioned me, punished me, fined and whipped me for everything else. But not this! Imagine that! This is the first trouble in the pueblo that has not been laid at my door! They are coming to their senses at last."

Martiniano went to bed unable to sleep for the satisfaction which possessed him. For the first time he had found peace. The crop from his new fields would pay off his debt; next year it would make him a rich man. By then he would have a family. And he had found a faith. All this accomplished by himself, alone! Triumph mounted within him.

He lay thinking, Never before have I really seen myself. Never before have I really seen the old stories truly. For one day these days will be in the dim past, and we who live now. Yes! And in them I shall be a legend!

Swiftly he built up the fantasy of his immense pride. One time long ago, the stories would tell, the pueblo was in trouble. The people's land, their Dawn Lake, was taken from them. White people and Mexicans intruded on their privacy. Then something happened. There was a poor young man whom nobody liked. Now this Martiniano killed a deer, was beaten and punished. But his act roused the old men about their Dawn Lake. A strange religion came. It was called the Peyote Road. This Martiniano ate this peyote, and was punished for it. But he had learned it was no good, and his action turned his people back to the good simple life. Now something else happened. This Martiniano beat a Mexican sheepherder off his land, the mountain slope that rose to Dawn Lake. He was whipped. But he took his whipping like a man for he had roused all the people to desire back their land. Ai! For all these he was fined, he was punished, he was whipped. No one spoke to him. He was called Martiniano the Trouble-Maker.

Life shows as the still surface of deep blue lake. But the impact of a thrown pebble causes ripples that beat upon all shores—that affect all men's lives, that travel from pueblo to pueblo, to Washington itself. And his was the hand which had cast the stone. This poor young man who in his wisdom and strength of will defied all men, suffered trouble, and so saved his people. And now he is no longer known as Martiniano the Trouble-Maker. He is a great man, a savior—he who in legend is known as the Man Who Killed the Deer. . . .

So dreamed his smug satisfaction in having for once escaped trouble, and his monstrous pride in having seen the first glimmer of faith.

It was interrupted from time to time by a certain faint rustle and crackle outside, and the queer sense of eyes peering in the open door. He thrust them from him and slept.

Next morning when he awoke and looked outside, he saw he had had a visitor. His corn, his beautiful new brave corn had been trampled. And there on the ground just outside the door, like a contemptuous refutation of his dreams, lay a few round balls of fresh spoor and the single imprint of a deer's split hoof.

A strange foreboding clutched him. His anger shook it off. He cleaned and oiled his gun, slept afternoons and kept vigil on his corn at night.

Carefully he selected his spot. On the pine slope above both the spring and corn milpa, and hidden behind a great boulder. Wrapped in his blanket he watched the moon rise, the shadows dissolve in a pale greenish effulgence that flowed unobstructed over mountain, sage slope and desert.

Rabbits played about him till frightened by the shapeless terror of a floating owl. Coyotes yapped far down the draw. Once he watched a small fox trot past. Aspens were turning in the high cañons; the small brown bears would soon be ambling down to frighten old women away from their berries. Night birds cried sleepily. At dawn he saw a turkey cock strut down to water in all its bronze, pristine wildness. . . .

Late the third night they came. Three deer gliding dream-like and noiseless out of the great trees to halt below him sniffing the breeze. A five-pronged buck and two small does standing behind.

Martiniano raised his gun, laid the barrel noiselessly in the hollow between thumb and forefinger of his left hand resting on the boulder, drew the butt up snugly against his shoulder.

Slowly the three moved forward—moved like shadows of clouds in the sunlight, having shape but no substance. Three ghostly gray dreams in moonlight. Aware of their wild pristine purity; self-possessive as masters of the earth they trod and which fell away, unbroken, down the sage slope and across the desert to the hazy blue horizon; and fastidious of every movement as patricians conscious of their heritage, they emerged into full moonlight. Martiniano drew a bead on the buck at the base of the brain.

He did not fire. His finger froze on the trigger; his mouth went dry; his knees trembled. Terror struck, he counted the five points of the horns, appraised the body of the deer. There was the same-toned gray though discolored by moonlight, the marking of black, and the little splotch of white under the left shoulder.

The deer had sauntered slowly across the strip of sage between the pines and the corn milpa. The buck was in the lead. He suddenly turned as if with a curt command. The two does stopped, the great petals of their ears thrust forward. Then suddenly—too swiftly to be remarked for mere motion—he was in the air clearing the fence around Martiniano's corn. It was as if he had been invisibly lifted and suspended in the air—as if his skin had been jerked off the wall of the hut and flung in the air to swell with life. His antlered head was up; his front legs curved gracefully under his chest, his hind legs thrust back; his white tail piece lifted. He lit lightly as a butterfly, bounded twice and disappeared in the corn.

The two does looked at each other, rubbed noses. Then like demure doves they too soared gracefully over the split aspens.

Martiniano gripped his gun with trembling fingers. Impossible! He had been betrayed by a foolish memory of the deer he had killed! He gritted his teeth; this time he would not lose his chance. Picking up a pebble, he tossed it into the dry stalks. Immediately, flushed like quail, the deer rose out of the corn. But lighting on the other side of the fence and standing quietly, gracefully and stupidly still, awaiting the message which had summoned them.

Again Martiniano had no power to deliver it.

He angrily kicked loose a stone. It rattled down the slope behind him, bumping dully against the protruding roots of a washed-out spruce and settling with a faint rustle upon a mat of needles. One of the big buck's ears twisted around in its socket to follow the noise. Then disdainfully lifting his nose above the horizon, and stepping high with his thin brittle legs, the deer walked coolly away, followed by his two meek attendants.

Martiniano stood up, banged the stock of his gun against the rock and began to shout. In a flash they were gone, as if erased with one sweep by the hand of night. Still he cursed them, the deer he had killed and himself, then curled up in his blanket for a sleepless night.

Twice later he saw them again, but did not shoot. Something about them from a distance, their untrammeled freedom and wild gentility, stayed his hand. Nor did he let them get close; he could not chance the possibility of being tricked again by a vision. So he settled down each night, shivering in his blanket, to frighten them away with mere noises and angry shouts.

He had not only lost the fleeting comfort of his immense pride, but knew himself a coward. He blamed the deer. And each morning after his vigil he rose stiffly and glowered at the dawn. "This deer I killed," he muttered sullenly. "I will be even with it yet!"

# 10

THEY STOOD in a somber circle about a lofty pine in the forest. Their faces were respectful and their dark eyes shone with wonder, but the blades in their hands gleamed bright and sharp. There were many of them, and it was Palemon who made the prayer-talk before they cut their brother down.

*We know your life is as precious as ours. We know that we all are children of the same Mother Earth, of Our Father Sun. But we also know that one life must sometimes give way to another, so that the one great life of all may continue unbroken. So we ask your permission, we obtain your consent to this killing.*

So they cut him down, he in their midst who had stood there tall and sound and proud before they were yet grown. And it was well with them and with him who had spiritually assented to their ritualistic request for his sacrifice.

They hacked away the limbs, stripped off the bark, adzed the trunk smooth and white. At night they snaked it down the trail to set in the middle of the plaza. A giant pine pole, glistening smooth white, too big to clasp at the butt and tapering at the top. . . .

Another group of men filed up into the dark cañon with rifle, rope and long keen knives. And when the sacrifice was made they laid the deer, their brother, with his head toward the East and sprinkled him with corn meal and pollen. Ceremonially they dropped drops of his blood and bits of his flesh on the ground for their one Mother Earth, and they sprinkled meal and pollen to their common Father Sun. It was proper so. For the deer, their brother, had assented to his sacrifice.

Then they brought him down with his antlered head hanging, his throat slashed open, his insides pulled out. They gathered together his small arrow-pointed feet and bound them to the top of the long pale pole. . . .

Still another group came bringing great green squash cold with frost, and ears of new corn whose yellow husks were wet with dew. And men brought a dirty flour sack full of fresh baked bread and groceries. All these likewise they lashed to the tapering end of the pole.

And then they raised it in the center of the plaza, and tramped it down securely. A tall, glistening white pine pole; and lashed to the top a deer with its throat cut, corn and squash, and a dirty flour sack full of new baked bread and groceries. . . .

Martiniano from his hut had watched the first group filing silently, without greeting, past him into the forest.

"They are getting ready for fiesta," he said to Flowers Playing. "I recognize Palemon. He is on the Committee which selects the tree."

Near dawn he heard the faint crackle of a rifle on the ridge, and knew it came from the Committee gone after a deer. Perhaps they had shot that certain five-point buck which he would no longer have to frighten away from his corn. Smiling with anticipation, he shook Flowers Playing awake.

"Come. Let us get up and do our work so we can see this fiesta. There is one thing about it I am going to like!"

How he hated it, this deer he had killed and which now had struck him through his false security. For like all men he could endure the blows of adversity but not the arrows which pricked his pride and vanity. And like most men he blamed the invisible marksman rather than his own vulnerability.

The late afternoon, the pueblo and the pole drew them all. Apaches had come like buzzards to a kill—both those known as the Llaneros and the Olleros. Big dark men wearing great black Stetsons and silver ear-rings, and women bulging in pink and purple waists and striped petticoats. Pottery makers from the pueblos down river had spread out on the ground their bowls and jars and little clay figures of skunk, deer, bear, rabbits and turtles. Some Uncompaghre Utes were down from the mountains; a lean Navajo had come from the desert with a load of silver and turquoise. Even a few Plains Indians, rich enough to come by train, stood beside Rena, their beautiful blankets draped carelessly over suits of wrinkled serge. They were talking sign-language with a tattered White River Ute—the expressive free-flowing gestures of dark, poetic hands that will always remain, unforgotten, the most expressive medium of their wordless souls. Everyone boasted his best clothes, his oldest buckskin. The sun gleamed on snowy boots and beaded moccasins, flowered shawls, silk shirts and colored blankets—all one vast blanket of color spread upon the plaza, and covering the terraced pueblo to the highest roof tops.

It had always stood between the lingering twilight of summer and the false dawn of fall which first begins to flame among the highest aspens. So they had danced the Sundown Dance after last evening's early Mass. Very beautifully, quietly, quickly, in all the wonder and the tremulous hush. A small group of old men filing out of the little church freshly whitewashed to reflect the pinkish glow of the setting sun. Standing in two lines, naked to the waist, in old buckskin leggings and new moccasins. Gently waving branches of green-leaved aspens left from summer, and the first branches of aspen leaves stained deep yellow, clear pink and spotted red. Singing softly, treading lightly, then quickly fading away into the dusk.

It had always marked the pendulum pause when the sun's summer race was over, and he began his winter journey. So early this morning the young men had raced down the long track in relays, toward San Geronimo watching from his shelter of green boughs at the finish.

For long too it had begun the great fall Fairs of a wilderness empire, and the plaza swarmed with travesties of lingering ghosts. Trappers in buckskin stepped out of long sleek automobiles. Mexican caballeros on spavined plow horses rode from La Oreja in skin tight black trousers embroidered in silver. Señoras in lace mantillas and high Spanish combs paraded, chewing gum and munching pop corn.

It was San Geronimo—an immemorial feast day whose roots were anchored deep in Indian earth, and whose branches held entwined the later traditions of Mexican Fiesta and white Fair alike. But its trunk was still a tall, stripped pine pole planted in the plaza of the pueblo; and hanging down from the top a deer with its throat slashed open, corn and squash, and a dirty flour sack full of fresh bread and groceries.

Martiniano squatted on the ground with Flowers Playing. Neither was in a holiday mood. They had brought dishes and blankets down to their winter hut, had killed and dressed a sheep, cooked chile and squash, baked bread. All to entertain two Ute friends of Flowers Playing and three Apache friends of his own with traditional and expected hospitality. Five big men gorging ribs and sopping up mole with hunks of bread had kept his wife busy at the stove for two days. True, they had all trudged into La Oreja and the Utes had taken her up in the rusty ferris wheel, and one of the Apaches had bought pink ice cream. But afterward Flowers Playing had looked a little wan, and back home she had vomited; she was still quiet and listless beside him.

Well, thought Martiniano darkly, it will soon be over, this foolish fiesta which has cost us so much. These guests of ours have been invited to the big feast tonight. Venison. From that deer! I will feel better when it is cooked, eaten and carried away from here. Then my trouble will have vanished at last.

With sullen resentment and bitter anticipation he eyed it hanging limply from the top of the pine. Yes, it was the deer which had trodden down his corn. But the deer he had killed, as if to still mock him, had made it resemble itself. So his resentment and anticipation was tinctured by a faint uneasiness.

There was a sudden whoop, a high-pitched yell. Howling and shieking, six Indians dashed into the crowded plaza. All were naked but for breech clouts and moccasins, their faces and bodies smeared with black and white clay. They were the Black Eyes, the Koshares, the Chiffonetas—the funmakers everpresent at most pueblo ceremonies. Really clowns, and very clever as they pranced around making horseplay, frightening children and pantomiming whites and Mexicans.

The Pueblo Indian is invariably patient and charitable to summer visitors. Yet in the antics of the Chiffonetas are revealed his acute perception and sly humor. One wears strapped to his arm a battered alarm clock. He looks at it. "It is time to be hungry!"—and he snatches from a bystander a bag of popcorn. Another owlishly puffs a pipe. Still another grabs a woman's hat for his own head, and as though on high heels minces off wiggling his naked hips. Civilization slapped on a savage who shows its ludicrous aspects.

But now their humor and pantomiming carried a touch of the malicious. The painted clowns strutted insolently as tourists into doorways. They jerked open women's handbags to loudly demand in English of the contents. "How much this handkerchief? How much? This Indian?" Squatting on the ground, they drew a tiny square and bargained for it in lewd Spanish. "This is Indian land. No good. We buy it for a drink of whiskey!" Two of the grotesque actors started off to the mountains to kill a deer. The other four set upon them, rolled them in the dust and gave them an imaginary beating. They were Government men, they shouted in their own tongue. And when the last one rose it was to snatch a kerchief from a spectator to wrap round his broken head, to spit upon it later and throw it down underfoot.

Most of the visitors sat forcing silly grins, knowing better than to resist and saving their cussing till later, or unaware of the meaning of this extravagant horseplay. But the Indians, seeing the ironic subtlety of the mimicry, smiled grimly at the howling, leaping figures.

Martiniano, suffering in silence this animated reminder of the trouble he had caused, endured stoically the eyes of both. In his immense and lofty pride he had bequeathed to the long memory of his people this very act. And here it was presented before him: not as the high drama of legend, but as mere buffoonery reënacted by grotesque clowns. Ai! In front of Mexicans and whites alike he was shamed. By the deer he had killed, who mocked him, who hung there in the skin of the substitute sent to plague him in his corn. What a fool and coward he had been for not shooting it! Well, he would soon be avenged. Look!

The fun was over. One of the gargoyle Chiffonetas had discovered something. Beyond the plaza. Down by the pueblo wall. Something in the dirt. He yelled. The others came running. They squatted around it, pointed, talked, then scattered like hounds to the four directions.

One of them loped into the plaza. He was bent almost double. The muscles of his clay-daubed thighs stood out like ropes. Every few steps he paused and sniffed the wind. His contorted, gargoyle face peered around. His eyes within their huge black circles were intent, aware. He was no longer the jeering fun-maker. He was wonderfully aware. The intent awareness of true aliveness.

The enclosing pueblo walls seemed to fall away behind him, letting the great pine hills move in, the wind and the fading September sun. And for a moment a forgotten past gave up a flashing vision.

He was a strange beast of prey as suddenly he leapt away, making queer animal sounds, and stopped again. This was mimicry, but of a different kind. Of life pure, untainted and cruel.

And all the time he was studying the ground, the unseen trail.

Martiniano saw what he was really doing. Unobtrusively, furtively almost, his closed right hand with forefingers protruding pressed into the dust regularly spaced deer tracks. He was making a trail for the others to follow.

Soon they came yelping behind him. Very slowly, bent double, stalking too. The leader returned. All six came together now, sniffing, prowling, whirling away and returning at a shout. One of them had found another deer track. They leaped into the air, baying deeply, then slid relentlessly forward once more.

The trail led them to the pole, the stripped, green pine pole. And hanging from its top, the quarry: the slaughtered deer with its gaping, red-slashed throat. Ten feet away they saw it for the first time. In an ecstasy of discovery they shrieked and dashed forward to surround it.

The pole was deeply imbedded in the earth, perhaps forty feet high and too big at the base to reach around. One of the Chiffonetas straddled it and yanked backward. How queer it doesn't pull down, exclaimed his ludicrous, painted face peering around.

Another hurled himself against it, and again. This was very funny to the silent watchers. A puny, five-foot clown trying to butt down a pine tree!

Hai! Watch the mighty hunters now.

Out came their bows and arrows: the bows of bent willow twigs hardly a foot long, and the arrows little yellow wheat straws which darted up the great smooth pole, broke and wafted away on the wind.

While the Chiffonetas were giving their painted grimaces of heroic endeavor and ludicrous disappointment, Palemon stopped beside Martiniano. He was strolling about in his best blanket and looking very proud.

Martiniano looked up and politely remarked the obvious. "You were on the Committee which selected this tree. My congratulations."

His friend acknowledged the bitter tone of his voice with a modest nod and stepped away.

Martiniano did not look after him. His face had set into a dark, sullen cast. Behind this curtain, at the back of his mind, seethed a growing resentment against something intangible and undefined. Whatever it was, the scene before him symbolized it perfectly. It was as if that tall, gleaming white pine stem held something of the pure, blind faith which had erected it; and those foolish, painted Black Eyes were but showing his own puny efforts to ascend it. The tall, stripped pine and the hanging deer on top, both in death more victorious than he. With smoldering impatience he waited to see them undone.

And at last the Chiffonetas got down to business: to shinny up the pole and let down the deer, the corn and squash, and the flour sack of bread and groceries to be used in the night's feast. One after another wrapped his arms around it, laid his bedaubed cheek against the smooth surface, and heaved up mightily with strong legs. Thigh muscles corded in the sunlight. Faces dripped paint and sweat. Moccasins scraped and squeaked on the shiny wood. And each in turn slipped down, leaving a smear of clay to mark his three foot rise.

The butt was too large. They gathered in a group, arched backs, and boosted a climber from their hips to their shoulders. With hands under his heaving buttocks, he went up another foot or two, hung panting, and then limply slid back down.

Defeated, the six stood ludicrously disconsolate at the bottom of the pole, rubbing sweaty hands on slimy thighs. No longer fun-makers, the jeering Chiffonetas. No longer hunters intensely aware, no longer Indians. Just six thwarted men who couldn't climb up a pole.

A murmur crept round the plaza. Through the patient throng men came with a short ladder. This was better. Placed against the pine it reached perhaps a fourth of the way up. A shout. Up went a climber. The pole was a bit smaller now; his arms and legs wrapped all the way around. But still he couldn't get up.

Martiniano gritted his teeth. The deer, head down, hung staring at the powerless men below with sticky, filmed eyes whose dull sadness yet seemed to hold an ironic gleam. Around him he could hear the visiting whites, bored to distraction, tooting their automobile horns. The Mexicans were grinning; these Indians couldn't get up their pole even with a ladder! And Palemon, he observed, no longer looked pleased and proud. He looked worried.

The old men around him murmured their own heavy wonder. It was a bad sign, this. They were interrupted by a sudden commotion which cleared the crowd—the trader in his automobile. Byers drove up beside the pole, got out and gave orders. But the top of the car was too insecure to support the heavy ladder, and the hood too low to serve the purpose, and after a time he drove it away.

This was serious. The old men huddled together in council.

Martiniano could stand it no more. Wild with anger and frustration, he rose and flung off his blanket. He stripped off his shirt, shoes and pants. Wearing only a loin cloth, he stepped forth and began to talk to the old men. One after another nodded assent. Then hurriedly they sent for a certain long, slim, notched spruce—an old-time pole ladder that Martiniano remembered standing back of the pueblo.

The sun was setting behind the mesa. The pine slopes flushed blood red. While he was waiting, Martiniano stared up at the tall pine gleaming yellow. Pride and confidence returned to him. This was his one big chance to show these old men, to vanquish the deer and ascend the pole.

He saw himself climbing slowly, carefully, an inch at a time, up the slick and shiny pine. Creeping to windward, left leg hooked in front, right leg bent back under him. Ducking his head under the squash and sack, squeezing up between the ropes securing the bound deer. Perching on top while carefully untying the knots and lowering the burdens to the ground by means of a small pulley.

Then—to a saturnalia of shouts, shrieks, hand-claps, whistles and auto-hoots—he saw himself balanced on top, his black, wind-blown head towering above the mountain ridge, his naked sweaty body gleaming redly in the setting sun. Hooking his legs tighter, he would lift and fling out both arms like wings, and scream one high peal of triumph like an eagle.

He had seen it so year after year. But this time he saw himself—Martiniano the trouble-maker who had saved the day for his people, and finally vanquished the deer. . . .

The boys came trotting into the plaza with the long slim notched spruce. They leaned it against the great pine, and the Chiffonetas standing on the shorter ladder underneath held it there. This would be the difficult task: to hold the tip securely against the smooth, rounded trunk while Martiniano clambered up.

Automobile horns letting out a continuous raucous blast of both encouragement and derision suddenly stilled as Martiniano started up.

It was even more difficult than it looked—this clambering up a slanting, sixty-degree spruce scarcely bigger around than a muscular arm. Martiniano looked like an awkward, hairless monkey. Bent double, head down, behind stuck up, he worked slowly upward. He held the under side of the pole with his hands while his naked feet pressed down in the small notches. It required all his strength of grip to keep it from turning, and to this was added the excruciating difficulty of evening his weight so that the tip end of the spruce would not be jarred loose from the smooth pine on which it so precariously rested.

Though accustomed to stooping while working in his fields, Martiniano could feel the muscles in his back strain and cramp. Sweat ran down his face until he had to close his eyes. He gritted his teeth, climbed on in a deathly silence.

It was suddenly broken by a blast of noise from the crowd below. At the same moment his hands ran into a smooth round wall. He had reached the slanting top of the spruce, nearly half way up the tall pine pole. His arms wrapped round it eagerly as a lover's. He rested his cheek against its smooth surface and clung there, resting, till the sweat dripped out of his eyes. He had accomplished a difficult feat.

Kicking loose the spruce, he began the still more difficult ascent of the vertical pine. Two feet up he knew he was done. The pole now was small enough to reach around. His arms were still strong; his legs maintained their hold; his desire flared with passion until he could hear the roaring in his ears. So he strained, heaved, tugged—but advanced no farther. It was as if an invisible weight pressed down upon him from above. Wildly he stared upward at the dull glazed sadness and the ironic gleam in the eyes of the deer above, and strained again. Now he hung there, half way up, his head flung back—the limp body of a man staring at the limp body of a deer suspended above him.

Then slowly, to a derisive blast of horns, he slid down. Limply, heavily, with many pauses, he slid back down. Without a word he staggered over to his seat, crawled into his clothes and blanket, and slumped down on the ground.

The sun had set. Dusk and a chill night wind were blowing down the cañon. The visitors were going home. It had happened; the disgraceful, the unbelievable, the thing that had not happened for years.

Martiniano, hunched over in his blanket at home, sat listening to a steady, resonant concatenation of sound coming from the dark plaza—the sound of axes chopping down the pole.

With it crashed the last cracked walls of his pride.

The deer he had killed had defeated him again—for the last time. For he knew now there was something about it not to be overcome, not to be escaped from; but which must be lived with and understood.

Chastened and contrite, he drove back up to the mountains to begin gathering his corn.

It is a deep truth and difficult to learn that the greatest

deeds must be done by him who is content to remain unknown lest his action be impeded by too ready acclaim.

*Life is like the still surface of a deep blue lake into which a stone is cast. Who knows how far, on what shores the ripples spread? But the stone, having been cast, has done its work. Let it sink, unnoticed and forgotten, into the blue, troubled depths. Until one day when the turmoil has ceased men may gaze into the placid face of the water and see there, still bright and shining, the stone lying at the bottom like a gleaming star . . .*

So mused Martiniano as he thought of the meaning of his people's traditional secretiveness and self-effacement, and of his own immense pride which had led him to put out his belly before the crowded plaza in a last boastful, futile effort.

As he worked among his corn, Martiniano wore his sheet not as a blanket, but as a bag knotted and slung under his left arm. It was tedious work filling the bag, trudging back and emptying the ears in front of the hut a hundred times a day. Flowers Playing sat beside it, shucking, though her face seemed to him a little strained.

"It is nothing," she said. "That ferris wheel and that pink ice-cream during fiesta. It made me vomit. Now sometimes I still remember that whirling in my head, the taste in my mouth and that awful coldness in my belly. And then I vomit again. That is all. I shall soon forget."

So now he had two things to worry him, his harvest and his wife. It was not enough that he had to hurry to pick his corn before frost in his mountain fields. He had to leave his ailing wife to guard it and finish shucking while he went down below to cut his grain. Martiniano knew better than to ask for the community thresher. He cut it by hand again; and heaping the grain on the floor of his clean corral, drove his horses around and around to thresh it. Then he hurried back up the slope to his wife.

Flowers Playing met him with a smile. She looked better and the corn was all shucked—a beautiful big heap. But colored: black, blue, pink, blood-red, yellow and speckled.

"Strange, is it not?" she asked. "It was seed of white corn we planted."

"But this is new land. Indian earth. And so it colored the corn. It made the seed its own. That is a good sign! Look! What a pile! And the wheat likewise was plentiful. I am anxious to measure and weigh it, to show it to the trader. It will almost repay him, I am sure of that."

Flowers Playing had had no visitors. Nor had she been lonely, having made two new friends.

"How is this?" he asked. "To me your tongue has spoken two ways."

"You will see tonight," she answered softly.

Toward dusk he saw—hidden in the dark hut where she bid him wait and watch out the doorway while she stood outside. In a little while they came. The two small does he had seen before with the big five-pronged buck. They stepped out from the great pines, ears up, sniffing. They drank at the spring politely, one at a time, and delicately licked the drops of water off their black lips when they were finished. Together they walked sedately to the fence and stopped. One of them muzzled the peeled aspen bars as if jerking a latch string for permission to call.

Flowers Playing was standing quietly in the gathering dusk. Slowly and gently she put out her hand. With a bound the deer cleared the fence and strode across the field.

A snake wriggled up Martiniano's backbone; his knees trembled. A vision clutched him by the throat. He had cut his corn stalks and stacked them in little, upright conical piles to shed rain. In the dusk they looked like a far, vast village of tepees standing on the plain. Striding between them, distorted and fantastically enlarged by perspective, came the deer—giant, ghostly figures looming above the highest tips of protruding lodge poles. For an instant, as the old myth-wonder and atavistic fear rose up and flooded him, he saw them as his people had long seen them, one of the greatest animalistic symbols of his race: the deer which had populated forest and plain in uncounted myriads on the earth, and gave their name to the Pleiades in the sky; whose hoofs as ceremonial rattles were necessary for every dance; who complemented at once the eagle above and the snake below; gave rise to Deer Clan and Antelope Priests; and lent the mystery of their wildness, swiftness and gentleness to all men. In a flash of intuition it all leapt out before him. And in its brief glimmer stood out a strange woman with the same wildness and gentleness which had first drawn his eyes to her as she danced—a woman no longer his wife, but as a deer clothed in human form and thus possessing the power to draw and control the great shapes that moved toward her.

The next instant it all was gone. There were only two small does standing before him and licking salt from her outstretched hands.

Martiniano stepped quietly out the doorway. At his first movement the deer were gone. Two gray streaks crossing the field, bounding over the fence, then stopping to look back. Flowers Playing rubbed the wet salt off her hands and stood watching them as they walked slowly back into the dark fringe of pines.

She had not spoken nor did Martiniano. But as he stood beside her, he sensed again the aura of mystery about her. And he knew, strangely, that henceforth she belonged to something greater than he. She was inviolable, beyond his touch.

Often during the next few days he furtively watched her. Her face was taking on a strange anonymity. Her movements were calm and assured. She seemed, without knowing she had done so, to have withdrawn from him.

The nights grew increasingly sharper. Each dawn the withered squash vines sparkled with frost. The clear days were dulled by a faint blue haze. Martiniano had finished his work up on the high slope; he thought they should be moving down to their winter hut just outside the pueblo. Flowers Playing shook her head.

"The mountains are my home. I do not mind this aloneness. There will be enough talk all winter. So leave me here yet awhile . . . But go down yourself, husband, and do your work. There is your grain to sell, payment to be made to the good trader. Our house needs preparing for winter—you do not forget that leak in the roof? And there is more wood to be brought and cut."

As if dismissed, Martiniano left her. To return every three or four days with fresh food and to replenish her wood.

Deer season opened. He cleaned and oiled his rifle with the indecisive intention of going hunting. One early morning he started out, stopping at his mountain hut. Dawn was just washing over the ridge as he arrived. While he waited for Flowers Playing to cook breakfast, there sounded a loud volley of shots and the crackling of brush up the slope.

They rushed outside. Above them, outlined against the sky, rode a group of white hunters from La Oreja. Below them, breaking from cover, dashed two gray streaks. Straight toward the hut they raced, leaping the fence—the two small does. Flowers Playing ran forward, turned and flung open the corral gate. The deer unhesitatingly raced inside the enclosure to stand wild-eyed, trembling and panting. Flowers Playing calmly threw down an armful of hay and closed the gate.

Rejoining Martiniano, she walked back to the door of the hut. They stood watching the hunters ride on across the ridge. "They came once before," she said quietly. "There was trouble getting them inside, but there was a dog. Now they know me well. But their days of fear will soon be over."

Martiniano had left his rifle in the scabbard hung on the mare. Without telling her he had brought it, he rode back to the pueblo. Down the slope he looked back. Flowers Playing was letting the two does out of the corral. A new fear beset him; he could not forget the power she had over the deer—the deer who had defeated him.

# 11

THE OLD MEN were still thinking of what lay behind the chopped down pole. It possibly had been a little too large at the base, perhaps too high and polished too smooth for ready climbing. Yet they did not censure Palemon; he had made the prayer-talk properly, followed through the ritual. They talked with the other committees; considered the deer, the corn and squash, and the fresh-baked bread which had hung on top. They discussed Martiniano's attempt to climb it. He was not a Chiffoneta, and had steadfastly refused to be conscripted for dances. But he had seen the impending failure, and had made an attempt against all precedent.

"He is a strange young man, this stubborn Martiniano. He refuses what we demand and offers what we have not asked," they said, dismissing him. "But clearly he was not the cause. We ourselves had already failed."

They thought of what lay ahead of the chopped-down pole. Its resistance to climbing clearly betokened a failure of their medicine. Now if their power was too weak to consummate their annual fiesta, did it portend an even greater failure? Were they balked at the bottom of their effort to save their land, their Dawn Lake? So they fortified their faith with renewed stubbornness and, as fall drew to a close, began careful preparations for the winter dances.

Meanwhile the Indian Superintendent and Strophy returned with groups of Government officials.

The representatives of the President of the United States, the Department of Justice and the Department of the Interior had made a quick examination of some five thousand claims. Their summary showed that compensation to whites and Mexicans for improvements on lands to be reassigned to Indians would amount to some $232,000, and to Indians over $100,000. The Pueblo Land Board was directed to continue investigations and make a detailed report with recommendations for each and all the pueblos. But to quiet the storm, action was necessary with regard to the pueblo which had started the trouble and still resisted arbitration. Hence the officials' visit.

Compensation to this pueblo would involve a consideration of over $84,000 to pay in part the liability of the United States to the pueblo and for the purchase of lands and water rights to replace those which had been divested from the pueblo.

This sounded very legal and difficult to understand. It required hours and days of interpretation. Through it all the old men were adamant. "Give us back our land in the mountains, our blue Dawn Lake. This is all we ask."

So early that fall the delegation left for Washington to draft one of the most astounding bills that the Congress of the United States ever had to vote on: an Indian pueblo proposing to surrender its compensation for lands taken by white and Mexican settlers in exchange for undisputed possession of a little mountain lake which was its "church"! What other community would forego nearly $100,000 to clear the title of its church and "keep it clean"? What other congregation believed that from its church "flowed all the blessings of life"?

The bill was drawn up for presentation, and with it the recommendation of the Secretary of the Interior who wrote:

"This bill, if enacted . . . will bring to an end the most vexed and ancient of land controversies affecting Indian lands under the jurisdiction of the United States . . . Failure to enact the bill . . . would have results vexing and possibly disastrous to several thousands of Indians and their white neighbors."

Remarked an old Congressman, "I have no personal interest in this matter, but for years I have watched these Indian bills come and go, and the result is that millions of dollars are dragged out of the Federal Treasury on one pretext or another. The United States Government has been humane with the Indians—and never fails to respond charitably to its wards. They come and say this is an emergency measure. Yet if payment is deferred many years nobody perishes."

Began another, "You can go to the city of La Oreja and there is not a single town lot or business property where the legal title is in the white man, though he and his predecessors may have occupied the land for many years—"

"Take La Oreja!" he was interrupted. "The white people pay taxes and exercise all rights of ownership. Are we going to pay them for that property and give it to the Indians? Why not make them pay for it themselves—let them adjust their rights in court? The United States Government has a fully equipped Department of Justice. If someone owns a lot that belongs to the Pueblo tribe let him pay for it. In court present claims and counterclaims—and let the Judge and jury say who shall pay and is responsible!"

But—it was pointed out—the alternative was to give these Indians possession of a certain lake in the mountains above their pueblo or village.

What! Part of the watershed for the city of La Oreja, and land included in a National Forest Reserve?

So the ripples kept spreading . . .

What was an Indian pueblo? What were these Indians?

Reports of Superintendents of Indians themselves were dug out of files and presented.

"While apparently the Pueblo Indians are law-abiding, it has come to my notice during the past year that in the practice of the Pueblo form of government cruel and inhuman punishment is often inflicted . . .

"The pueblos, however, are very insistent upon retaining their ancient form of government. As long as they are permitted to live a communal life, and exercise their ancient form of government, just so long will there be ignorant and wild Indians to civilize. The Pueblo form of Government recognizes no other form and no authority. The returned student who has been five years at boarding school is compelled to adopt the Indian dress upon his return to the pueblo; he is compelled to submit to all the ancient and heathen customs of his people. If he rebels he is punished. He therefore lapses back and becomes like one who has never seen the inside of a school."

Another confirmed this view.

"There is a greater desire among the Pueblos to live apart and be independent and have nothing to do with the white race than among any other Indians. . . . They really care nothing for schools. The return student going back to the pueblo has a harder task before him than any other class of returned students. It is easier to go back to the Sioux tepee, and lead a white man's life, than to go back to the pueblo and retain the customs and manners taught in school.

"In pueblo life the one-man domination—the fear of the wrath of the Governor of the pueblo—is what holds the people down. The rules of the pueblo are so strict that the individual cannot sow his wheat, plant his corn, or harvest same in the autumn without permission of the authorities. The pueblos under my jurisdiction adhere religiously to old customs and rules—Taos, Picuris, Santo Domingo and Jemez, and none of them has made much progress away from the ancient and pagan rites."

These reports from Government Indian Superintendents had been upheld by the United States Supreme Court which held in general that the Indians of the pueblos were "essentially a simple, uninformed and inferior people."

In the opinion of the court it was the consensus that: "Until the old customs and Indian practices are broken among this people we cannot hope for a great amount of progress. The secret dance, from which all whites are excluded, is perhaps one of the greatest evils. What goes on at this time I will not attempt to say, but I firmly believe it is little less than a ribald system of debauchery. The Catholic clergy is unable to put a stop to this evil, and know as little of the same as the others. The United States Mails are not permitted to pass through the streets of the pueblos when one of their dances is in session; travellers are met on the outskirts of the pueblo and escorted at a safe distance around. The time must come when the Pueblos must give up these old pagan customs and become citizens in fact."

Was this the time?

Here the developing controversy stuck in argument. For if it were, they were going to have to vote a hundred thousand dollars out of their vote-casters' and taxpayers' pockets. Or else they were going to have to give a group of these stubborn Indians a tract of National Forest Reserve containing a lake around which they could continue to carry on unmolested and in secret their ancient, ribald and pagan rites. . . .

The leaves had changed color, dulled and fallen before Flowers Playing moved down from the mountains. Martiniano had not urged her; it was evident she preferred the companionship of the two deer to his.

Now with him again, she seemed to have brought with her some of their qualities. Her big brown eyes held their liquid luminosity, her movements the same gliding, dreamlike ease. She was wider across the hips, heavier, more mature. Like them she was tamed, domesticated—and yet showed more clearly than ever the intangible, illusive strength and wilderness of her heritage.

Winter had come. The time of the great ceremonials and dances drew near. Martiniano, walking across the plaza, was called by one of the old men. Politely but warily, Martiniano followed him inside his house. They smoked a cigarette in silence before the old man spoke.

"You have had some trouble. It is life that has punished you for not understanding, though it has used our hands. But you are one of us. You will understand. No?"

Martiniano studied the old face before him, its leathery cheeks, deep wrinkles, the sharp clear eyes and firm wide mouth. It was at once kind and indomitable.

"We have observed you of late," his host went on. "There are things you are coming to understand. So now we ask again. About these dances, this our work. Are you ready to assume your duties?"

"My Grandfather," Martiniano answered respectfully, "it is like this. I cannot tell myself what these dances mean, but something in my heart tells me they are good. But this also I think and say. A man's religion is in his heart. It speaks out from his heart in action. But freely. It cannot be compelled. Now if there is a dance and my heart tells me it is good, then I shall dance. Freely, without compulsion. But when my name is called out from the housetops, and when

I am punished because I do not obey the summons, then my heart is no longer free. It takes no joy in action. My faith is false. So I say leave me free to have my religion in my heart, and not at the call of authority."

"How can one heart be free? There is only one great heart. Of our pueblo, our tribe. Of the whole world. We beat as one with all around us."

"Yet I would not be forced, Grandfather," said Martiniano stubbornly. "I would rather continue to thresh my wheat with horses' hoofs, the old way, without benefit of the community machine. To live outside the town wall like an outcast. To suffer injustice for no wrong."

"So you will not take your turn in our dances, our work? You will maintain the illusion that you are separate and alone? Well, perhaps understanding will come later. Now about your wife. Does she too refuse that participation which is also required of women?"

"How can I answer for my wife, Grandfather? I would let her heart speak for her, as mine for me." And he had walked out respectfully, still stubborn, but vaguely worried.

Christmas Eve and Day came, beginning the winter ceremonial dances which here were the most important, powerful and beautiful of all. With the deep snow the small herd of buffalo was brought in from the Big Pasture, and milled closer to the pueblo under their shaggy shawls. Martiniano stood one afternoon, huddled in his blanket against the falling snow, watching the Buffalo Dance. A small group of men with great brown buffalo hoods thrown over heads and shoulders, their little bare bodies painted red, and glowing against the adobe wall. But the heavy buffalo heads shaking back and forth, the pale horns tossing gently up and down, and the drum sounding the thunder of invisible hoofs while the icy moccasins kept time. It all sent out a peculiar yellow warmth like that of the stamping bodies of the great beasts farther off.

One dawn he rose to watch the Turtle Dance. The plaza was still shrouded in dusk, bitterly cold and deserted save for two or three dark ghosts like himself shivering against a wall. Then suddenly, with the first shaft of day, he saw a faint line of men filing out of the far kiva. They crossed the frozen stream, and walked between the snow banks to stand in front of the church wall. About thirty dancers garbed in short kirtles with a fox skin hanging at the back, their upper bodies and legs bare to the acid cold, and unpainted save for a white streak extending across their faces from ear to ear and passing under their lower lips—an elongated turtle mouth. Each wore in his hair two eagle feathers sticking up, V-shaped, like a rabbit's ears, and between them a small, colored macaw, quail or parrot feather.

Behind the single long line, unseen, stood a man with a drum. And in front, marking step, the leader wrapped in a blue blanket and holding an armful of blue spruce boughs. It was one of the rare dances in which the dancers themselves sang instead of an accompanying chorus. A beautiful song rising in the terrible dawn-cold, as if out of the steam of their frosty breaths. Rising like the lifted gourds and spruce branches to the blue and white peaks which, like themselves, rose out of the dark primeval water-world to the earth-world of beast and man.

Thus they sang, while dancing, and then filed back across the snowy plaza and down into the kiva before sun-up. Something that had emerged in the dawn-dusk with the memory of another emergence long past, not yet forgotten but dissipated by the rising light of day.

These dances. They all had a faint, lingering aliveness that stirred awake something deep and sleeping within him. Martiniano could not evaluate their meanings. They were like symbols long familiar but whose outlines were peculiarly blurred. But he watched them with a strange fascination.

That afternoon as he entered his hut Martiniano saw an older woman sitting on the floor with Flowers Playing. Around them lay strewn a length of white cotton, soft buckskin and a pair of snowy deerskin boots. Their talk hushed, slowed, then stopped. The visitor gathered up the articles, bade him good-bye politely, and left. A strange visitor, this old woman who had never come before! Martiniano waited until night for Flowers Playing to tell him what she would. She spoke casually, as if it were too natural to be explained.

"They are giving the Deer Dance this year. I have said I will take part."

Martiniano grunted—a little apprehensively, as his glance roved swiftly over her heavy body.

"They were very kind when they asked me, those old men who remembered my dancing in the grove, who remembered my teaching those children our Sariche. That is why they asked me. Because that old woman who has always taken this part has died. So I assented to be a Mother with her who remains."

A Deer Mother! Martiniano controlled his surprise. It was a very sacred part in a very sacred dance. It required a good dancer and a devout woman. Indeed, the two who had served had not been replaced for years.

"So Josefita came to bring me dress and boots to try on before they are put away in the kiva till the day. She will come, moreover, to teach me my part. Perhaps it will be wise if you are not present, husband." Then rising and stretching her tall, full body, she added lightly, "I shall dance well. I feel inside the power and the grace already given me."

Martiniano looked at her in amazement, then slunk out to putter in his shed as if dismissed. The husband in him could not censure the wife. But the man in him was stirred against the woman. For he felt in her a strange female power that sought to dwarf his manhood, and against which he had no means to rebel.

And so it went. Dutifully she rose and made the fires, cooked his meals, kept the hut clean and swept the outside walls of snow so that they would not crumble. She was respectful, submissive, even tender at times; he could find no fault with her. Then of an afternoon when Josefita came or they went off together, Martiniano retreated before a stranger. A woman who seemed no longer his wife, but a symbol of something in all women he could not but resent.

A Deer Mother! He remembered her as he had first seen her, with all the grace, timidity, power and wildness of a deer. He could not forget her with the two does up on the mountain. He thought of the deer he had killed. It all came back to him; all, as the old men said, drew together in one unbroken whole.

"That deer I killed!" Martiniano muttered low, alone. "Has it bewitched her? Is it striking me at last through my wife, herself?"

He was tormented, a little frightened. But he did not rebel. He had learned that there was something about it not to be overcome, not to be escaped from; but which must be lived with and understood.

He could only wait until the day of the dance.

The sun had risen high and clear of clouds, leaving the mountain and the pueblo below sparkling with a light fresh fall of snow, when he saw them emerging from the kiva. A long file of strange figures, part man, part beast, and led by gods in human dress. They crossed the hand-hewn logs over the icy stream, passed between the banks of drifted snow, came silently across the still, dazzling plaza toward the waiting throng. As out of the white shrouded forests they came with all the wonder and the mystery and the power of unseen forces now made visible to all eyes.

Two tall, dignified leaders beautifully garbed in loose white buckskin shirts, long fringed leggings and moccasins, and carrying arrow quivers of white buckskin decorated with colored beads. Two Deer Chiefs also dressed in snowy white, with antlers branching from their heads. And behind them, in single file, all the animal forms of plain and forest: men wearing the heads and skins of deer, antelope, buffalo, wildcat, coyote and mountain lion. They stalked slowly forward, bent over, a short pointed stick in each hand to serve as forelegs; heads and horns raised proudly; their lower bodies bare and unpainted under the drooping skins and pelts. Behind them, small boys as fawn and cub, followed by the grotesquely painted Black Eyes carrying tiny bows and arrows.

Martiniano watched closest two figures which had been carefully arrayed and painted in the kiva, and were being escorted across the plaza so no one could touch them. Two women attired similarly in white, ceremonial buckskin gowns with the left shoulder and both arms free, and walking through the snow in high white buckskin boots. From the back of their freshly combed heads rose two tall eagle feathers, and on top their heads was fastened a small bright tuft of parrot feathers. On their cheeks were painted black spots, and around their jaws ran a black streak. They passed him slowly in quiet dignity, with lowered eyes—close enough to touch, but inviolable. Two women, both tall and heavy and anonymous, no longer separated by human years, but bound together by that which recognizes no time. No longer recognizable as a certain Josefita and Flowers Playing, but as the sacred personages, the Deer Mothers.

So they all passed before him in the dazzling white silence, white figures against the snow, neither beasts nor men, but forces made visible to portray this great blood-drama of their common heritage.

Martiniano drew back respectfully and let them pass,

as the people let them pass, and in their reverent stares shone too the wonder and the mystery. They saw the mountain walls close in, the gray skies lower upon the snowy clearing between two cliffs. In it two lines now of waiting animals. And then, slowly, at first, the beat of a drum.

One by one, from the two long, opposite lines, the animals began dancing forward and back. They were all dancing, the deer, the antelope, the buffalo, the coyotes, wild cats and mountain lions. Bent forward, horns tossing, the short pointed forelegs stabbing down the snow. Then down the aisle between them, down and back from each end, came the Deer Mothers. Tall, impervious, silent, they came dancing. Slowly, as women dance, their white boots never lifting above the clinging snow, their heavy bodies moving rhythmically within the loose, supple buckskin gowns. At the turn they paused, shaking the gourd rattles in their right hands, raising aloft the branches of spruce and the two eagle tail-feathers in their left. One saw, as each approached, the impassive face made stern by the black streak around her jaw and the spotted cheeks. As she turned one saw the glimmering sheet of color on her back, the skin of a wild mallard duck with all its iridescent feathers. And above it the tall clean eagle feathers rising above her head.

They all gave way before her, down and back. The wild deer and graceful antelope, the massive buffalo, the wily coyotes, the snarling wildcats and mountain lions, and all the fawns and cubs. They all drew back shudderingly, with strange low sounds, from the sacred, inviolable Deer Mother. And when after a time she turned, eyes down as if unconscious of their presence, they followed her in great circles, spirals and diagonal lines of dancers. Followed her in the soft, powdery snow, uttering their strange low cries of resentment, their snarls of defiance, but unable to resist and being led back again into a long oval.

Within it the drum kept beating. Outside it prowled the Black Eyes horribly streaked and bedaubed with gray and clay blue, their eyes large gawking disks of black.

The dancing oval slowly constricted as the cub lions, coyotes and wildcats drew back from the prancing deer and antelope. With wild, frightened eyes, one of them timidly touched a deer. A loud whoop, a chorus of shrill yells. The Black Eyes came scrambling and leaping through the snow. One drew his tiny bow and shot the boy lion with a yellow straw. Then flinging him over his shoulder, he ran off through the snow.

But the two beautifully garbed leaders, the Deer Watchers, were watching. And one of them leapt forward out of the circle and pursued the escaping Black Eye. Across the plaza he was caught. The boy was let down, his animal hood straightened, and he was led back, panting.

It was great fun, the swooping Black Eyes, the kicking captive boy, the pursuing Deer Watchers. There was a mad scramble and fall in the snow. There was clever concealment behind one of the large ant-hill ovens, much dodging and twisting. Sometimes there was a show of violence. And rarely a Black Eye escaping with his burden, trotting across the hewn-log bridge to the kiva.

But the people did not laugh. They saw it as a violation of that inexorable power which held unbroken the circle of sobbing, defiant animals—as a rare escape that if consummated must be ceremonially atoned for in the kiva afterwards.

So it continued in the snowy down-trodden clearing between the adobe cliffs, high on the pine-forested backbone of a continent—this silent, tense blood-drama of the forces unleashed and controlled in all its children. The leaping, clutching Black Eyes. The swift escape foiled by the wary Deer Watchers. And all the while the Deer Chiefs tossing up their branching antlers beside the drummer as, up and down, the sacred Deer Mothers danced softly before the animals in bondage.

They gave way before her as the male ever gives way to the female imperative. They tried to break free of the circle only to be irresistibly pulled back as man in his wild lunges for freedom is ever drawn back by the perpetual, feminine blood-power from which he can never quite break free. And all the time they uttered their strange, low cries, the deep, universal male horror at their submission. Out of them it welled in shuddering sobs of disgust, of loathing and despair, as still they answered the call. On all fours, as the undomesticated, untamed, archaic, wild forces they represented, impelled to follow her in obedience to that spiritual cosmic principle which must exist to preserve and perpetuate even their resentment.

The two Deer Mothers kept on dancing; impersonal, impassive, with lowered eyes, as if oblivious of the power fatefully bestowed upon them as of the obedience they commanded.

Martiniano watched them with a hypnotic horror. He felt himself cringing before that manifestation of the blind force which had pulled him back from his own strivings toward a new and resplendent faith—back into that warm flow of human life of which he was still a part. His own revolt, his anger and his fear; it all came out of him anew and was echoed by the sobbing, tortured cries of the deer before him.

Now, for the first time, he sensed something both of the conscience which turns us back, and the intuition which illumines the forward step, and so holds us on the upward road of self-fulfillment. Sensed dimly, as one only can, the invisible, undefined and irrational force that has no meaning outside its living truth. It stood before him, silent, inscrutable, clothed in loose white buckskin—in the anonymous shape of a woman who had been his wife, and was now the commanding mother of all men.

And when they left, the Deer Mothers leading the animal shapes silently away across the snowy plaza, it was as if they all withdrew into the white-robed mountains. Embodied forces discarding their assumed shapes, but leaving in all men the truths of their existence, the magic, the wonder and mystery of their portrayal.

The dance was over. It was dark. Flowers Playing was back home in her shabby old clothes.

"Supper is ready," she called from the kitchen, laying out their cracked cups, a tin pie plate and a shallow earthenware bowl.

Martiniano still crouched down in front of the fireplace where he had been for two hours.

"Supper, husband! It is ready. Come!"

He stirred with fright at the tone of her voice, rose and walked as if drawn to the kitchen by a rope tied about his neck. The woman was standing at the stove. He cringed past without touching her, sinking to the edge of the bench where he sat in a posture of abject fear. Flowers Playing dished up beans and chile, laid a hot tortilla beside his plate.

"I am not hungry!" He got up and stood staring at her with wild, troubled eyes. "It is my chores . . . I must finish them!" He rushed out into the winter night.

*The deer he had killed, the two deer sisters of Flowers Playing up in the mountains, the deer dancing in subjection to the Deer Mothers. . . . The dead deer, the live deer, the pantomimed deer . . . Who could say now which was dead, was alive, was flesh, was spirit, as they ran around him crying out that dead flesh is impregnated with living spirit, that all living forms are but the embodiment of powerful unleashed forces which must be neither feared nor mastered, but simply understood?*

*He did not know. . . . He did not know. But within him he felt something stirring awake. The power within him that knew what he did not know. It was like a great coiled serpent sleeping within him. Like the legendary earth-serpent of his people, heavy with wisdom and power, that someday would awake, uncoil and strike from the torn and tortured flesh the rending, screaming eagles of desire.*

*Awake! Awake! Awake!*

# 12

THROUGHOUT the weeks that the controversy in Washington flared and died down to be resumed again, Byers alone in La Oreja kept following all the speeches and arguments against the bill. They sounded superficially reasonable, and he concurred in most of the facts. The world was moving on, and speedier every day. The Indians he saw being left far behind, and himself shut up in one of his own glass show-cases. A pretty museum piece! The Devil take them all! In a continuous ill-temper he neglected to shave for days and railed at the perpetual snow.

Whenever his blackest moods assailed him he slapped on his moth-eaten fur cap and trudged into La Oreja to drink cheap Bourbon in a little bar. He stood in front of the big-bellied stove, back to a group of Mexicans wrangling over a game of cards, and stared out into the snow-stung plaza. A thin, intermittent trickle of Indians flowed in and out, on foot, burro and horseback, or huddled in their creaking wagons. He watched them stalk into a store with a sack of grain and a half-hour later amble out with a bit of meat wrapped carelessly in a newspaper, a little paper sack of ginger-snaps, a head of wormy cabbage.

One late afternoon in January as he stepped outside and leaned against the portal, he saw an old Indian coming slowly across the deserted square. His skinny brown hand held his tattered blanket close, his feet plodded up and down in soggy wrappings of gunny sacks. A geyser of compassion spurted up inside Byers. The sight of old toothless Sun Elk hurt him, and he attacked it with a malicious joviality.

"Hello, Grandfather! What a day! Pues. What a day!"

Sun Elk, arrested, grinned toothlessly at the strange white trader, his friend for many years. He let down the blanket from his face, and sniffed the whiskey in the air.

"Well, Grandfather," joked Byers, "those officials in Washington are pointing their fingers at that pueblo of yours and laughing. You are going to lose your Dawn Lake!"

The old man's face cracked into a wrinkled mask of tolerant good humor. "Indian she no lose Dawn Lake. How you think know, this big talk?"

Byers jerked a thumb over his shoulder toward the town's small telegraph office next to the bar. Both turned and looked through the frosty pane at the clattering relays.

"They tell me. Those machines and the wires that go all the way to Washington to carry talk. You will see."

Sun Elk stared through the window as he had stared a thousand times before, and with the same suspicious non-belief.

"Those talking machines! Those wires that carry words! Some of our young men believe them but I do not. Ha! If white men have so much power, so good medicine, why she use noisy machines and long wires to carry their thoughts? Ignorant Indian she no use and know just as quick. We no lose our Dawn Lake!"

He turned and quickly hobbled away, and in a little while Byers too trudged back to his post. Half way down the road he was stopped as if by a sudden obstructing query.

"By God!" he muttered, thinking of the old man's words. "One of us is a damn fool! I wonder which?"

The sun was setting when Byers arrived home. The sight of Angelina in her best silver and beaded moccasins reminded him of an uncomfortable fact. Once each winter he gave a dinner to his few close friends. It was a lot of trouble; he dreaded and damned it—and had the best time of all. Tonight was the night.

Byers grumbled, scraped off his stubble of beard, then cursed his way into a clean shirt and black necktie, white socks and black shoes. But back went on the dirty, limp buckskin jacket.

In the kitchen he got out Scotch, gin and vermouth with a Westerner's contempt for everything but the bottle of cheap Bourbon he added to the tray. Buffalo-Old-Woman shook with laughter and lifted the lid of a black kettle; she had had another child and still seemed just as fat. Byers sniffed, prodded inside the kettle. Great slabs of his yearly elk simmered in a thick red mole, pungent with herbs he had had specially gathered in a certain mountain glen. It was his own dish—Picuris Stew.

Most of the guests had already arrived when he walked out. Dwarfed by the lofty room, Benson prowled about looking at paintings. "You haven't sold it yet!" he exclaimed stopping. "My first big oil! Just after I came out here for the first time. Wish I could afford to buy it! Not bad, but a little romantic. Look at all that blue, that garland of green leaves, that flute!" Gray-haired, he still laughed like a child. And then sadly, "But they were like that then, sweet and unspoiled. Eh, Byers?"

A well-tailored woman sitting beside his wife smiled primly. To understand Indians you've got to dig. For artifacts, old foundations, pieces of basketware. For the real structure of daily life. It's the culture that really matters. "Don't you think so?"

Byers snorted into his Bourbon, and led a shy, slim Indian lad into the corner with the old artist. "I want you to see some of this boy's water-colors," he said kindly. "This corn plant—the spots on this running pinto, stylized designs of running rain clouds—the manes of these buffalo worn like blankets over their humps. I'm trying to keep him out of school before his drawin' is ruined."

Angelina stood with a wheezy scarecrow of an old Spanish family and his oily wife who was wearing a lace mantilla that smelled of moth balls. They were looking at the cloth of Spanish lace covering the massive, hand-carved table in the middle of the room. It was set with silver, crystal and candles. Above it hung a great round chandelier of twisted willow over which was stretched, like a drum end, a buffalo hide scraped thin enough to show a yellow even light. It shone upon the long, square, carved vigas supporting the roof, the alternating plank lattias of white pine and red cedar.

"Ay de mi, Doña Angelina!" sighed the lady. "From up the Chihuahua Trail, no doubt. A treasure. A miracle. It warms my heart to see a bit of grace in these vulgar times. You should show it more often. Now—"

There was a sudden soft knock. Byers got up and opened the door. The last guest was standing outside, head turned, listening. Byers' greeting stopped at his lips; he merely stuck out a hand. Across the snowy pastures came the faint but resonant sound of a drum that had just begun to beat. Both men, arrested by the sound, stood listening a moment. Then Byers stepped back in, followed by Manuel Rena.

The Indian walked across the room and sat down alone on the seating ledge beside the fireplace. Despite the roaring fire he kept his beautiful wine-red Chief blanket drawn up close around him. One corner folded back over his broad shoulders showed dark blue. The blanket was of double thickness, of pure bayeta brought up from Mexico. His coarse black hair, parted in the middle, shone with oil; the long pig-tails hanging down in front were braided with white and green ribbons. His broad dark face with its Roman nose and plucked eyebrows held a look of impassive dignity. The tips of two expensive riding boots sticking out from under the lower edge of his blanket lent his silence a touch of haughtiness.

The woman Mrs. Benson had brought flipped open toward him the lid of her cigarette case. A short, wordless conflict ensued. It was she who rose and went to him. He took a cigarette, put it in his mouth.

"No! The cork end!" she laughed maliciously.

Without changing expression, he changed ends, stooped to light it in the fire, and sat back to puff in dignity.

Dinner was served. Cómo no? "We have been waiting for it all year," said Byers drily.

So they sat in candlelight and flamelight, at lace, crystal and shiny silver—Spanish, Indian and white: Byers and Angelina, Benson and his wife, Señor and Señora Trujillo, bashful Luis in store clothes, Manuel Rena in his red blanket, and the strange visitor, Mrs. Anderson.

Buffalo-Old-Woman waddled in and out steaming like her trays. Young Luis, sitting stiff as a poker, spilled red sauce on the lace tablecloth and visibly cowered under the old woman's scowl. Manuel muttered to her in dialect to bring in more pepper. Señor and Señora Trujillo exchanged "Que sabrosas!" in Spanish with Angelina. Benson, smacking his lips, reminisced to his visitor, Mrs. Anderson.

Only Byers, elbows free at the head of the table, sat eating in silence like Manuel. But his eyes were never still.

"Luis! Use your spoon. Or better yet—sop up that gravy with your bread." . . . "Hey!" he shouted at Buffalo-Old-Woman. "Bring in to Mr. Rena that nice piece of elk you're hiding in the kitchen!"

There was even wine. Benson's face grew red under his graying hair. Doña Caterina fingered the stem of her glass with thoughtful fingers. "Ay de mi!" she sighed. "There was the day when these old wrinkled fingers were soft and plump, and covered with rings."

"And doubtless with kisses—my own, querida mia," answered old Don Juan laughing. "Or was it other lips—or other fingers?"

"More! More, Manuel!" urged Byers once again.

The red blanket slumped back in its chair. A limp brown hand, palm in, thumb and forefinger drooping, lifted slowly from belly to throat, then decisively and horizontally drew the line of satisfaction.

All nine rose and grouped at the end of the big room; Byers threw on another log. How heavy, how filling that elk. But Madre de Dios! Que sabroso! And the wine. It effervesces in the stomach yet. Lifting a word, a thought at a time, to break gently on the surface silence.

"How hot it is in here especially after such a heavy dinner!" said Angelina, rising. "Do you mind?" She glided across the room and opened a window.

A soft, murmurous pulse-beat stole in the room from across the open pasture toward the pueblo. Byers stirred, a little apprehensively, and glanced furtively around the room. No one else appeared to hear it.

Manuel Rena, slumped against the wall, seemed sleeping with his eyes open. Yet after a moment the eyes casually focused on Byers. He was silently staring into the flames, listening also to the faint sound of distant drums.

It was dusk and still snowing when a young boy had emerged from the pine forest and paused on the mountainside. He stared eagerly down the cañon. As the indistinct but solid shape of the pueblo stood out behind the curtain of whirling flakes a gleam of relief and triumph brightened his black eyes. He had been running. Gasps shook his thin body inside its blanket; with his chest lifted and fell a small buckskin sack dangling from a thong looped round his neck. Regaining breath and composure, the boy walked slowly down the trail. With quiet dignity now he crossed the plaza to one of the kivas and descended the ladder.

The glow of a small fire shone on a few men seated before it, and cast their hierophantic shadows on the circular wall. As the boy came down the ladder, one of them rose to meet him. With an outward motion he brushed off the boy with eagle feathers, sprinkled him with corn meal. Then dribbling a line of meal across the floor, making a road for the boy, he conducted him to a seat across the room. Four other small boys were seated against the wall. Like them, the newcomer was given a small steaming bowl to drink, and left to warm and rest.

The wait began anew.

The boys—even the last—could not wholly conceal an obvious anxiety. From time to time each looked quickly and furtively at his companions as if to reassure himself of the unaccountable absence of a sixth. Then he returned his gaze to the ladder.

Only old men came down, one at a time, to glance briefly and searchingly at the incomplete group of boys and then seat themselves silently on the floor. There was no need to remark the obvious. Yet their dark wrinkled faces showed no anxiety nor impatience.

An hour passed, perhaps more. The old man seated in the valuable place, the place beside the fire, gave a short grunt. He, and all, raised their hands before their faces, palm in, and breathed deeply, partaking of the essence of prayer. Then one took up a drum. The room, like a well, filled with its slow, muffled beat.

Above, around the plaza, one could hear it only as a faintly perceptible, underground pulse. It was as if the sleeping earth had awakened beneath its thick white blanket. The night priests had drawn their dark curtains. There was no moon. The communal pyramids rose lifeless and still as solid stone. But now a door opened and then another. A man stepped out of each momentary rectangle of light and faded into darkness as he walked swiftly to one of the six kivas.

The deep, underground pulse was beating faster, stronger now. Soon it was joined by the power of a second, in another kiva. The swiftly closing pueblo doors had let in the beat which still continued, inaudibly, inside. The walls pulsed imperceptibly in and out; the pueblo itself throbbed in tune.

Martiniano, sitting in his hut just outside the town wall, heard it too when the third kiva joined in. He flashed a quick glance in lamplight at Flowers Playing who did not look up. *Something is wrong! Listen to the kiva drums!* Early that afternoon while returning with a burro load of wood from the mountains, he had glimpsed a small boy passing on the trail above him. One of the kiva initiates sent out on one of their strange missions. Who else, so small and ill-clad, would be heading alone into the snowy mountains? Perhaps he had not returned.

Martiniano rose and walked outside. It was growing late. The earth was white; the sky, emptied of snow, was beginning to clear. Against them the clump of naked cottonwoods, the pueblo and mountain seemed etched, like iron, by the acid cold. It was a bitter night to be out in, yet no one seemed to be going after the lost boy. No lights shone from the terraces. No lanterns gleamed in the corrals or on the plaza. There was only the desolate emptiness of night filled by the dull but resonant throb of drums.

He shivered. The more he thought, the stronger grew his conviction that the boy he had seen was Palemon's son, Napaita. Something in the quick, apprehensive lift of the head, the furtive haste . . . Yes. He was sure, sure, too, the boy had not returned. He stood there indecisively in darkness and the corrosive cold. There was warmth and assurance, there was power in the muted rumble of drums. For him there seemed also a strange tone of warning. Both expressed that dark, impenetrable mystery of a faith long shut to him, but which beat invisibly around him.

He gave up his thought of Palemon, and dismissed the faint idea of tracing Napaita with horse and lantern. He returned to his hut, went to bed.

At Byers', Mrs. Anderson angrily flipped open her cigarette case again, but did not pass it around. For a half-hour she had tried vainly to get a word out of these Indians. Rena remained slumped down in his blanket, with invisible shutters drawn across his open eyes.

This mask of sluggish indifference! This impenetrable wariness! Who knew what it hid or why? Even young Luis lay face down on a bearskin shamming death or sleep. Agh! How dull they were, really.

But Benson was in good form. He had come West as a young illustrator for the Santa Fe. The color, the raw newness of the life had caught him; he stayed—nearly five months of every year, even now. He became a well-known painter. A little romantic, a bit sweet, old style for nowadays. But N.A., originals in the best galleries, and reproduced in magazines and on calendars. Really a fine, unaffected fellow, better than his work.

"Now I'm not running down the Indians, their surface color and the romantic appeal they had before the roads came in—they've made a good living for me," he was saying. "But I've been wondering if they ever had anything else. Real values, an inside life to match the paint and feathers. Something worth while behind all this fasting, chanting and praying, ceremonials and dancing—this kiva stuff. Something we've never bothered to learn or knew there was to learn. You know, one does hear strange things."

He winked at his wife. There was no derision in it; it was simply to let her know he was trying to get Byers started on one of his stories. Byers was gradually reminded of this, Benson of that. They bantered back and forth.

"Tie this one," said Byers carelessly, but with a sharp look at Manuel who seemed practically asleep.

"It was thirty, maybe forty years ago—what the Hell's the difference! It was when I was young, starting in to trade, and went with a bunch of the Pueblo boys here down to the Indian Territory, down in Oklahoma. None of them had been there either.

"We all rode horseback—maybe twenty of us. But we took along a wagon full of grub, blankets, the boys' drums, feathers and dress-up clothes, and presents to the Cheyennes, Arapahoes, Kiowas, Osages and so on.

"Sure there were some fences and once in awhile a squatter's shack or lonesome ranch house, but nothin' more. It was comin' fall. Wind and plenty of dust. That's all. Just those brown rollin' plains of crinkly buffalo grass. Ever' day. In a week some of the boys began to get lonesome sickness. You know, no more mountains hangin' on the horizon, no trees, no runnin' water, no nothin'. Just brown crinkly plains risin' and dippin' down again in one swell after another.

"These boys were pretty young, some of 'em younger'n me, as I'm sayin'. But they'd never been away from home before. So I kept tellin' them to cheer up: they'd be braves when they got home. We beat the drums at night and sang war songs. Nothin' did any good. They just kept pinin' away, not eatin', like lovesick women. Well, a bunch of 'em left. They weren't ashamed. Said the feelin' of the place was bad, that it was gettin' worse, that the spirits told 'em to keep away.

"From what? The rest of us kept on, and in a couple of days we got there. Maybe it was the Canadian, the Red, or even the Big Skin Bayou—I've forgotten. Anyway, a creek. We could see the line of trees and brush a long ways off. The first we'd seen in a long time. I can tell you it looked mighty sweet—wood, water, brush full of game, trees stickin' up.

"And then again it didn't. I don't know why we slowed up, and the closer we got the slower we went. Nobody said a good God-damn. Just nervous. Well sir, we might have been on the warpath the way we rode up and down that creek, and back and forth, before we made camp. There was nothin' there but a scrubby corn patch some squatter had forgotten. Nothin' within miles.

"The place was full of rabbits though. We had us a big stew, piled up wood on the fire like tenderfeet, and rolled in. Then it started. Damned if we could sleep. My hair kept pricklin'; my backbone tingled. I had the nervous chills. I got up.

"The other boys were already crowded round the fire. They weren't beatin' the drum and singin'. They weren't relaxed like, rollin' cigarettes. They weren't talkin'. Just breathin' fast, rollin' their eyes around, and scroogin' in their blankets.

"Pretty soon we heard a coyote howl on one side, and then a wolf on the other. Then an owl, and once in awhile night birds all around us. Leastways good imitations, the kind only Indians can make, the best there is. They kept closin' in. Not too often, not too far apart. Just steady.

"By now the moon was up. We were in a big glade. Scrub oak, some big cottonwoods. The muddy creek, and across it in the dip the scrubby corn patch nobody had tended to. And the rollin' prairies all around, showin' through the trees bright as day. By God, there wasn't a movin' soul around within miles!

"But we could hear the dry corn stalks rustle, and then grow still. And rustle again. It wasn't the wind.

"The horses whinnied. One of them kicked the single-tree —slap-bang and a rattle! We took off the hobbles, tied 'em fast. We loaded up the wagon, built up the fire. The boys took out their rifles. The oldest sat humped in his blanket, his gun across his lap. A knife was in his mouth. All of us just waitin'.

"Still those brittle corn stalks kept rustlin'. And then we heard voices. Not imitation birds or animals. Real voices. Indian voices. The oldest boy—the one with the gun in his lap and the knife between his teeth—stood up and let his blanket drop. He was naked to the waist, and he had on his fancy dress moccasins. But I didn't think of that till afterwards. He looked too natural.

"Just then there was a long, shrill, waverin' cry from the corn field. Then another from down the creek. And then another from the brush behind us. They were like three long lances of sound stuck up suddenly in the sky and the feathers on them shaken.

"I thought they had split open the sky, and the stars were fallin' down. All Hell had broke that loose. The air was full of yells and cries; the brush crackled; the dry corn stalks went crashin' down.

"In a minute—I reckon—it was all over. We stood there shakin' and listenin' to a low groanin' voice in the corn. Pretty soon it stopped. There was some cracklin' like a body was draggin' through the stalks. We figured we heard hoof beats out on the prairie, and then a long time later a single far-off yell. And that was all. . . .

"Well no—not quite," Byers said, after a moment. "I can tell you we made tracks out of that creek bottom. But at daybreak that oldest boy and I rode back alone. There wasn't a corn stalk down, not a track, not a sign anybody or anything had been there but us. . . .

"Well, that isn't all either," he continued. "We finally got back home. The boys reported on the trip to the War Chief, delivered their presents. I had picked up some pretty good stuff myself—I got a fair piece of change out of that Pawnee rope of human hair that's up in the State Museum now. But we got to talkin' to one of the old men; he's dead now. He could describe that place as well as we could. He said that when he was a young lad a party from the pueblo had gone out buffalo hunting on the Plains and had camped in that creek bottom. One night a Cheyenne and Arapahoe war-party had come up and killed them all. All but an old man and a younger one who had carried him away on his horse with his head split open."

There was a long silence. Manuel had drawn his blanket across his face so that only his eyes showed, and they were hidden in shadow.

Benson grinned delightedly; a teasing sparkle leapt into his eyes.

Byers, sprawled out on the floor between them, was suddenly, acutely aware of both. There was something groping in this man, he thought of one, beneath that artistic childishness he still affected—if you could pierce his armor of continual banter. But what it was, pure, undefiled and undefined by reason, was in that other. Would they ever meet, he wondered.

Benson chuckled, rubbing his hands together. "What a story! What a story! Possible, yes, possible. But highly improbable, really."

He watched Byers rolling a cigarette. This man, he thought, was something of a sham to all but his friends—the biggest hoax he ever knew! That dirty buckskin jacket, the whole life that covered him as well, hid something he had never penetrated. But the way Byers relapsed into the vulgar grammar of his youth didn't hide a mind that could jump out of ambush clear and bright as a naked blade. An essence truly Indian was in this man: for twenty years he hadn't been quite able to make him out.

"Come, come!" he continued. "I don't doubt your story's possible, not even uncommon. We all believe in auric emanations, in psychic disturbances. But I do say it was highly improbable just the way you told it—simply because you all, and at once, had the same experience. For it to happen to one of your boys, yes. To you alone, yes; you're a queer chap, something like that is always happening to you. That's what I think, really. You got it, were so caught up in it, that you imagined everyone else experienced it too, instead of just participating in the general nervousness. Besides, you're a good story teller!"

Benson watched his friend's face; they had played poker together. But Byers remained imperturbable. He rose to no bait. He refused to play. After a moment he curtly shrugged his shoulders. "Maybe so," he muttered curtly, and remained, head tilted, ear turned toward the window, but gazing into the fire.

The drums were still beating. The sound was not loud, but deeply resonant and powerful. It seemed to flow into the room like the murmurous wash of a distant sea. The low undertone of tremendous power beat at his ears, crawled into his blood, made him nervous and apprehensive.

Damn these people! Were they all deaf and insensible? Even Benson, the so-called sensitive artist, with his talk of auric emanations and psychic disturbances, was stolid as a post. How could he believe that tale when right under his nose something else was happening and he wasn't aware of it?

He affected a yawn and rudely stretched; he was suddenly tired of them all. Everything had conspired to spoil the evening. Everything wrangled out of tune. The presence of that stranger, Mrs. Anderson, whom he had never seen before, Benson's attempt to get him into a long, intellectual harangue, and above all the sound of those drums. He could not imagine what it meant this time of night, this time of year.

Manuel Rena had not uttered a word all evening. Nor did he do more than nod and shake hands when the guests began to leave. Señor and Señora Trujillo, bundled in their moth-smelly finery, and rattling away in an old buckboard to a little adobe hut. The Bensons driving away that Mrs. Anderson in a shiny new automobile. Luis happily trotting his borrowed nag across the fields; Benson carrying away a stack of his sketches. Byers watched them all go.

Angelina was taking off her heavy silver to put back into the case in the morning, and soon went off to bed.

Manuel hunched up his blanket. "Well, I go now," he said abruptly.

Byers walked with him to the door. The night was cold and frosty. The stars trembled as if floating high on the surface of an invisible vibrating sea of sound. The two men halted a moment and stared searchingly into each others' faces. What was there to say? Silently they shook hands and parted. Byers watched his last guest go—the oldest boy who had been with him on that trip across the plains so many years ago.

They were all gone—everyone, all the jangling human vibrations in the room. There remained only the one, clear and powerful, which rolled in steadily, stronger, from the night. Byers, unable to sleep, blew out the lights and squatted down in front of the dying coals.

In the darkness, from Angelina's room, he heard the faint chime of a clock. It was midnight and the drums were still beating.

# 13

THE KIVA, each kiva, was now itself a vibrating drum. A single star visible through the aperture at the top quivered as if painted on the vibrous, skin-tight membrane of the sky stretched overhead. In the middle of the round floor, like a dot within a circle, was another symbol—a little round hole, the opening to the center of the world, the place of emergence. The circular walls quivered.

The inside of the room was dim and faintly pungent with the smell of burnt cedar. Occasionally, when more was thrown on the fire, the faint glow leapt up into a flicker. For a moment the rude altar stood out from shadow: the cloud terrace design of white corn meal, a bowl of medicine water from one of the sacred springs, the prayer sticks of red willow dressed in feathers, an obsidian knife brought up from the lower world, and an anthropomorphic fetish of white stone. Then again it drew back into darkness. Only the men remained visible. They sat in a circle around a small drum, all within the greater. Quiet and with bowed heads they sat, but with intense concentration and a single purpose.

From time to time an old man withdrew from the squatting circle, rising and walking to the altar along a line of white meal, along the road of life. His body seemed boneless, his face was immobile and his eyes held a peculiar fixity of expression. Little by little as he rested, strength flowed back into him. His body grew lighter, animated with life. Blood again darkened his face. His eyes came into focus. He sprinkled corn meal to the directions, laid a branch of cedar on the fire. Then again he became part of the silent circle squatting about the softly beating drum, in the great drum of the kiva.

The others did not stir. Sweaty and naked except for breech-clouts and moccasins, each sat cross-legged on the floor. Heads bent, chins down, they stared unseeing at the small round hole before them.

*From the place of the first beginning, where the deer stands, we have come. From our fathers, the life-giving priests, our roads have come forth. Perpetuating the rite handed down since the first beginning, we have sat down quietly before it.*

*The sacred fire burns before us. Holding our cupped hands before our faces, we draw into our bodies the breath of life and add to it the essence of our prayer. On our altar we observe our house of massed clouds. Our bodies attest the earth, so do our Corn Mothers, the flesh of the white corn with which we have marked our roads. We are mindful of that grace of the spirit above us, which transcends us. We are mindful of the sleeping serpent of wisdom and power below us, which we now summon forth. Blue, rattlesnake yellow, red, white, many-colored, black: the priests of all these: take us to be your children. Desiring our fathers' medicine, hither we take our roads.*

*Perpetuating the rite handed down since the first beginning, we sit down quietly before it. Cross-legged, heads bent, we sit in this our prenatal posture, and are mindful of the directions around us, that above us, and the one below. We are body, mind, spirit, undifferentiated. We are indivisible, unrestricted, unbound.*

How simple and strange it all looked. Less strange and more simple than perhaps a big room somewhere on the earth above, silent too but for the monotonous pulsation of a monstrous dynamo: its circular, revolving drum cutting lines of magnetic force induced in the outside laminated wheel, generating electricity and transmitting it far across mountain and plain. It was wonderful, unbelievable, yet simple too when its laws were understood—this cumbrous, frightening mechanism of modern science wherewith man artificially transmits thought and power. He has yet to learn to disintegrate material substance, to transmit it in its electronic form, and reconstruct it at a distance in its same material shape. But will he ever learn again that the mind of man which has created such monstrous artificiality of means may accomplish the same ends by natural means?

Who doubts the great magnetic currents of the earth, or the psychic radiations of man? The flesh of the earth and the earth of the flesh are both similar bodies obeying the same laws of the greater whole which envisioned them alike into being from its own universal mind. From the depths of the human organism, as from the core of the physical universe, the vital life force stems up into the lakes and reservoirs of the nervous system; is called up into the one directing nerve center of the brain. Here, conjoined and transformed, the vital physical force and the psychic power unite to be diffused throughout the whole awakened body, to be directed at will. Who then can doubt the efficacy of prayer, when once the psychic-spiritual process is envisioned and utilized, like that of the material-mental, for man's good?

So hour after hour this human dynamo, these old men sat silent, bent over, through the night. Calling up through the little round opening in the floor the warmth and power of the sleeping earth-serpent. Calling up from the depths of their own bodies, from the generative organs, the navel center and the heart, their vital life force. And each calling down through the open skylight the infinite grace and power which pervades all things, and the consciousness and will of his own stimulated mind.

And all this infusion of strength and power, grace and will, they loosed as if from the sagittal suture on the crown of the head, covered by the scalp lock—from the corresponding aperture at the top of the kiva. As one powerful, living psychic flow they directed it upon the focus of their single concentration.

He lay in the mountains above, within a great cave. Imprisoned, in freezing darkness, he lay in a dreamless torpor —he who had been known as Napaita, son of Palemon.

Early that afternoon he had left the kiva with five companions. All were thinly clad in dark, earth-colored blankets, wearing small medicine bags around their necks, and carrying short red-willow sticks peeled and painted and dressed in feathers. At the mouth of the cañon they separated: one to climb up the crags to a small, lofty shrine, one to a bank of red medicine clay, one to a sacred spring, one to strike sparks from the flinty base of the mountain—each in a different, designated direction and painted its corresponding color. They were a little frightened but resolute, and hurried away to return before dark.

Napaita struck out over the rounded piñon slope, then turned right along the ridge to avoid being seen from a scatter of remote huts. A thick gray mist obscured the world below. As he climbed into the fringe of pines it began to snow. The flakes fluttered down slowly upon the becalmed forest. The trees grew thicker, taller. The boy, dwarfed below, was oppressed by their age and stature. They were like a multitude of old men hoary with age standing in a deep meditative hush as he wormed between them.

He had never been here before—till now he had been warned against coming, but he knew where he was. It all had been carefully described to him. There where the pines at last stood back to let him pass, he saw rising before him the two rocky points of a parted cliff, and between them a steep, narrow defile. Carefully he felt his way up the old, almost obliterated trail rising crookedly beside a small stream. Then suddenly it loomed before him—the cave to which he had been sent.

The mouth was a narrow rectangle. Over it, from above, during summer rains, poured a noisy waterfall. The entrance was now covered by an icy curtain of flaky white feathers and icy eagle-down clinging to the rock on each side. But for one day each year the shadows of the dark cañon covered it completely. Then, on the day of the winter solstice, the sun sighted squarely through the narrow cañon; the icy feathers gleamed and ruffled; the cave was opened for once to the miracle of diffused light, as if in memory of that first emergence of the Old First Ones from their dark, elemental prenativity in the ancestral womb of time.

The boy approached it with awe. The fall of snow was lessening. The sun was sinking, but still obscured by a thick gray mist. The curtain was a smoky gray. He found a narrow slit between it and one side of the cliff, and squeezed inside.

In the dusky translucence he planted prayer sticks in the rocky, ice-encrusted walls and beneath the ancient symbols dimly outlined on the ceiling. Then, breathing rapidly and shivering, he faced the receding interior.

The floor was heaped with fallen boulders and debris.

Climbing upon a narrow, waist high shelf which ran back into the cave, Napaita cautiously felt his way along the slimy wall.

A tall, dim shape appeared. Somewhere far up above in the lofty dome there was a tiny crack in the rock. Water seeped down, dropped and froze, gradually building up into a tall stalagmite, a natural phallus of ice. The boy knelt and planted his last feathered prayer plume at the base.

Somewhere, deeper inside, a pebble fell from a crumbling wall. The echo of its rebound from rock to rock roused eddies of sound in the well of silence. Napaita stood up trembling. Then quickly, a little frightened, he stumbled back toward the mouth of the cave. Abruptly, without warning, his moccasins slipped on the smooth stone. His feet flew out from underneath him; he fell heavily, twisting in the air, head toward the opening, and clutching at the ledge.

There was a sudden reverberating roar behind him, a violent blow, as if he had cracked his head open in falling. Slowly the broken silence mended together about him. Quivering with pain and fright, Napaita raised a hand to his throbbing head. A thin trickle of blood ran down his face; he had merely gashed his scalp. But worse, one of his feet was caught. Sitting up, he felt around in the darkness. His feet had struck and loosened from the jutting wall a crumbling talus of decomposed rock, and this had released an avalanche of stones.

The boy's fingers and patience were soon worn out trying to pull his foot free. It seemed clamped securely in a crevice between two rocks he could not see to dig out, and one resting on top too heavy to lift off—not crushed, but throbbing painfully and beginning to swell above the ankle. As he stopped struggling, the cold began to eat through his blanket. He shivered until he shivered no more, and lay quietly numb. Now fear wracked him. Frantic with his predicament, he could do no more than lie there in dark and cold and silence, imprisoned in a taboo cave far up the snowy mountainside above the world of men.

As he lay there he saw death. It came out of the depths of the cave in an endless line of dim anthropomorphic shapes, of strange beast-like men walking on all fours, inarticulate and with eyes yet unopened. Death in the shapes of life yet unborn to a greater life. Imprisoned within the mindless void of the primordial uncreated, condemned to await in dark unreality the glimmer of that light which might lead them out of bondage. They paraded about him, tongueless, eyeless and unwhole. Shrouded in the wonder and the mystery, but without grace. Treading the trail of their bound existence, the dark unborn.

The ice-sheeted mouth of the cave had been steadily growing darker until it was now but a thin, barely translucent membrane. Then suddenly, far to the west, the dipping sun broke free of mist. For an instant only a last ray struck obliquely, like an arrow, through the curtain. As it fell, shattered on the floor and crumbled into darkness, the figures fled.

A faint glimmer of the clear, resplendent promise of the life they refuted and fled revealed to the boy something of their vast, overwhelming futility. But even as he himself roused to hold it, with all its invigorating clarity and promise of freedom, they vanished. It all vanished—the gloom of night and the brief dawn of the clear light, and he sank down again clutching his little medicine bag.

Outside, the great trees moaned. The evening wind screeched down the defile. And then as it fled before dark, even these sounds ceased. Only silence roared in his ears. An impenetrable blackness closed round him. And in deep winter and night, the boy lay in a dreamless torpor.

But strangely now there seemed to begin inside him the beat of a drum, faintly at first, then stronger. It seemed to pervade his body with warmth, his heart with courage. If it had a meaning, a message, he did not know it, but was content to feel its presence. And huddled in his blanket on the cold stone he lay there, hour after hour, through the night. Holding tight to his little medicine bag, clutching fast the memory of the clear light. Waiting for it, as it must, to burst again through the thin membrane that stretched between this ancestral womb and the greater life outside—the clear light of awakened consciousness which once glimpsed must never be let go.

No, Martiniano could not sleep. As he lay through the bitter wintry hours preceding dawn, listening to the steady murmur of the underground drums, he remembered that other night when he had lain in the mountains with a broken head before one had come miraculously to his aid. Now it seemed strange that no one had gone to find Napaita—even stranger that a warning in the drums seemed to forbid him to go. There were dark matters here, beyond his knowledge. He suffered from incomprehension.

Yet shortly before dawn he rose and dressed, walked quietly into the plaza. The snow was deep and trackless. Only a thin line of smoke and the rumble of a drum still came out of the kivas without pause.

Seeing a light in Palemon's house, he knocked and was admitted. Estefana had been nodding in the lamplight, sitting fully dressed beside the stove.

"You are up early," she said politely.

"I am going up to the mountains to see about some more wood," he answered her easily. "Such cold nights have used more than I thought."

They were silent, listening to the drums. Martiniano looked carelessly across the room without appearing to notice the empty bed beside Batista.

"Will you have coffee?" asked Estefana as if reading his thoughts. "I have been keeping the pot warm for Palemon. But he has not returned this night. There is some little trouble or other, no doubt."

"No doubt. Well, I must be going. I will not stay to drink up my friend's coffee. Let it remain for him when he comes."

Thus he answered, knowing as well as she that Palemon was continent, fasting, and would not return that night.

He went out and saddled his horse, riding slowly around the town wall. It was as he thought: even Palemon had not gone after Napaita, nor had Estefana been told that anything had happened to her son. The feeling rose within him that the boy was given over to something beyond all of them. Nevertheless he continued on. Dusk still held when he reached the spot where he had seen the boy. Under the thin crepuscular light the snowy slope rose wan and desolate toward the fringe of pines. It was the disconsolate gray hour when man falls most easily into discouragement, when he forgets that this is the dusk which gives birth to light instead of darkness. There was no hope of tracking the boy, or even keeping on the obliterated trail. Martiniano was not sure he had intended to. He kicked his horse to plod forward where he would through the snow. Half-heartedly he unslung his small-bore rifle; a rabbit or two, then he would return home.

They had reached the fringe of pines when day came. The mountain tops began to rise like black islands out of a still sea. The air lightened to a dirty gray, like sheep's wool. Along the ridge the pines stood up like hairs on a cat's back, grew phosphorescent; then suddenly the forested rim began to flame.

Martiniano stopped and looked back. Far down the slope he could see smoke rising from the pueblo chimneys. Suddenly conscious that he could no longer hear the sound of drums, he felt happy and free of their spell. In the miracle of light he spurred his sweating horse through the thick pines toward the wall of cliffs standing beyond—to give him a drink in the stream emerging from a narrow defile.

And there, just across the stream, on the snowy trail, lay Napaita. He lay on his side, his wild eyes staring up at the sun breaking over the mountains. Martiniano washed the dried blood off the boy's face, and rubbed his frost-bitten hands with snow. Then he bent to the boy's foot. The moccasin was gone, and both sides of the ankle were stripped of skin as if he had pulled it between the edges of two saws. Perhaps it was broken; he could not tell, the flesh was so swollen.

Without waiting longer, he gathered the boy in his arms, clambered up into his saddle, and rode slowly back down to the pueblo. Napaita babbled feverishly. Martiniano closed his ears. He had stumbled upon a queer thing that belonged only to the old men of the kiva.

This feeling of chance participation in something strange and secret still persisted as he approached the pueblo. On the snowy housetops an old man wrapped in white had taken his post as usual, but the underground drums were still beating. Martiniano rode slowly along the outside of the wall until he came to the opening nearest the first kiva. He hesitated until the plaza was clear of the first women who had come out to fill their water jars. Then he clambered off his horse and carried Napaita to the kiva. There, very simply and without a cry to those within, he laid the boy down in the snow at the bottom of the ladder and walked back to his horse.

He rode quickly across the plaza on his way home. As he passed Palemon's house the door opened. Estefana stepped out with a water jar.

"You have seen about your wood? You are back already?"

"Yes. I have seen about my wood," he answered her simply, and rode on.

The freezing cold broke. The snow began to melt. Plaza, fields and roads became pools and rivers of slimy mud which slowly drained and hardened. The wind came. Then for weeks the tableland was enveloped in clouds of yellow dust swirling up from the desert.

Martiniano repaired a harrow, sharpened plow, scythe and all his knives, soled his boots, made a wooden bench and a rawhide-bottomed chair. And still thoughts of things there was no use thinking about swirled in his head. Thoughts which of their own accord must settle like dust before he could see clearly. So he let them be, and continued to rivet, pound, hammer, scrape and whet the lesser shapes around him—anything to keep busy.

He needed more than this.

There was little companionship with Flowers Playing, somber and absorbed in the mystery to which she gave herself wholly. He went to see Palemon and was surprised at what he found. There was no husband to provide and care for Estefana and Batista. They cut and gathered their own wood, but were long out of wheat flour and had not tasted green food for days.

"Palemòn is working for the sun," said Estefana delicately. "It is the time when he has his duties to perform."

Martiniano brought her flour and a few heads of cabbage, and said nothing. He no longer questioned such matters.

He went to the trading post. The adobe-brick walls of Byers' new room had been laid and settled. The big pines for vigas cut last fall had seasoned all winter. Now Byers needed help in carpentering and carving. Martiniano was glad to accept the employment he offered; it would give him money and work for the several weeks remaining until he had to prepare his land for spring planting.

Both men worked silently and slowly, without shirking, but with time out for cigarettes and coffee, and for frequent trips to town after more material.

"This strange white trader!" thought Martiniano. "No wonder the old men trust him. No wonder I like him. He understands. He knows much, thinks well and says little. That is the mark of a good man." But there was nothing to say to him.

Byers, rattling around, was as conscious of the one who worked beside him. But in the one there were two. There was a jim-dandy carpenter and craftsman who knew tools and how to use them, a young fellow who had been to school, spoke English and Spanish, was intelligent and matter-of-fact. There was another, dark-faced and somber, with long hair braids down his back, who squatted patiently, hour after hour, beside the long roof support he was carving. He worked with a mindless preoccupation. His toes dug into the ground, his thigh muscles corded. A gentle tremor flowed up the red-brown torso revealed by his gaping shirt. It passed down his arms; through his tender, sinewy fingers; out into the sharp steel blade and into the wood. Meanwhile he sang softly of gathering clouds and of the tall rain walking through the corn. And the tall rain walked round and round the wooden post, and the clouds gathered on it in terraces to mark the rhythm at frequent intervals. It was all one flowing whole, passing from toes to finger-tips, into and up the wood—a simple design springing evenly and effortlessly from nerve and muscle and bone. Byers noticed suddenly that the heels had been knocked off Martiniano's worn boots.

With a small frown he turned away and resumed work. What he had seen prevented him from asking about those drums beating in the kivas all night many weeks ago, about that mysterious medicine made for some boy or other lost up in the mountains.

Bah! he snorted. This stuff and nonsense, this perpetual medicine-making! He had known too long the tricks of Navajo medicine-men making feathers dance on the ground in front of a squatting crowd. Yet something in the casual, guarded way it had been mentioned to him roused a vague uneasiness.

He remembered what had happened when this Martiniano killed that deer. He remembered many other things throughout his years of trading. Discounting all the parlor-tricks, all the hokum, all the childish sincerity in believing in ghosts, all the superstition and nonsense, there still remained—well, for example, the simple, appalling and incontrovertible fact that an old, weak medicine man attired only in moccasins, breech-clout and blanket could go up into the snowy mountains in the dead of winter and remain there all night, without a fire, keeping himself warm by bringing to bear his medicine-knowledge on the functioning of his own bodily processes while he prayed. Byers himself had seen it.

There is a difference between races, he thought. A difference down to the tissues, nerves, integuments and bone structure, the chemical composition of the blood-stream, in the very rhythm of life. Who really knew what this race was? A race that had raised pyramids by ways now unknown to man. Which had evolved a time calendar more accurate than the one now in use, and were trepanning skulls while the barbarian tribes of Europe were still breaking theirs with stone hammers. A race whose tribes had overspread a continent and developed a civilization whose ancient mysteries still defied the probing of modern minds—and whose pitiful remnants still carried untouched the secret core of their inner life.

What an appalling difference, really, between this race and his own which had supplanted it. No man knew what it was, because his vision of another, his vision of the life around them both, was compacted of the sum total of the very things which differentiated him from his fellow.

Byers thought of the world of nature as the white man sees it: the sparkling streams and turbluent rivers as sources of potential electric power; the mountains gutted for the gold and silver to carry on the commerce of the world; the steel and iron and wood cut and fashioned, smelted, wrought and riveted from the earth to bridge with shining hulls the illimitable terrors of the seas—a resistless, inanimate world of nature to be used and refashioned at will by man in his magnificent and courageous folly to wrest a purpose from eternity. And yet what did he really know of the enduring earth he scratched, the timeless seas he spanned, the unmindful stars winking at his puny efforts?

And he thought of the world of nature as the Indian had always seen it. The whole world was animate—night and day, wind, clouds, trees, the young corn, all was alive and sentient. All matter had its inseparable spiritual essence. Of this universe man was an integral part. The beings about him were neither friendly nor hostile, but harmonious parts of the whole. There was no Satan, no Christ, no antithesis between good and evil, between matter and spirit. The world was simply one living whole in which man dies, but mankind remains. How then can man be lord of the universe? The forests have not been given him to despoil. He is equal in importance to the mountain and the blade of grass, to the rabbit and the young corn plant. Therefore if the life of one of these is to be used for his necessity, it must first be approached with reverence and permission obtained by ritual, and thus the balance of the whole maintained intact.

What then is a pine, thought Byers, the potential mast of a ship, a life that stands and breathes and dies like man, or the carven image of a thought? What is the world we see? It is as each man sees it, and his vision is compounded of the tissues and blood-vessels of his eyes, and the blood that feeds them, and the nerves that lead into the nerve-center of his brain, and the sensations that stimulate an image in his mind. And there alone it truly exists—in the mind of man which sees it as only he can see it, according to his conception of the life of which he is a part.

So Byers looked at the wooden post and at the man who carved it, and knew that each saw there a different thing.

The brotherhood of man! It will always be a dreary phrase, a futile hope, until each man, all men, realize that they themselves are but different reflections and insubstantial images of a greater invisible whole.

There are those who have eyes and cannot see, who have ears and cannot hear. They are blind, they are deaf, they have no tongues save for the barter of the day. For which of us now knows that awakened spirit of sleeping man by which he can see beyond the horizon, hear even the heart beating within the stone, and speak in silence those truths which are of us all?

A means, a tongue, a bridge to span the wordless chasm that separates us all; it is the cry of every human heart. And Byers looked at Martiniano but neither spoke.

# 14

FOR TWO DAYS he had been up in the mountains felling young aspens. He cut off the tops, trimmed them of branches and peeled off the smooth green bark. White, naked and a little damp, like a new grub, each lay stretched out drying on the floor of the forest—slim, straight lattias perhaps four inches thick that would be laid across the vigas of Byers' new room to form a herring-bone pattern on the ceiling.

Now, as he quit his work early and rode back to the pueblo, Martiniano's heart swelled. He had plowed his fields. By the time he had delivered his aspens to Byers, the day of planting would be at hand. It was a wonderful thing, this progression of seasons, this coming of spring. It was like a great river that caught up and carried all men. He could feel himself being swept along in its wonderful, powerful tide.

The fresh-plowed earth heaved, the wild plum buds puffed and broke. Springs and streams leapt up singing. He could hear the distant roar of the river swelling in the gorge. The clear blue skies stretched out above him like the skin of a puffed fiesta balloon. The whole earth strained and stretched with new life. Martiniano began to sing.

At home Flowers Playing too was swelled up, fat, huge, monstrous. She looked bigger than Buffalo-Old-Woman. Soon she would explode. Then there would be a son. It seemed very simple. He did not question or anticipate it.

Now this was a peculiar thing, his strange feeling of dis-association from her. For as she had steadily swelled and bloated with pregnancy, and grown more vague of look, she left behind in his memory the slim, cheerful girl he had known as Flowers Playing. She was just a huge, taciturn woman shuffling around in his hut, rattling her pots and pans. He was glad to keep away from her, completely separated.

So Martiniano himself was a little vague about this woman lately. She was no longer personal. She was an impersonal part of that earth around him which heaved and strained and broke open in long fresh furrows, the lambing ewes, the bursting buds. So he thought more of his new seed, and rode on singing.

But as he clattered through the pueblo and approached his house, he saw that the door was closed and smoke was spouting from the chimney. This was strange on such a warm, sunny day. He was oppressed by a mounting uneasiness. An instant later the whole heaving earth stood still, the bright-ness faded, the air seemed sucked away as if by an immense and invisible siphon.

Martiniano came to with a jerk. He had dismounted from his horse before the hut, and was clinging to the saddle-horn with both hands. His knees were trembling, his throat dry. He was staring wildly at the closed door.

Even as he took a step toward it, conscious of its meaning, a sound from inside tore through the hut and struck him. A single, faint but high-pitched cry—the first cry of a new-born child . . .

Perhaps there is no sound on earth so compelling, so symbolically expressive of the stark, naked reality of life. In that one cry is at once all the triumph of the freed flesh and the despairing shout of the soul plunged into the depths from which it will have to climb out again so slowly, with such agonizing effort, throughout all the length of its imprisonment. Never again in life does the tone of man reach this high key-note; thereafter, like primitive music, it lowers little by little in a descending scale.

To the Indian, breathing is an act of blessing; to partake of the essence of prayer he places his hand before his mouth and breathes deeply from his cupped palm. It is a gesture by which he affirms the living essence of the universe about him. So that the first inhalation of a child is not only a beginning of a life of physical matter, but an initiation into the life of spiritual essence. With his first breath, through the cosmic air which he inhales, he relates himself to the whole universe. In him is impregnated the whole of the universe, the solar system, all of life.

And the child reacts to this impress by a violent cry. It is a great moment. He has, as an embryo in his mother's womb, absorbed the elements of physical growth, and recapitulated the life of race. Now he has been born into a personal life, in which he must be developed as an individual. But also he has received the seed of fertilization of the greater, cosmic life that in time will also come to birth.

And all this, in one instant, hung quavering in the air, in a single high-pitched cry.

Martiniano rushed forward, halted, and walked slowly into the room. The midwife had finished with Flowers Playing: she lay in the bed, covered up with blankets, apparently dead or asleep already after labor. The partera's assistant was bent over a tin wash-bowl and a small thing laid beside it. This thing she wrapped up in a towel and blanket, and carried to the middle of the room. Here she turned about, murmuring, and heading it to the directions—the six directions which had contributed to its first breath.

Martiniano gritted his teeth and tried to maintain a stolid, impassive shell around the tormenting unrest within him. Unobtrusively he peeked over the woman's shoulder to see the thing she held. It was too much. He walked dizzily across the floor and sat down weakly on the threshold, trying to roll a cigarette.

The two women shuffled around unconcernedly talking.

"An easy birth," said one. "She was not stingy and tenacious of small presents when children passed her house. Therefore neither the child nor the afterbirth stuck. Did you look over the child? It has no marks, no blemishes? Good. She was a careful woman. She did not mock the deformities of others."

"But still a Ute," answered the other. "Or she would not have gone to see those moving pictures in La Oreja. It is evident she did so. I thought I saw the child twitch. Just like those strange pictures."

"I thought she had peeked out of the door and then reëntered the house," went on the other casually. "But the child did not stick. No, it was an easy birth . . . What? Now what is this man doing here?"

It was Martiniano who had stood up and stalked back tremblingly into the room. "It is my wife of whom I inquire," he said in a low voice. "And this child. You say it is a son?"

"A boy?" The woman looked at her assistant coldly. "Can you imagine such a question? A man with such hips and loins who dares to imagine he has begotten a son! A son the first try!" She broke out into a peal of laughter, then harshly drove him out of the house. "A son. A son. Ai. A son. . . . But out! There is work to do!"

There was work to do for four days—small, important tasks done unobtrusively and in proper silence, lest words rob them of power. The afterbirth and the cord were carried out and buried in the field. At sunrise following the birth the child was carried outdoors, meal was sprinkled and the Sun was asked to give him long life. Flowers Playing stepped across the fire, and then it was taken out of the house, to take away the sickness. The house was swept and cleaned. The midwife and her assistant were prepared a meal, given presents. Palemon and Estefana were invited, and a few friends including Byers and Angelina who brought gifts. The district nurse came on her rounds and left advice. The village priest called to collect baptismal fees in advance.

It was all very confusing to Martiniano. A child had been born. But to whom? He could hardly believe it was his own.

But the day soon came when Flowers Playing was up and about her tasks again. And the night came when they sat alone before the fire. The child, already fed, slept in a pine log cradle. Its small round head and broad little face glowed fresh and pink against the blanket. The woman rubbed the sore nipples of her breasts with grease and tucked them back inside her shabby dress. The man sat silently rolling a cigarette. It was all as it had been before, but better. They had a son. Imagine! The wonder began to fill him.

But yet there had been another strange change of values between them. Flowers Playing during pregnancy had been huge, taciturn, vague, impersonal. Now, her work done, she was herself—her body a little heavier, but still lithe and alive; her face cheerful, aware, content. Flowers Playing as she had been before.

"A beautiful son, no?" she murmured delightedly like a child, continually smoothing his blankets. "I can hardly wait till we take him to the priest! What will you name him before God, husband? Pomosino. Donaciano. Juan de Jesús. José Maria. They are all good names. . . . Now I like those red ribbons for him the best. Those that came off the candy boxes, which the store-keeper gave me for a present the day we complained of the stale meat he sold us. Still, those blue ones are nice. A little faded perhaps. But it makes them the color of the sky . . . And I must make him his first moccasins too. With many beads."

Martiniano sat silent before her chatter.

"That deerskin hanging on the wall. The skin of that deer I killed," he said after a time. "You may use that. I don't know why I have been saving that old skin so long."

What a strange woman, he thought. But none of them can see ahead of their noses. You would think that having given birth to a son her work was all done. Perhaps it was. But his was just beginning. He felt suddenly very old, very important, very much a man. The weight of his responsibilities oppressed him. This business of having a son involved things he had never thought of before. There was a Spanish name to select for the papers and the priest—the name by which he would be commonly known to town and authority. There was his real name, his Indian name, to be confirmed at the summer solstice ceremonies. Should the child be taken for adoption into one of the kivas; should he be later stolen away, hidden away from school to receive spiritual, tribal instruction like Napaita? Or should this be discounted and ignored, the white way, in favor of mere manual-trade and instruction such as he himself had received? What is my son? he wondered. Is it the greater life of the spirit I want for him, with its inward peace and outward poverty, or the more comfortable, material life of those who learn the ways of the life encroaching upon our people? I will wait for a sign, he decided. Meanwhile there were his fields to plant, his summer hut in the mountains to prepare. There were three mouths to feed. There was the long life ahead of a family man. A family man.

Flowers Playing had smoothed down the child's blankets again. Now she rose and kissed him; he could feel for the first time in months the warm pressure of her breasts and full body against him. And suddenly all his thoughts flew away like eagles. Before long they would be man and wife again, as was proper. It would all be as before, but better.

So he felt happier every day of these few quick days that sped like arrows toward the Day of the Holy Cross, the day of planting corn. It was all as before. The willows burst into green along the stream. The wild plum thickets, in full blossom, hovered in the moonlight like fragrant, low, white clouds. The boys began to sing. He had a wife, a son, new seed, new courage. Life was a new song he felt the need to sing.

But he felt a little twinge when he heard the voice on the housetops announcing a rabbit hunt next day. And in the morning when they rode away he seemed left with his own joy unsung and his vigor unspent. He watched them ride naked and bareback toward the Big Pasture where the buffalo were kept. Men and boys dashing wildly through the brush, without firearms, leaning from their horses to club and spear the twisting running balls of fur that leapt from stone and bush. And that night he heard the drums in the kivas, the singing, and knew what the rabbits were being cooked for.

He went to the old men.

"I have not participated in any dances this year," he reminded them respectfully. "I did not like to have my heart ordered to a duty it did not feel. But now I feel its need. I would do my duty in the races tomorrow."

And the old men answered shortly and softly, and Martiniano went home content.

It was a beautiful May morning when he took his place in line. Palemon had helped to paint him. His body was bare save for a colored scarf wrapped round his loins for a breech-clout, streaked with gray clay and stripes of red and yellow. His hair was gathered in a knot, plastered tight and stuck with tufts of eagle-down. He wore no moccasins, but around his ankles were tied strings of fur. The wide, dusty race track, immemorially worn down below the level of fields and sage-plain, ran east and west, the way the sun travels. It led from a quarter of a mile beyond the town into the breach of broken wall, past a kiva, and across the plaza along the south pyramid of the pueblo. The terraced walls quivered with color in the bright sunshine, a solid blanket of spectators. The plaza was filling with more visitors. And up and down the long, stone-pitted course the old men paraded with their green branches keeping back the crowd.

At the far end of the track around Martiniano waited one group of racers. Fifty men and boys or more, all painted, plastered and bedaubed. And at the far end, against a jutting pueblo wall, waited the other group. Suddenly, at a signal, the first two runners started. Relay fashion, they hurtled down the track, heads up, straining forward like two hounds. To release at the far end two others who came stumbling and panting back up the course.

So it kept up under the brilliant climbing sun, between the shouting visitors and the silent, blanketed throng. Two naked boys down and two back. Whipped along by the old men with their green branches, their anxious shouts. Bruised feet, a stumble on a protruding stone. A boy, sick with over-exertion, vomiting in the brush. Then an old man kneading his belly with curative fingers, and pushing him back into line for yet another effort.

There have always been races. The long distance races in the old days when young men ran fifteen, twenty miles through the snowy mountains—the race around the world. And still there are the shorter spring and fall races. They are the valiant expenditures of man's puny efforts and unfaltering courage to meet and run forward with the everlasting wonder of creation.

And so, one after another, the young men hurtled forward over the stones with bare, bruised feet; with naked bodies painted red and yellow, black and gray; with their plastered hair stuck full of tufts of eagle-down to catch the power of the air. Running not to win from one another, but extending all their strength to the sun for his new race, that once again he might return it to them, the creative power to carry the tribe forward another year. Running in panting bursts of speed while the old men along the track urged them along still faster with their green branches, their wavering, anxious shouts of encouragement. "Oom-a-pah! Oom-a-pah!"

It is the race of the individual against the limits of his own flesh, and it is the unending race of all humanity with the wonder of creation. No man wins. No man loses. But as each walks away, his broad chest heaving, his knees trembling, it is with the ecstatic look in his eyes of one who has spent himself to the full and, before he faltered, seen over the horizon the sunrise glow of his final victory.

How good it felt! thought Martiniano walking weakly home. To have felt his personal life stripped off him with his clothes, to have taken on the robe of earth with markings of fire, air and water, to be crowned at last with that symbol of the wild earth's nobility and his people's badge of immortality—a feather, if only a tuft of eagle-down. To have been one with men who for a time were not men but less than men and symbols of more than men. To have expended his joy, his hope, his worry, his prayer in one frantic, clean-limbed effort. He felt emptied, cleansed and whole.

Now he sat in the sunny doorway of his hut, drawing the biting smoke of a cigarette deep into his lungs with pure enjoyment while Flowers Playing tediously plucked the small, fluffy specks of down from his hair. Then she would wash it for him, cleaning out the clay with suds of soapweed. After that he would have a big meal of meat and onions and beans and chile. He could smell the pot already simmering. Life, he suddenly discovered, is a simple thing when once accepted wholly. . . .

The next day Martiniano began planting the field behind his house. And on Sunday they went to Mass, and afterward the priest baptized their son as Juan de Bautista.

"It is a good name, our little John the Baptist," said Flowers Playing. "And look! I have used both ribbons, the red ones and the blue."

"It will do," said Martiniano soberly. What concerned him most was the boy's real name that would be confirmed at the summer solstice ceremonies, and whether he should be adopted into a kiva.

A week later he went up to his mountain hut to prepare it

for summer occupancy. What he really wanted was to be alone, to see his son's road straight and true.

The roof leaked; he mended it. Winter snows had clawed the adobe off the walls; he replastered them. He dug out his spring, cleaned out his ditch, began to harrow and plant. At night he lay alone under the naked skies, on the high, heaving breast of the earth that turned under the steady stars.

The deer he had killed. It no longer troubled him. It no longer existed to give him a sign. There was only that power within him that knew what he did not know, upon which he could rely. He lay and stared into the sky. And it seemed to him that in these illimitable immensities of space, these unfathomable depths of dark time, all of man's life was but the brief glimmer of a candle, a single faltering step in darkness. There was no road, predetermined and secure, that he could lay for his son. There was only the faith that his life was the courage of man to make his own step in darkness, his single glimmer, and pass on unafraid.

They had gathered in Palemon's house. Palemon, Estefana and Batista, uncles, aunts and relatives of two dozen sharply distinguished ranks and degrees, Martiniano, Flowers Playing with Juan de Bautista in pink ribbons, all the old men, Byers and his wife, and still more friends—all gathered to welcome him who had been known as Napaita. For the boy had completed his long initiate in the kiva; the ceremony was over. He had been formally adopted into the tribe and now he had a new name.

The day was warm, but a small fire burned to give life to the room. The walls had been freshly whitewashed with tierra blanca. Against them gleamed the best blankets, brightest shawls and gaudiest shirts of the crowded guests. Between the two rooms paddled women carrying benches and dishes, setting the long plank table upon which all, taking turns, the men first, would feast on meat, chile, rice, beans, fresh coffee, canned tomatoes, stale store cake, fruit, cheap stick-candy, and more potatoes and meat. It was all very cheerful, completely relaxed in tone. Men murmured and smoked Byers' cigarettes. Women worked and giggled. Children stared hungrily at the passing platters of food.

But he, the object of their guarded attention, the focus of all their congratulations, the guest of honor in his father's house, stood silently in the corner and hitched up, as if cold, his new blanket. He wore it proudly, but familiarly and unobtrusively too—this robe of his new manhood, a cheap, bright-patterned blanket from Montgomery-Ward. He had grown a little in the year and a half, but was still small. He limped slightly as he moved aside to let a woman pass. Napaita, a small boy, who had returned home to that which was too small now to constrict him.

Estefana could not keep her eyes off her son. She beamed at his new blanket, at the little, new, store-wrinkled yellow shirt that showed, the beautiful beaded moccasins on his feet. Drawn as if to a magnet, she stopped to speak, to touch him. The boy imperceptibly shrank back from her touch, and listened to her and all the solicitous women no more attentively than to a flock of magpies.

Byers stepped up and congratulated him. Napaita nodded casually, like a man, but with wary black eyes which looked on the white trader with probing sharpness.

To the old men his manner was respectful but confident, as if he met them alone on equal grounds. A boy so accustomed to fasting and frugality that he looked on the spread feast with curious, disbelieving eyes. A boy upon whom the hold of mother's destructive pampering had been forever broken, a man henceforth.

It seemed at once both pathetic and magnificent, this small boy already bereft of his foolish boyhood, so soon whetted like a small, sharp blade to his task. But in it was the truth of his heritage—a race which out of necessity had learned so well to sacrifice the lesser for the greater that there was no hesitation before the true values of their lives.

Byers frowned slightly. It always comes out, he thought. You think they're getting soft and are done for, then bang! They are all little flint knives, these children. Then laughing good-naturedly, but deeply appreciative of the honor showed him, he walked to the table for first serving.

Finished, and taking his leave, he stopped for a moment beside a small group standing in the doorway. He shook hands with Napaita and spoke to Martiniano, struck suddenly by the same calm assurance of their faces. His ex-carpenter, the stubborn trouble-maker, had changed since he had had a child. Byers noticed that he was wearing moccasins. The fellow, he knew suddenly, had gone back to the blanket. Byers bent over the child in Flowers Playing's arms, the little round Mongolian face worn like a flower at her full breast.

"I've got a little pair of Arapahoe moccasins that'll just about go on this man's feet," he said gruffly, in his low, kind voice before going out. "You better come over after 'em, huh?"

"What a wonderful, manly little fellow, Napaita," said Angelina as they walked across the plaza.

Byers jerked down the sloppy brim of his big hat and began to whistle through his teeth.

Yet in the three who stared after him was the truth of his own and all men's lives.

The child born by woman out of the formless mystery of everlasting life into the narrow confines of human flesh, linked to the boundless universe with the first breath he draws, but constricted for awhile within the personal, individual image.

The boy born by ceremonial out of the long initiate wherein he has been awakened out of the narrow world of the flesh into the greater world of the spirit, into that conception of his oneness with the cosmic whole, the breathing mountains, the living stones, the young corn plant and the deer, all that life which has gone before and will follow after, and which exists at once in one perpetual time.

And the man reborn, as men are ever reborn out of their dead selves, by life itself. For as there are many faiths and many conceptions of the one paradox by which man exists as transient flesh and enduring spirit, all these faiths stem from the one faith, the one wonder and mystery of which we are an inseparable part. Let each man, though bereft of teacher, priest and preceptor, but depend upon this faith, and so be reborn by life itself into the greater whole. And so see before him at last, through the cycles of his widening perception, the one road which is his to tread with all.

*"Indeed, even while I call myself poor,**
*Far off on all sides,*
*I have as my fathers life-giving priests.*

*"Asking for the breath of the priest of the north,*
*The priest of the west,*
*The priest of the south,*
*The priest of the east,*
*The priest of above,*

* Lacking "religious" instruction

*The priest of below,*
*Asking for their life-giving breath,*
*Their breath of old age,*
*Their breath of waters,*
*Their breath of seeds,*
*Their breath of fecundity,*
*Their breath of riches,*
*Their breath of strong spirit,*
*Their breath of power,*
*Their breath of all good fortune whereof they are possessed;*
*Asking for their breath,*
*Into our warm bodies taking their breath,*
*We shall add to your breath.*

*"Do not despise the breath of your fathers,*
*But draw it into your body.*
*That our roads may reach to where the life-giving road of*
*our sun father comes out,*
*That, clasping one another tight,*
*Holding one another fast,*
*We may finish our roads together;*
*That this may be, I add to your breath now.*

*"To this end:*
*Reaching to Dawn Lake,*
*May our roads be fulfilled.*
*May we grow old*
*May our peoples' roads all be fulfilled."*

Early in June a terse paragraph in the newspaper caught Byers' eye. He read it through carefully: certain appropriations had been authorized by Congress to provide compensation for sundry Indian lands. Byers scratched his buckskin jacket, and wondered if it referred to the passage of the bill proposed last fall. For months the thing had been a dead horse. The arguments for and against it had dwindled and finally vanished from the press. Even the Indians seemed to have forgotten it. As usual with the closing in of winter the old feuds, controversies and grievances flared up; and then with spring, when they got out into their fields again, all trouble vanished. A people like a barometer; they reflected every change of weather.

Three days later a batch of papers came from the city. The

vague paragraph had blossomed into concise pages. The bill had passed the House of Representatives and the Senate and had been finally approved on the thirty-first of May. As amended, it provided for appropriations to the total of some $762,000 for compensation to Indians for land divested from the various pueblos, and some $232,000 to compensate white settlers and non-Indian claimants "who had occupied and claimed land in good faith but whose claims had not been sustained" and whose occupation was to be terminated. These sums, he read, were to be appropriated from the United States Treasury in three annual installments, beginning four years hence.

Byers whistled in astonishment, then rapidly skimmed down the columns to locate the compensation allotted his own pueblo and neighbors: $85,000 to the pueblo, and $57,000 to the non-Indians around it. A perplexed frown gathered over his face. He read a peculiar thing. Approximately 30,000 acres of national forest land were to be set aside by the Secretary of Agriculture ". . . upon which land Indians depend for water supply, wood and timber for their personal use, and *as the scene of certain of their religious ceremonials*" . . . and to "thereafter grant to said pueblo, upon application of the governor and council thereof, a permit to occupy said lands and use the resources thereof for the personal use and benefit of said tribe of Indians for a period of fifty years . . ."

Dawn Lake! The land in the mountains around Dawn Lake! "Jesus bless my soul to hell!" muttered Byers. There it was in a nut-shell, for all the fusty phrases. These damned stubborn Indians had got back their Dawn Lake. A nice little present from Uncle Sam! Just listen now to Sanchez and his forest rangers howl. Listen now to the Mexican sheepherders when they were kicked out of their mountain pastures, and the white tourists when they were turned back from their camping and fishing grounds. He knew what they all would say. The thing seemed utterly fantastic, impossible, inconceivable: that a bunch of poor, ragged Indians in this day and age of haste and reason were given thirty thousand acres of national forest, right on the watershed, for the practical purpose of jumping around the shores of a tiny lake in an annual orgy of dancing.

He didn't believe it! But there it was in print, in detail, the whole act of Congress. And gradually it was confirmed. Teodor Sanchez, stalking surlily around with a glum face, had given orders to his rangers to accept no more grazing fees from Mexican sheepowners, and to refuse white visitors permits for camping in the area. A week or two later Byers glimpsed the District Indian Superintendent and Strophy in town—come to get the required papers signed by the Governor and the Council. But the Indians gave no sign of victory. No celebration, no bragging, no talk at all. They went around as usual, quiet, secretive, impersonal.

Old Sun Elk hobbled into the post for a nickel sack of tobacco. Byers slid it across the counter.

"Well, you got back your Dawn Lake!" he growled.

The old man undid the sack, rolled a cigarette with wrinkled hands, carefully secreted tobacco and papers, silently borrowed a match. He puffed a time or two, then suddenly looked up with sharp, probing eyes.

"Cómo no?" he asked serenely. "Why not?" and hobbled slowly out with his stick.

"Mother of God!" muttered Byers, still thinking in the idiom. "Why not indeed!"

He was a little amazed at his first reaction, his intangible resentment. He had reconciled himself to view these Vanishing Americans as circus performers parading in remote rings for the benefit of gawking tourists, and himself as an old fogy, way behind times, and quickly going to pot. Now, like a condemned man reconciled to his fate, he was confused by receiving a sudden extension of freedom for fifty years. He realized that it would cover the rest of his lifetime. This post and his livelihood from it would endure. There would always be for him, as there always had been, the distant sound of a drum, the flicker of flamelight on dancing ghosts, the faces calm, dark and inscrutable that had surrounded him since childhood, and the impalpable mystery of their simple lives—the life to which he too was confirmed in the midst of the forest of steel and stone inexorably pressing in upon him.

Byers saw its falsity. There can be no oases in the desert of ever-shifting time, no idyllic glades of primitive culture in the forest of mankind, no ivory towers of thought. We are all caught in the tide of perpetual change. These pueblos, these reservations must sometime pass away, and the red flow out into the engulfing white. The Government had only postponed the inevitable. His resentment gave way to a faint sadness. The victory, even for the Indians, seemed a shabby makeshift.

For it was predicted upon the differences between men, upon the outward forms of their lives, their ethnological behavior, and not upon the one eternally groping spirit of mankind. It was maintained by the white who was content to set the red apart in his tiny zoo, and by the red who with traditional secrecy and stubborn obduracy to change, himself held aloof. So both must sometime pass: the Indian with his simple fundamental spiritual premise untranslated into modern terms, and finally the white with his monstrous materiality.

But perhaps there would still be time, thought Byers, to learn from these people before they pass from this earth which was theirs and is now all men's, the one truth that is theirs and shall be all men's—the simple and monstrous truth of mankind's solidarity with all that breathes and does not breathe, all that has lived and shall live again upon the unfathomed breast of the earth we trod so lightly, beneath the stars that glimmer less brightly but more enduringly than our own brief lives.

And as the weeks passed and midsummer approached, he noticed a faint but perceptible change in the pueblo and in town. There were less men working in the fields and loafing in La Oreja. Visitors were unable to find guides and horses. The trails to the mountain were carefully guarded. Then suddenly one early evening he knew the time had come. It was early August, when the ceremonial year reached its climax, when all the boys let out of the kivas, the young men and unmarried girls and all the kiva people made their annual pilgrimage to Dawn Lake.

Byers rode up the cañon a way before he was stopped. The end of the procession was just vanishing from sight between the trees—the bright blankets, the flowered shawls, the black heads wreathed with green leaves. It brought back to him, for one instant, a vision of the idyllic strangeness, the wild barbarity, the childish sweetness of a life yet untouched, that he remembered. With it came too the wonder and the mystery—the everlasting wonder and mystery that must never be allowed to depart.

Martiniano had moved up into his summer hut. He still had seed from last year's crop, money for supplies, and credit with the good white trader besides. His corn was in. With his blanket tied round his head, turban-fashion, he walked up and down the rows, carefully weeding. Flowers Playing sat with Juan de Bautista in the doorway. She was watching her bread in the adobe oven outside.

In a little while he came in and put up his hoe; it was late afternoon, his day's work was over. He knelt at the spring and drank deeply, letting the water trickle down the corners of his mouth upon his shirt as he raised his face. Ah! How good! he thought. The coldest, clearest water in the mountains!

Flowers Playing had taken out her bread. Four huge brown loaves sat on the table. He broke off a piece of crust, munched it hungrily. Bueno. Que bueno! he thought. There is nothing like good bread. Wheat bread at that!

Waiting for her to cook supper, he sat in the doorway smoking and watching his son. The child, almost naked, lay on a thick saddle-blanket on the floor. Flowers Playing had given him a piece of sweet fat to suck on. Around it she had tied one end of a string. The other end was tied to one of his big toes. The child half-swallowed the cube of fat, began to choke. He rolled over, threshing out wildly with his legs. Plop! The meat jerked out of his mouth. Then after a time he located it again and was content as before.

Martiniano grinned and turned back to watch the sun sinking over the desert, down the sage slope and across the river gorge. Soon Flowers Playing put the child to sleep. They ate.

His wife was not a difficult woman, he thought contentedly. Of course, like all women, she wanted a few things now and then. For one, a piece of colored oil-cloth for the table. Also she mentioned the possibility of a stove—for the second time.

"Am I a squaw who must cook in a fireplace?" she asked him cheerfully. "I who was taught to cook bacon on gas, and to have ice in the summertime? I think, Martiniano, you had better bring up our stove from our house in your wagon. I have no place here for my pots. You understand. With a family it is more difficult."

He nodded and went on eating. Finished, he leaned back and hooked his thumbs in his wide, brass-studded belt.

"I wish," said Flowers Playing, "that you would bring up some more ginger-snaps when you come from town. And perhaps a big can of tomatoes. What is better than a cold dish of tomatoes after a hot supper in the summertime! And a ginger-snap to eat with it. Besides," she added casually, "that child likes cookies. They are not too hard to hurt his gums."

So they talked, listless and unhurried, while dusk strode up the slope. In a little while Flowers Playing would light a lamp and wash the dishes. The boy would wake up. She would sing to him awhile, a Ute song, an Arapahoe lullaby, the Corn Dance Song. Then they would go to bed and he would lie there, his wife warm on one side, and the night breeze cool on the other, wondering how it was that now he had no more worries and if he should fix his fence tomorrow.

But now he stood up and reached for his blanket. "I am going for a walk," he said a little curtly, as a man speaks to a wife when both have learned their proper place. "For the while you do those greasy dishes. For perhaps a little more."

Slowly he sauntered out to the trail above the spring, then swiftly climbed up through the pines. Already his quick ears had caught the faint sound of drums.

It was dark when he reached the crest of the ridge and squatted down in his blanket. They were there below him as he had known they would be. The people on their pilgrimage to Dawn Lake, stopped here as was customary for the first night. Already others had gone ahead to gather wood and erect the tepees. At daybreak small boys and girls would leave early, in advance, wearing garlands of green leaves and singing as they climbed.

Martiniano had never gone; he was not a kiva member. But he knew what it would be like. The little mountain lake, the pale conical tepees erected along the shore, and behind them, the dark curtain of pines. All standing out in the faint pink glow of fires while the people danced, their skins rose-red in flamelight, black in pine-shadow and greenish-gray in moonlight. All returned, as was proper, to the source of their beginning—the little blue eye of faith, the deep turquoise lake of life, their sacred tribal Dawn Lake.

One must not forget one's beginning, thought Martiniano. And that was why he had consented to the adoption of his son into a kiva, with Palemon for the boy's godfather, his preceptor. Times were changing, and his son should know something of the old before he was confronted with the new. Martiniano had not told Flowers Playing. Let her have the boy ten years first, perhaps twelve, before it came. Perhaps it would not come at all, it was getting so difficult to keep a boy from the Government's away-school, and secreted in the kiva. But if it came! Ah, then would come the night he sat here and saw his son below, like Napaita.

He peered forward and down the steep-walled cañon into the little glade below. The pilgrims were through eating. The fire leaped steadily higher. He could see the sparks flying like fire-flies above the great limbed cottonwoods and against the opposite wall of cliffs, the shimmer on the stream and the feathered falls. The drum-beat sounded stronger now. He could see them fringed round the circle of light, the bright blankets, the dark faces. Then one by one they stepped out. A great circle, men and women, boys and girls alternating and clasping hands. They began to dance, right knees flexing, left feet sliding a few inches away, then the right drawing up beside them for the next step. The men bending at the waist, heads up. The women shuffling upright, their hips, knees and shoulders keeping time. And all of them, in the great circle, slowly revolving clockwise round the fire. A Ghost Dance, a Round Dance. Very slow. Not serious. Pure enjoyment.

Then slowly, still dancing to the beat of the drum, they began to sing. Low, slow voices lifting out of the deep glade between the cliffs, out of the dark cañon along the singing stream. Rising like smoke into the star-stung summer sky.

Martiniano lay back and wrapped his blanket around him. Sound came clearer now, the rising chant, the beat of the big belly drum, the pop of a piñon log. The murmurous undertone of the falls and the stream singing whitely over the rocks. Far off, a coyote yapped. And then it was all one sound, one song, the song of night and summer and Dawn Lake and his people who did not forget; and he lay on his back, listening, and staring upward at the stars.

The Deer were up. He watched them twinkling in the immemorial, indestructible pattern against the inky blue. There were the long-stemmed legs, the upflung antlers. There was the pointed nose and the lifted tail-piece. It seemed suddenly to be one great deer, the body of all deer, climbing overhead. He counted the points of the horns. Five, all five! He appraised the little splotch of white where the star dust lay thick under the left shoulder, down toward the belly. He saw the marking of black where the sky shone through. And suddenly he knew why the deer he had killed troubled him no more. And he knew now that there is nothing killed, nothing lost, if one looks far or deep or high enough to see how its transmuted meaning is imprinted for all men to read and understand. Ai. A man drops but a pebble into the one great lake of life, and the ripples spread to unguessed shores, to congeal into a pattern even in the timeless skies of night.

So he lay listening to the singing, content and free of worry: Martiniano, the trouble-maker, the man who killed the deer.